Squashed Tomatoes and Stew

Michelle Mina Scowcroft

ISBN: 1-4819-0376-4
ISBN-13: 9781481903769

Dedication

In memory of Sam Scowcroft

1980

Acknowledgements

Thank you friends and family for supporting me in my two year venture creating this novel. I appreciate the editing and technology help I received from Jane Chilton, Debbie Geldart, Abi McGovern, Miranda Robinson and Pauline Whitaker. I highly recommend Willber G. Force for his meticulous proofreading services. If any errors are spotted in the text please let me know and I can pass on the blame!

A lot of research has gone into making the story. I really appreciate the information given to me by the late Richard Parkes of Corvallis, Oregon. His enthusiasm and great knowledge helped 'Stella Hurtigrutensson' complete her circuitous rail journey from La Junta to the Grand Central Terminal with relative ease!

I consider the front cover an important aspect for setting the mood of a novel. I am very fortunate in having permission from the wonderful artist, Anita Klein, for giving me permission to use her 'Evening with Maia' as a front cover. To see more of her delightful art work please look at her website at www.anitaklein.com

Many of the stories in this book are based upon factual incidents although the characters are fictitious. However, names and places, apart from those of the Chamel family, have been changed.

Michelle Scowcroft was born in London in 1956 to non-British parents. Over the years she has lived in many places but has chosen to settle within the wild beauty of the Yorkshire Dales. In the past she has travelled extensively but is now content to stay where she is. Originally trained as a social worker, she has experienced a variety of careers in her life. Mother to Abi, Sam and Peter and is wife to Alan, a mountaineer.

Prologue

"Shhh! Quiet, George. Shhh! Stop clattering! Can't you see she's asleep? Forget the coffee. Let her be. I can fetch her up another soon enough."

"D'you think she's okay, Delph? She's looking a bit chilly to me. I'll get her another blanket. I can feel the wind's picking up. It's not that warm out."

"Okay! Go on then ... but, shush, keep it quiet. Pick up those big feet of yours. You're not marching off to war!"

"I'm doing my best to be quiet. I've not got fairy toes like you!"

"Too right you haven't! Now just get that blanket, without knocking anything over this time and, while you're at it, pass that red cardie of mine. It's just there ... look, over by the door. No, George, the other door! I think, before too long, you may be in need of a new pair of spectacles."

"There's nothing wrong with my sight, nothing whatsoever, Delphine. I think there's something, more likely, gone wrong with your tongue! Snap, snap,

snap! You turning into a crocodile, or what? Here, is this the cardigan you're wanting?"

"Yes ... that's better, thanks. Sorry, dear. — You're right, there is a bit of a nip in the air. Summer's definitely on the turn; I bet autumn won't be long in coming. Hand me the blanket, dear, and I'll put it over her legs. We don't want her picking up a chill, now, do we?"

"Hey, you two!" Kitty laughed and opened her eyes unnaturally wide. "I'm just fine. I'm not asleep. I was just checking the insides of my eyelids; see what I could find hiding up there."

"Sure! So how d'you account for the snoring, then?"

"I wasn't snoring, was I?"

"Uh-huh."

"Oh! You spoil me somethin' rotten, you know. Am I that old that I need two nursemaids now? I'm only, what, seventy-nine ... and a quarter. You know, it's not as if I'm a hundred and seventy-nine and a quarter, well, not for a few more years yet, anyhow."

"Well, Kitty, we're just practising for when you are one hundred and seventy-nine years old. And, by the way, just for the record," Delphine continued, "you're eighty-three ... and three quarters, if you're being so very particular with numbers. You know full well that you can't hoodwink us now, not after all this time. We got you pretty well sussed. In fact, we got you sussed right from the very first day we met. And when we think you deserve a proper spoiling, you'll get one, whether you want one or not. Now, how about that nice milky coffee?"

"Not at the moment."

"A tea?"

"No thanks. You're a dear but I'm fine. Just come sit with me awhile. Keep an old girl amused."

"Okay, just for a minute or two. It'll be nice to take the weight off my feet, but then, Kitty dear, I'll need to do some shopping. I don't want you complaining we don't feed you up properly."

"I don't think I could ever complain about that."

"Glad to hear it — Ahh, that's better! Nothing like a little sit down every now and again"

"True."

"But we do need to get a couple of things in for tonight. Trouble is, Kitty, now I've sat down I don't feel like getting myself up again. Sitting down's so very nice. I do like this sitting down business. I know, here's a thought, I s'pose I could get on with the mending before going into town. I've still got all that hemming left over from last week, and then there's those buttons which could do with fixing back on your coat. I've been putting it off for far too long."

"That'd be really nice, Delphine. I feel like a bit more company today. Don't know why, just one of those days."

"Okay, then, my darling. You chat away. When I've finished this pile I'll pop down to the shops. You tell me a story or something. It'll make that mending a little less painful. I never enjoyed stitching. I'm sure you can tell!"

"I sure can. Happy to help out."

"Hey! Tell you what, Kitty, I've got an even better idea. I know what we'll do."

"What's that, then?"

"Well, just thinking, I'm sure George could manage the shopping on his own. He doesn't need me around to tell him what to buy; there's not that much we need in. Just some bread and fruit, and some other bits and bobs. We could then get down and have a right good natter. How's that sounding with you, George?"

"No problem. That's fine with me, ladies."

"Oh! Just hold on a moment. Oh dear, maybe it's not just so 'fine'." Delphine raised an eyebrow. "Now, Kitty, do we actually trust George after yesterday's little escapade?" George grimaced. "Not too sure we should let him out on his own. I think that Lucia, down at the bread shop, may have an eye out for my handsome husband. I reckon she's big enough to eat him all up and more. D'you think we can trust him not to fall for her voluptuous charms?"

"Now, listen here. You two ladies are my only loves. You know that fact perfectly well. I've eyes for no other. I was only smiling because she was smiling at me first. You're just winding me up. You're just teasing again. Now, you two settle down and have a nice little chat. I can manage the shopping perfectly well. In fact I'll leave the car and walk to town and get myself some fresh air. If you want I'll switch on the percolator before I go, and I may even leave you a slice or two of that rum cake I cooked up this morning. It might sweeten your tongue. But mind you, only if you're both good and promise not to make fun of an old boy like me."

"Now you're talking. Okay, we'll try our very best, sweetest one."

"Well, I'll finish up in the kitchen and hurry down to town. See you later, alligators."

"In a while, crocodile ... that is, if you escape Lucia's clutches."

"Now, Delph, what did I just say? No more teasing!"

"Oh, Delphine, he's such a dear man." Kitty squeezed Delphine's hand. "I'm so lucky to have you both here living with me. How many years has it been? Seems like a whole generation has passed us by."

"Believe it or not, Kitty, it's probably more like coming up two now. Must be well over forty years. Doesn't time fly? But no, it's George and I who are the lucky old things. Where would we've been without you? Anyhow, enough of that soppy stuff. How about a little story?"

"What d'you want me to tell you?"

"Let me think ... hmm. Tell me about when you were little, you know, back home in Colorado, down in that, what you call it now ... whatever that God-forsaken hole of a place was called."

"You've heard that tale so many times before. You sure you want me to tell it over?"

"Course I do. You've only told me little snippets before now. This time let me hear it out. I sure love listening to your stories, Kitty. You know that. I don't mind where you start. The beginning, they say, is the best place to start off from."

"Don't know about that. Not in my experience. Where you start off in life is not always the best of places."

"I s'pose not. Okay, then. How about when you were living along with your ma and pa down on that old ranch of a place close to the border with ... was it Kansas? You said the winds never ceased blowing. And nothing grew, did it? It was just like sitting in a big bowl of dirt and dust."

"Uh-huh, you remember that? Your ears listen well! You're right, nothing could grow, nothing would grow, not even a child." Kitty raised a hand to her mouth and let out a sigh. "Not like around these parts." She stopped and, smiling, gazed into the distance. A roll of gold-green hills lay beneath the terrace where they sat. Little patches of honey-hued vineyards graced their slopes, and tall grey-green cypress and even taller towers, the colour of terracotta, danced their way across the valley floor. A blush-blue haze was swirling the heights of the Sibillini, and Kitty, hearing a lullaby of mothers' voices ushering the coming night, clasped her hands and laughed out aloud with pleasure.

"But that was quite some time ago, Delphine," she murmured, "another country, another people. That was a whole world away."

"I know, it sure was, but I'd still like to hear it ... that is, if you want to tell."

"Okay, but stop me when you've heard enough. I don't want to bore you to death."

"You could never bore me, Kitty."

"You bet?"

PART ONE

I

A large shiny beetle was crawling over my palm. I tickled it with a blade of dry grass. It stopped in its tracks, its feelers flailing wildly. I turned my hand and the bug kept going along and along its endless journey. Across the fence I could hear giggling and yelling. It was coming from the yard at the big house. I put my hand back down on the ground and let the beetle carry on its way. There was a gap in the paling and I pulled myself up and hurried across to see what was going on over there. From my hideout I could spy the Brigham children playing 'Piggy-in-the-Middle'. The kids were having fun and running about like crazy. The three girls were 'little pigs' and their two elder brothers were launching the ball far too high. They were never going to catch it. Lincoln, their dog, was yapping and helping the boys hound the ball away from the girls, wrestling it out of their hands whenever the sisters chanced to grab it. They were protesting that it wasn't fair but the boys just jeered. I saw my ma walk out on to the Brigham's terrace. It was one of those blistering hot days again. She was carrying out a tray. Drinks and cookies piled high.

4

On seeing her, the Brigham kids, like starved vultures, flocked their way towards Ma. They snatched and pecked greedily and knocked back the lemonade. I waved to her. She didn't wave back. She didn't smile. I knew she wouldn't.

❄ ❄ ❄

"You know, Delphine, I was only about four then but I was well aware of the rules going; Ma was not permitted to take notice of me. That's how it was then. The Brighams had their ways. Nobody questioned them. They were the bosses. They ran your life for you. There was no choice. Choice, ha, that would have been some luxury! If you complained you were right out, there and then, on your butt."

"That wasn't nice." Delphine looked up from her mending. "What with having your ma so close and yet you weren't even allowed a wave!"

"No, Ma'am, they were not nice. No, they were not! You know, Ma had been with that family since she'd been a mere slip of a girl. She worked real hard. I bet those Brighams didn't appreciate her one iota. Pa worked up in the big house too. They both did. Together they kept the household going real nice for that family. The Brighams treated them tough. Later on I found out how very tough the Brighams were with them. You know what?"

"Tell me."

"When Ma fell pregnant with me, she was scared witless. She was terrified she'd lose her job; it was custom then. It happened all over, not just with the Brighams. Back in those days live-in domestics were got rid of for simple human things like marrying, or getting pregnant, getting sick, or just old. Once employed your personal life went flying out the window like an old boot. Eventually Ma got the courage to own up to her 'sin'. You can just about imagine Mrs Brigham was none too pleased with Ma. Poor Ma was left to stew overnight wondering her fate."

✳ ✳ ✳

Next morning Mrs Brigham cornered her in the kitchens. "Ellie, you've done wrong. Lucky for you we're good Christians ... not that you'd appreciate any of that. We see ourselves as God's representatives here on earth and our duty is to watch over ignorant little girls like you. You have done wrong. We do not condone what has gone on but we've decided, this one time, and only this one time, we won't punish you."

"Thank you, Ma'am, truly grateful."

"Mr Brigham and I are certainly not happy with the disrespect you've shown us. We expected so much better from you. We've treated you well and you've taken advantage of us and our good nature. I hope you're thoroughly ashamed of yourself."

"I'm truly sorry, Mrs Brigham."

"You've disappointed us, Ellie. Y'understand? Others would've been out the back door before they knew what'd hit them. No discussion there."

"Yes, Ma'am, thank you."

"Round these parts most families would have long ridden themselves of bungling girls like you. Most helps accept the rules as they are. They're truly thankful for what they receive. Not all helps, you know, have good Christian families like the Brighams to look over them. They don't all get a good solid roof over their head."

"I know, Ma'am, we're truly obliged to you and Mr Brigham."

"But you, you got the best and how d'you pay us back? By breaking our trust! We expected loyalty from you, Ellie. It's what we call honouring your betters. But, of course, you always want more and more. You wanted to marry Frank and, charitably, what did we do?"

"You let me marry my Frank."

"And, we let you stay on. We didn't have to, did we? And see what happens; is this how you go about repaying us for our generosity?"

Ellie lowered her head and put her hand over her mouth. She stared at the sink, stink-full of pots and pans. Her stomach heaved. She swallowed it back. "Now that you've fallen, do you appreciate," Mrs Brigham continued, "that it's only out of the goodness of our Christian hearts that Mr Brigham and I have decided to keep you both on, eh? You're more than fortunate having me as your boss. You got that?"

"Thank you, Ma'am, We're truly grateful."

"However, I want you to understand something, okay? You listening now, girl? From this precise moment onward we don't want sight nor sound of you. You stay out of the family's way. Y'understand?"

"Yes, Ma'am."

"Oh, one more thing. Now listen here right careful, girl. If you fall again, you'll be out on your own. Have you marked my words? Out on your own along with your Frank. Both of you O-U-T. You'll have neither home, nor money, nor work, and no ref-er-ence. Nothing. That way you'll soon learn what's what in life. Just you remember that, missy, remember that right well. The Brighams don't give second chances. Do you understand that? Yes?"

"Yes, Ma'am. Thank you."

"You're a very lucky girl, not that you know it. Now, getting down to practicalities. You won't have had the common sense to think things out for yourself so I've done it for you. Now, see here, more likely than not the infant will die at birth, if not before, God willing. In fact it could happen any time. Girls like you aren't made to be mothers. However, if God wills that the infant survives then the Church Union will relieve you of the burden. They'll find it a place down at the Holy Cross. Some of the orphans get adopted: some into good Christian homes like ours, others farmed out. It depends if they're lucky or not."

Ellie opened her mouth as if to say something. She shut it again.

"Now, no need to thank me. As I said, it's my Christian duty to God to help those who can't help themselves." Mrs Brigham turned to go.

"But Ma'am ... but I was ..."

"What's the matter now? Why you hopping about?"

"Ma'am, please ... er ... my sister; Mae's her name. Can she ... can she come help look after my baby, please, if it lives that is? Please, Ma'am, please? She don't want no money. She can live with us. Help round the place, too. It won't cost you a cent more. I can keep it then. It won't take up no generous space down the Holy Cross. And, Ma'am, please, I assure you, you won't have no trouble with us. You'll have two maids then for the price of one. Please, Ma'am. It won't be no problem. I'll vouch for Mae. She's good, a good girl. She's twelve now, same as I was when I came, so she's still real strong. She could do all sorts. She could help Bet with the linens and then ..."

"For crying out loud, girl! Stop your snivelling. Enough, I said, enough! Let go of me! Let go! I've taken more than I can stand. You've got some cheek begging me like that. Why, doesn't it just show how ignorant you trash are! Tell me, then, how can y'afford to feed another two mouths? Eh? Why, only the other day your Frank came pestering Mr Brigham 'beggin' a raise'— as if he was actually worth half of what he's getting! Now you're telling me you can afford yet another mouth to feed. What a load of bunk! To be honest, now that you can't work the same I should be telling Mr Brigham to cut your pay. I notice things, you know. I'm watching you. And I can see you've been slacking of late. Your sort are all the same. Next y'all be wanting time off for being sick. I've seen you throwing-up in the yard and being sick is wasting my time."

"Sorry, Ma'am, really sorry but ..."

"My time and my money. Get it? As you very well know money don't grow on trees. Or maybe you don't! Mr Brigham's just too soft with y'all! But, luckily, I wasn't born yesterday. I know your type well. I think I'm just going to have to have some words with Mr Brigham about these goings-on. Now before

I change my mind get out of my sight, and get on with whatever y'are s'posed to be trying to do. Stop wasting my precious time. And never ever, ever, ever tell me what I should do again, or you'll be out of here like a shot. Now, git!"

✳ ✳ ✳

Kitty turned to Delphine. "Wasn't she some nasty bit of work? I bet Ma must've gone through some hell. It wouldn't surprise me if that woman made Ma go crazy like she did. Looking back I can now understand Ma and why she did what she did. Too late now. I s'pose Ma went along with it until, eventually, she just cracked, couldn't take it anymore. I'm surprised she lasted that long. I wouldn't have. She put up with all the Brighams' demands as well as coping with the heat and the winds. It was always blowing, blowing. Blowing hot. And then the dust! Dust everywhere, suffocating everyone, everything. Poor Ma, she'd it going so hard. You know, I bet she was only 'bout sixteen, or seventeen at the most, then."

"And that Mrs B calling herself a Christian lady. Not that I think she was; not in my eyes, anyhow. And how could she be so lacking in her understanding? I mean, goodness sake, she was a mother herself! How can one woman treat another like that?" Delphine shook her head as if in disbelief. "At least you weren't bundled off to that Holy Cross."

"That's right ... and nor did I die at birth! But, I'm telling you, at times I really wished I had. That's sad thinking for a little girl; unnatural. You know, out in that dust bowl, hundreds and thousands died. They reckon must've been around sixty thousand or more folk passed away just from the effects of the dust. They say it's the world's greatest man-made disaster. Don't know if it's in the *Guinness Book of Records* or not, but it was some mass killing. Not that I s'pose the land owners really knew what the outcome would be when they cleared off the topsoil."

"No, I'm sure they didn't."

"Of course, it was mainly the old and young that suffered the most. Animals perished, too. They all died, one after the other, from starvation and this illness they called the 'dust'. Some called it pneumonia but it was, more or less, the same thing. It was lurking about us all the time. I survived. I was one of the few lucky ones."

"Glad you did."

"Me too! Those years weren't good for anyone, or anything. Back in the thirties, there wasn't any work going: no work, no money, no food. As I said, nothing grew."

"Bad times indeed."

"Summers burning hot. Hardly a drop of rain fell. Then those winters. Real bitter. Real icy cold. The winds whipped their way through everything. People just dropped down dead, weakened from hunger or smothered by dust. It choked up the lungs, you see. It gunged up the eyes, leaving them red-raw with infection. People went blind. Cattle too. Folks were too poor to buy food let alone buy medicines. Sometimes whole families went. Dust to dust. Charities couldn't cope no more; there was no cash to spare. Times were wretched."

"Sure were."

"Even the Brigham children got the sickness. They were retching for weeks on end. But being the Brighams, they could afford the doctor. Pa told me that one night he had to drive round a 'twister' to fetch the doctor up for one of the girls. It was a lucky break for me because, just as the doctor was about to leave, Ma went into labour. So Ma and I got the best medical care money could buy ... that is if we'd had the money. The doctor didn't charge us farm hands anything if he was already out on call. I bet my poor ma was crazy with fear thinking that, at any moment, I was going to be snatched away and hurtled down to the Holy Cross. Anyhow, as luck would have it, things went in my favour. You see, Delphine, there were just so many orphaned or abandoned that the mission had to close its doors. It couldn't take in any more kids. So, as things turned out, Ma was allowed to keep me with her and Mae was sent for. And then luckily everything fell right into place."

"Well, they say good things come out of bad."

"You make me laugh!"

"Hey!"

"But sadly, many people had it just too bad; luck wasn't on their side. And, the Great Depression that hit us back in the '20s and '30s caused problems for just about everyone. Me, Ma and Pa were caught right up in the middle of it; it was like being in quicksand. You couldn't move. If you tried to do anything to help yourself, things just got worse. You were stuck and slowly sinking in a great dust desert."

"Didn't your folks try moving on then?"

"No, we couldn't. There wasn't any way. No way out. We belonged, you see, to the Brighams. In many a way we were just like slaves tied to our masters. We couldn't survive without them. They couldn't survive there without us. They kept us poor on purpose; it was in their interest. We kept on plodding this never-ending rut, going on and on. Did you ever see that film, *The Grapes of Wrath*, Delphine?"

"No. I read the book, though."

"Those people Steinbeck goes on about were rich as kings compared to the likes of us. Many of those 'Okies' had the wherewithal and resource to escape their lives whereas the folks down our way had nothing, nothing at all. We had to stay. No transport, apart from our feet. Every cent we earned we were owing someone else. And even if we had had the strength to walk, there were still hundreds of miles of smarting desert to cross."

"Imprisoned in your own backyard."

"Like a chained dog! And the air in that backyard was always sour-heavy with dust. It was acrid. Foul. I can taste it now!"

"D'you want a drink, Kitty, to take away that taste?"

"No, I'm okay really, thanks dear. I'll just drink in the sweetness of this fine, clear air. — Ah, that's better!"

"And to think I go about complaining how much dusting there needs doing around this place!"

"I know, well times have changed, thank goodness. But, let me tell you, the dust back then didn't just pile; somehow, it stole its way inside absolutely everything. Even with doors and windows rag-jammed shut it burgled its way through. It just kept crawling and creeping in, and on, and under. It's surprising I survived at all."

"You must have been hardy stuff, Kitty. You still are."

"That's true. Ah, is that George I can hear downstairs? Is he back already? That was a quick shop. Maybe he was running away from Lucia."

"No, don't think so. Just the wind banging. Time we went in soon. Now, how about a little hot drink? With all that chatting about dust in the air my throat is dry as the Sahara."

"Go on then. I suppose I could do with a coffee now. By the way, how's the stitching going? I'm glad you're doing it. I could never be bothered with mending. I can tell you don't like doing it either. Now, if you're getting us a drink, I wouldn't say no to a small piece of George's rum cake, that's if you're asking. It would be so rude not to eat it if he's gone to the trouble of making it for us."

"It would indeed. Right-e-o, I'll put this down and go and get us some straight off. I could do with a break from stabbing my finger. Now, wait 'til I get back before you go on with your story. No talking to yourself, now!"

"Yes Ma'am! Would you like me to finish that hem off for you whilst you're gone?"

"No I would not! You're worse than I am. Leave it be. I'll only be a couple of minutes. In fact, it's getting rather chilly. Let's pop back inside and shut the door?"

"No, not yet. I like that freshness. I love the smell of the early evening air. I'm not cold."

"Well, that was lovely, Delphine. Thanks. Nice cake, nice and sticky. Now, where was I? D'you want me to go on?"

"Of course I do. Let me see, ah, you were looking through the fence, looking at the big house, waving at your mother."

"Oh yes. I'm drifting a bit, aren't I? Pull me up if I do it again."

"No, you say it how it comes. It comes from the heart and that's good."

"Okay, then. Well, aside from being forbidden contact with Ma, I wasn't allowed, of course, to mix with those Brigham kids. I think they thought I was tainted with poverty or something and would give them some awful disease. I knew no different. I didn't like it but I just accepted that's how things were. Children do, don't they?"

"They do indeed."

"Our little house, or shack I should say, was bang next door to the big house. Just a picket separated us. From over the fence, during the summer months, I could hear the squeals and squeaks of delight as the children played outside. They had some fun! I could see the sisters bouncing on their pogo-sticks, throwing their hoops, trotting and cheering their pony around the pasture. I could hear the yells from the boys frolicking in the pool, splashing each other and having water fights, or playing 'Cowboys and Injuns' with pop-guns and wooden arrows. I would press my face through the slats in the white fencing that divided their world from mine and watch their jollity. Oh, and I'll tell you something, the parties they had! And you thought mine were wild when I was younger, Delphine!"

"They were! They were certainly wild upon many an occasion, Kitty."

"Not in the same way. Shiny cars would draw up to the big house and whole families would jump out and shriek and laugh until darkness fell. Fireworks would be let off. Air heavy with tobacco or frying chicken or spiced squash would drift across, and the honey-sweet smell of cakes and warm fruit tarts baking in the ovens would waft through our door. I so loved to smell it.

I was alone much of the time. I played by myself with whatever I could find. I was only about four or five when Mae went to work full-time in the kitchens. Ma, I think, had been promoted to being in charge of the children ... as well as the housework. I saw her less and less. The nursery maid, I think, had run away, or got sick, and Ma just took on all her jobs. Pa's work was to help around the place. He kept the yard and stables going, you know, chopped the wood, worked wherever he was needed. Did I tell you Pa had been born on the ranch?"

"No, I didn't know that."

"I think his parents were, too; they never left the place, except to fetch provisions in from town. He kept the gardens and lawns just fine. I can still see them. He definitely had green fingers."

"That's where you probably got yours."

"Maybe. Pa really loved to garden, but it was too much for him, far too much for him to manage, particularly as his health was never too good. He was a sick man. His coughing would often keep me awake at night. Sometimes, I'd sit up in bed and see my father leaning against the porch staring out at the mountains. He was always trying to get his breath. I'd watch him for a bit and try to see what it was he was actually staring at. I'd scramble out of my cot and tiptoe across. 'What you looking at? What's over there, Pa?' I'd say. He'd look down at me and whisper in his wheeze, 'Another land, Kitty-Kat, another land.' And reaching down he would gently take hold of my little hands in his big gnarled ones and swing me high onto his shoulders. 'It's a lifetime's journey away,' he'd say. 'Too far for the likes of us.'

✳ ✳ ✳

About once a month I'd go on an outing with my father to town. We'd pick up provisions and mail from the rail depot. I loved those outings. If it was Ma's day off, the three of us would go along together. We'd sit high up on the buggy and Vladimare, the pony, would trot the road to Elkhorn. It must have been about ten miles or so but Ma and I would snuggle up on that bench and we'd sing away in full throttle. Neither of us had a voice but it didn't matter one jot.

First we'd go and wait for the mail train to arrive. People came from all over the area. Families of all ages shouting and laughing. Children running amok. Street vendors gathering crowds. Some came, like us, to do errands or pick up their parcels; others just for the excitement of it all. People dressed up as best as they could: women wearing hats, husbands with hair shined and parted dead straight, combed sleekly to one side or the other. Children with red-scrubbed cheeks playing games of tag. Skipping. Kicking balls. Hop-scotching. Playing school. I just joined in with anyone and ran along with the chase. We all did that. Whilst the train waited to be unloaded, a man with a monkey in a cage would sometimes clamber down from it. He would entertain the crowd with dance and song. Sometimes the monkey wore a little railroad suit and at other times it would be dressed like an old lady with a lace bonnet pulled down over its ears.

Once he had a bear with him, or rather, it was supposed to be a bear. Struggling, he'd lift down a battered, shaking container from a wagon-car. I don't think anyone actually saw the bear but we all heard it roar and heard it scratch the inside of the container with its long sharp claws. There were streaks of blood and rips on the clothing of the bear-keeper's body. Sometimes people would toss a few coins into the man's cap on the ground. Other times there were no coins for the throwing. The monkey man would shout insults and holler that the people of Elkhorn were the meanest folk he'd ever seen, unlike those good people of the previous town. He warned the crowd that he would not stand for misers and, as punishment to the folk of Elkhorn, he would set the bear loose to eat up their children. The gathered crowd would laugh at his threat. We children all wished that he would let the bear free but, disappointingly, he never did get round to it.

At other times travellers would get off and sell their wares. Often there'd be a cure for pneumonia or blindness, or even a potion to make a lover return to his, or her, beloved. People would jeer, then cheer, it was all very good natured. My mother loved it. She loved the razzmatazz of it all. And I loved to see her smile and hear her giggles. I would laugh too. She would pick me up high and swing me around and around until I was so dizzy that I couldn't stand properly when she set me down again.

Pa was more restrained in town. It was his job, after all, to fetch the mail. He was quite a bit older than Ma, and he took his role most seriously. But he was happy enough to see Ma and me enjoying ourselves. Sometimes Ma would chat to complete strangers, asking them where they were going and where they came from. She loved to hear their tales, their life tragedies and their hopes for the future. At other times Ma would meet up with a friend or a relative from her home town for a good gossip. Proudly she would introduce me and boast how well she was doing, about our 'fine' life and the luxurious parties in the big house.

There were a couple of bars in town but neither sold alcohol. It was Prohibition at the time. Sure there were drug stores where alcohol could be got for 'medicinal' reasons but most people acted civilly and soberly. Pa would stay by the pony, chewing gum or tobacco. He was a quiet man. He was not one for chatting. How Ma and Pa came to marry, I really don't know. They were like chalk and cheese. I suppose there was not much to choose from.

If there was women's shopping to be done for the Brighams, Ma would let me go along with her to the store. She would wander along the reels of cottons and materials, delicately feeling each one between her fingers or scrunching them up as if she was actually going to buy the 'red silk', or maybe the 'blue velvet', for her own personal use. She would lift up the soaps and the powders to her nose, breathe in their violet or rose scent and sigh a deep contented sigh with her eyes half closed. Whenever she passed a mirror on a wall she would stop, pout, ruffle her hair, give herself a sideways glance. I thought she was beautiful. I can see her now, posing like a film star at the ice-cream counter and winking at the boy serving. I remember her lifting me up on to a bar stool and smiling sweetly like Clara Bow right into the lucky boy's eyes. Some-times in return for her smile, the boy would hand me an ice pop to suck or a frothy cup of soda to sip. I don't think money ever changed hands.

But at other times Ma would go and chat with one of her town friends. She had a friend, Ruby. She was a seamstress who had a little workshop off the main drag. Ruby and Ma grew up together. I wanted to go visit with her but Ma said no, I'd be bored and become a nuisance. She said it was only talk of the old days, way before I was born or even a twinkle. Neither Ma nor Pa ever talked to me about the old days. I didn't like to ask. I knew she was sore about something and she didn't want to talk. Pa said to let Ma be. I never thought about grandparents. The idea that I had some family somewhere, you know, people that were related to me, never even crossed my mind.

I still don't know even to this day where my folks came from.

Just before the train pulled out of the station at Elkhorn, the driver would signal the departure by trumpeting its horn. All the children would gather along the line in an excited group and when the train started to move they would race alongside the carriages waving and shouting. Eventually only a few children were still left running alongside the track; one by one they would drop out as the engine gathered its momentum. I used to run alongside too and with my long legs I could keep going further than most of the other girls. Sometimes there was an open end carriage and passengers would stand there and cheer and even throw a few cents out to the winning child. With those few cents you were rich. You could buy sweets ... and of course with that currency you could then buy loyal friends. I ran with the fastest but I was never the first.

But on one occasion I found a coin that hadn't been spotted by the others. What excitement! Back at the store I bought my treasure; three large jaw-breakers in red and pink and yellow, garish and nasty-looking, but so, so delicious. I gave one each to Ma and Pa and on the way home we sat in the buggy, silently sucking and dribbling, totally unable to speak. I remember thinking that I had wished I'd got one to give to

Vladimare to suck. That would have been so funny.
I let her lick my fingers instead. Thoroughly satisfied
we wiped our mouths on the backs of our sleeves and
Pa looked right happy. I felt like a princess having
owned such riches.

You see, we had no money of our own really to
spend at the stores. Maybe Pa bought some tobacco or
gum and Ma may have bought some paper or envelopes
to send letters, or swap a film-star magazine with a
friend. We hardly ever bought any provisions for ourselves. Our daily food was generally provided from the
waste food left over from the Brigham family's meals.
They conceded that we could eat their scraps. But with
our buggy chock full of provisions destined for the
Brighams we felt like real rich folk. Those monthly trips
were so good. Then something changed my life forever.

❋ ❋ ❋

Delphine squeezed my hand. "Hey, let's go in
now. It's getting a bit on the chilly side for us two old
ladies."

"Whatever you say."

"I think George's home now ... not been eaten
up this time by that Lucia! You sit over there in the
armchair. I will make up a fire in a bit. Nice and cosy.
Tomorrow we will have more stories."

2

Mae went. I think I must have been around about four or five. Her services no longer required. The Depression had affected everyone, even the Brighams. The children's ponies, beloved, long fringed and shiny coated, were auctioned off. I heard the girls' squeals and protestations. The pool was sealed over, emptied of its cooling content. The raucous night-time parties and opulence of dinners ended. The day of Mae's departure arrived. We drove to Elkhorn. Mae bought a ticket going somewhere. She stepped up into the carriage. That was it: no tears, no hugs, no forwarding address. On the platform we stood and stared. The train pulled away. I didn't run alongside. Ma waited unmoving, caught still like a statue of Ruth alone amid the alien corn. Without stirring she watched as the last remnant of her past chugged away. The remembrance of a childhood fading in the grey of steam and smoke. Eventually the train, a mere shadow, hovered on the horizon. Mae's departure had cut Ma's last connection to a life once lived.

Before long other farmhands and domestics started to leave. Finally, apart from the Brighams themselves and a couple of the old stock men, we were the only ones left to work the ranch. The land parched. The resplendent green and gold of the pastures soon turned to grey grit. The air didn't smell good. It became dry. It braised the insides of your mouth and nose. Everything hung tired and heavy. The bones of the cattle became prominent through hides that swung loose. Some just dropped dead right in front of us, their legs crumpling underneath them. Crops failed to grow and the hens became feather-light and scrawny. They scratched themselves an awful lot. The abundance of melon, golden peaches and rich-red cherries of previous years was not forth-coming. There was not even enough fruit on the trees to bottle and even fewer left-overs for us to feed on. "There's work for the asking in the big cities," Ma said. But Pa would not hear of it. "The ranch is my home. I was born here and like my mother and father before me I will die here, God rest them. Anyhow," he continued, "next year everything will be just fine again. Mr Brigham said as much. It's just a bad patch we're going through."

Pa did his best around the place but he wasn't too well. His breathing was getting heavier and bad sounding. Some nights I'd wake up and the room was strangely silent. I'd get up and find him gone from his bed. He would take a gun off with him and try to shoot down some rabbits. I don't ever remember him bringing anything home to eat.

As I got taller I was able to look right over the fence at the Brigham children playing their games. They all seemed more fractious, more petulant than before. One day I was poking my nose across when a big pebble hit me right on the cheek-bone. The children had obviously seen me watching them and had decided I would be a good source of amusement. As it was my fault for being there spying I didn't tell Ma or Pa. I told them that I'd fallen over some dead wood and gashed my face. But it happened again, and again. It became a ritual to them. I was their 'injun' and they were determined to hunt me out. Sometimes they catapulted stones, other times bits of splintery wood flew through the air. They yelled at me, mocked me and delighted in hurling insult with words I didn't understand but knew in my heart were bad. I hurled those words back, not knowing what I was yelling.

The end of the summer holidays came and the Brigham children were sent back to school. I was relieved; my peace returned. By that time they only came home once or twice a year. I was safe again. There was no schooling for me, of course. Too far from anywhere. But Ma could read good and even write her letters. It looked like magic when she did it. I loved watching her. She was so clever. Sometimes, when the Brighams were staying up in town, she borrowed books from the big house. Once she brought me over a children's book belonging to one of the girls. I cried when she took it back the next day. It had pictures of bunnies dressed up in ladies' clothes and bonnets. On the pages there were words and those words told a story about the rabbits. I wanted it again. But Ma said she wouldn't bring it over again because I got so upset. I think she was probably afraid I would damage it, or even hide it. Sometimes she brought over some scraps of old paper and she'd draw me some squiggly lines. These, she told me, were words and she said what they meant. Then she would mix all the squiggles up and I had to guess which squiggle was which word. It was a good game. She clapped when I got it right. She told me about other countries; a world where kings and queens still lived. I didn't know there were so many other places apart from Elkhorn and the big house. I wanted to see them. But I knew I couldn't because Pa said that they were over the mountains, in another world, another lifetime; they were not for the likes of us.

When it was too cold I'd sit inside and look out of the windows. I'd press my nose up against the cold glass and draw squiggles and pictures on the misted panes with my fingertips. Each pane was a different picture. The real mountains outside the window were the backdrop and I would draw, in the foreground on the wet glass, little figures and animals and houses and trains. I could make up all these imaginary worlds, each in its own frame with its own story. In my mind I walked through those scenes with two leg-like fingers; sometimes to the mountains beyond, but no further. I would get to the top of the ridge but I could never see over. I didn't know what there was to see. Were queens living there, swathed in rubies and emeralds, and winged dragons of purple swooping about? Were there people-sized mice dressed as washer women chatting to each other, and shiny green frogs kissing princesses on lily ponds, and wolves eating little girls in red cloaks? I had no idea what I would see. I could go no further. It could be dangerous. There could be lions.

One year, after the snows melted, we all went off to Elkhorn for the monthly mail and provisions. Ma was really eager to go. She had letters saved up to be posted. She'd hidden them but I knew where they were. I really wanted to read them but, without pictures, I couldn't do the big words. I don't know why she hid them because Pa couldn't read either; bad sight, he'd tell me when I asked. Ma was now working very long hours at the big house. Dark big smudges of purple sank deep under eyes. She was tired. She'd asked Mrs Brigham if I could come and help work alongside her as a kitchen maid ... free of charge, of course. She told her I could be learning domestic skills. Apart from needing an extra pair of hands I think Ma was probably lonely working by herself. Surprisingly, Mrs Brigham agreed but on the condition I never left Ma's side nor spoke to anyone unless spoken to first. At first I loved working alongside Ma.

This day I helped Ma unpack all the provisions out of the buggy from our trip into town. There were such luxuries like I'd never seen before: shiny tins of biscuits, a pair of sweet-smelling leather gloves and a blue and gold bottle of *4711* cologne. I unpacked while Ma sorted out the mail. I saw her stop mid-way through the sorting and carefully slide an envelope into the pocket of her apron. I'd just finished putting away when I saw Ma half-hidden in the larder cupboard. She was reading something, head bent low. "What you doing, Ma?" I asked, peeping around the door. "Nothing to do with you," she snapped. "Mind your own business!" She glowered at me and clicked the door shut. I stood and waited. A few minutes later she brushed straight out and passed me without a downward glance. I didn't understand what I'd done wrong. I just knew Ma was upset and I didn't know why.

In the following weeks Ma seemed to change. She became more and more silent, more reclusive, more secretive. No more reading and writing games. I just trailed around after her in the big house, dusting and waxing and dusting again, and again. I tried to do exactly what she told me to do. I didn't want to upset her any more than I had done. There was no more chatter or laughter. No more clapping of hands, or skipping. She acted just the same with Pa. When he dared speak to her she snapped him back ferociously.

"Is Ma sick?" I asked Pa one day. I was frightened she might die.

"No," he said, "she's just a bit down. Bit out of sorts. She'll crack out of it soon enough."

But with the weeks passing her anger increased. She looked grey like the land; deep frown lines rutted her brow. Her lush hair of which she had been so particular and so proud was stringing greasy and unkempt down her back. I wanted so much to make her better. One night, after she finished work, I asked her if I could brush out her hair for her. I thought it would make her happy. She turned upon me with such savagery. She yelled that there was nothing wrong with her hair and that it was mine that needed a thorough brushing. She hit me with the brush at every stroke she tore down my long plaits. Then, yanking, she dragged me across to the sink where, from a drawer, she got out her rusted scissors and, without any to-do, mercilessly cut through my braids right there and then. When her rage subsided I fell to the ground crying and crawled under the bed. Pa must have heard the commotion and came striding in. "What are you doing now, woman?" he hollered. It was the first time I'd ever heard Pa raise his voice.

Ma never said sorry to me. In fact I don't remember her ever speaking to me again except to order me to finish some job for her. With my hair sticking out oddly I skulked around the house behind her. I felt bad just being close by. She made me feel as if I had done something really, really wrong. I felt I was being punished for something but I didn't know what it was. Terrified, I couldn't speak, let alone ask her what I'd done. I hung about Pa most of the time. Pa and I would look at each other, eyebrows raised when, in silence, she'd walk straight past us. She didn't seem to want to eat, or even care about feeding me. I helped myself to food from the scrap bowl in the big house and brought some home for Pa.

"Maybe you're right, Kitty. Maybe Ma isn't too well," Pa confided one day. He looked worried. "Next time we go to Elkhorn I will try and pick up a tonic or something from Doc Wadham. Maybe it's the dust in her lungs. I've heard them say it can go to the mind. But don't tell your mother I said that, though. Promise?"

✳ ✳ ✳

"You'd some pretty rough time with your ma, didn't you?" Delphine smiled at me. I nodded back and gently patted her hand.

"I s'pose so. It wasn't easy. But, you know, it was a bit like that nursery rhyme. How does it go? Oh, 'when she was good she was very, very good, and when she was bad she was horrid.' That's how I remember her. Shame, isn't it? Shall I go on now, or finish there?"

"Let's have some lunch first. It must be getting on one o'clock. My stomach here is telling me that. I don't need no fancy watch on my wrist."

"What's George getting us today?"

"Don't remember. Oh yes, I do. There's that gnocchi you like, with sage and butter sauce. Nice and filling. Warm you up for this afternoon."

"Nice, but I think it may put me to sleep as well."

"That's good too. Nothing wrong in that. A sweet dream never hurt nobody."

"How about a nice little glass of rosé as well after all that talking?"

"Now you're talking! I'll fetch the glasses. I won't be a moment."

"Delphine?"

"Yes, Kitty?"

"Changed my mind about that little glass of wine. I'll have a big one instead."

❉ ❉ ❉

You know that low feeling you get when you wake up some mornings? The sun can be beaming a welcome but you know that its warmth and light are not there for you. From the first moment I opened my eyes that day I felt something ominous was about to happen. I felt it in the marrow of my bones. If I think about it I can still feel that foreboding now. I don't really want to think about it.

The three of us were getting ready for our trip to Elkhorn. Pa and I kept looking at each other and then glancing nervously across at Ma. That day she seemed more vital, more spirited, and also a bit on the fidgety side. She seemed to be making an effort to tidy herself for the outing. She scrubbed at her face and, with a stiff brush, she fiercely scoured her clothing. Looking in the mirror she closely examined herself and repeatedly combed and preened her hair. She spat on her shoes and gave them a quick wipe-

over as if that was something she did every day of
the week. I was ready to go and I climbed up on to
the buckboard. Ma quickly followed me up and, for
a frightening moment, I thought she was chasing me
and was about to snap at my ankles. I flinched and
pulled myself tight down on the seat and Ma slumped
down heavily next to me. She sat close to me. Far too
close. It felt odd, as if she didn't notice I was sitting
there next to her. She stayed like that, for the whole
journey mostly staring forward and clutching her bag
like a new-born to the breast. Vladimare trotted out
of the gate and I noticed Ma turned to look back;
she looked back as if there was something she'd left
behind, something she'd lost. Pa kept peering at her
out of the corner of his eye. A death-like stillness
settled about her body. We arrived in Elkhorn, solemnly, as if in cortege. Pa had hardly pulled into the
yard when Ma seemed to waken from her trance, and
before we'd even come to a halt she was scrambling
down. We watched her scurrying towards the depot.
She looked back and yelled, "Wait there!" Pa and I
did what we were commanded. We sat silently, hands
in laps. Apprehensive. Vladimare too, head bowed,
stood respectfully to attention.

Ma returned. She was carrying letters for the
family and some parcels from 'Sears' for Mrs Brigham.
Normally we would try to feel through the brown

wrapping to gauge what was contained within. But that day she just dumped the packages as if she didn't care one way or the other what was hidden inside. She turned to Pa. "I'm spending the afternoon round at Ruby's. Don't disturb me."

"Bye Ma," I shouted. "See you later!" But she was off like greased lightning. She didn't turn around. She didn't wave good-bye. "Say hi to Ruby for me! Have fun!"

Pa and I wandered about the town. His hands were deep in pocket. He doffed his hat and nodded in recognition at people we knew. He tied Vladimare to a hitch post and both of us squatted down on the edge of the walkway. Pa bowed his head into his hands. He stared into the gutter. One foot he scraped backwards and forwards in the dirt. Backwards and forwards. I stood up.

"You go play with the other kids."

"I'm fine, Pa. I'd rather stay here. I don't feel too great either."

Every now and again he raised his hand and wiped the back of his head. I heard him sigh, loud and long. His hands trembled. Maybe he knew something bad was going to happen that day. I sensed his fear. This was not the cheery outing to town I had grown to expect. The sky was darkening. We chewed our gum; we chewed it slowly.

After a while I squatted down again and looked Pa full in the face. Minutes passed. I don't think he noticed I was there. "Shall we go get Ma that tonic from Doc Wadham now?"

He looked down at me. "You know, Kit, you're a right good gal, right good." He ruffled my hair. "But I don't think that will help Ma no more."

"Well, s'pose that's kind of true. Ma seems loads better today. Maybe she's getting out of those dumps." I tried to sound reassuring for Pa. But I wasn't believing what I was saying myself. On top of that I didn't quite understand Pa's drift about a tonic not helping Ma no more but I didn't like to ask.

Suddenly Pa stands up and smiles. "I think you've got a good point there, Kitty-Kat, maybe she's on the mend. Up you get, girl. Let's go get ourselves an ice!"

"Really, Pa?" I couldn't quite believe what I was hearing. "An ice-cream?"

"Why! Don't tell me you don't care for one? If you don't want your share I could always eat it up myself. I've not had one for that many a year that I've a mighty hunger. Don't worry; I'll eat yours, no problem!"

"No, Pa, I can eat one up, no problem either. Wow! Pa, you're the greatest!" I clasp his hand tight in mine and skip alongside him to the store. I scramble on to the stool and Pa pays straight up front, there and then, for a whole ice-cream soda. I don't have to smile like Clara Bow to get one. A tall fat glass of ice-cream appears. Two long silvery spoons swing from the rim. The boy squiggles red sauce on the top and flashes some brightly coloured sprinkles down the sides. It's so beautiful. I put my nose close to and breathe in its perfume. It smells so strawberry-sweet and ice-cool. You can't imagine how good ice-cream feels when your throat's all shot up with the dust. I don't know where to start but Pa just digs in. He is slurping cream around about his mouth and making such contented sounds that it makes me want to laugh. I stand up on the bars of my seat and I dive right in too. It is the best thing I've ever tasted. I can still smell that sweetness and taste that gooey creaminess right now. I can feel the tingle of ice crystals bursting cold on my tongue. I scrape the spoon up and down the sides of my glass. I want to gain the last moments of joy. I give Pa a big hug. "I love you Pa, I love you so much."

"More than strawberry soda?"

"Nearly, Pa."

"Off with you now. Run off and play with the other kids. I'll see you back at the buggy after the train pulls out."

"You sure, Pa?" He nods. I am already half out the door with excitement and ready to tantalise the other kids about the real ice-cream soda I'd just been eating. The bounce is back in my step. Some kids are playing leapfrog and I stop their game to brag.

When the whistle sounds we all gather by the departing train ready for our race. That day I really want to win some pennies to buy a soda for Ma when she's back from Ruby's. I'm so excited. So happy. I jump up and down, waving at the passengers, whooping, running on the spot. Then, 'hoo-hooo', we're off. The train's dragging slowly out of the station ... and, as the cars pass me by, a terrific sadness seems to envelop me. I am running with the others, trying to keep up, but without enthusiasm. The other children are all yelping and 'hoo-haaing'. Passengers are waving from the windows and others standing on the end-platform are laughing and cheering back. And all I feel inside me is a growing emptiness as if somehow I've been set adrift. My pace slows. I watch the train disappear, further and further until it evanesces into a pyre of dust and smoke smouldering red and black on the horizon. I am no longer near the front of the race. My legs come to a stop. Like birds of prey, the other children ravenously pick at the candies and pennies strewn haphazardly across the desert sand.

Hands deep in pockets I shamble back to where Pa is waiting. He sees my face. "What's up, Kitten? No pennies today? Never mind. Maybe next time. We can't all be winners." I shrug my shoulders and climb back into my seat to wait for Ma. After an hour or so Pa turns to me and says, "Ma's taking her time. Run across to Ruby's for me and tell her it's time we got going. Most likely she's chatting so much she's forgotten what time it is. Let's hope she'll be in a better frame of mind now she's had a good old natter." I do what I'm told but I do it with reluctance. I sense something is not quite right long before Ruby answers the door. When she sees me skulking there she does not seem that surprised. "Tell your Pa, Ellie's not here. She left ages ago."

"Where'd she go?"

"I don't know. She just went. Didn't say. Just upped and went."

I walk over to the store. Closed. I look through the windows of the diner and the ice-cream parlour. She isn't in there either. Nor the drug store. Where's Ma? Nobody has seen her around town. I wend my way back to Pa. When I tell him he looks down at the ground. Nothing is said. We tarry a few minutes. Silent. Then with a sigh Pa takes hold of the reins and Vladimare automatically moves forward.

"No! We can't go yet!" I yell. "What about Ma?"

"She'll come back when she's good and ready. You'll see."

That was the last time we ever spoke to each other about Ma's disappearance.

3

"Well, what am I s'posed to do about dinner, then? Eh? Tell me that? I'm not putting up with this behaviour no longer. Where is she?" Mrs Brigham was yelling at Pa. It was already dark. "What's Ellie doing?" she snapped. "By now I thought she would have had the chicken on the roast." Pa's face went red. He clutched his cap tightly in his hands, twisting it from side to side. He stared at the ceiling. He was rasping loud and slow.

"Well? Where's Ellie, then?" Mrs Brigham repeated.

"Well, Ma'am, I don't rightly know." Pa's face was screwed up.

"You don't rightly know where your wife is?" Pa looked real uncomfortable. He was shifting his weight from leg to leg. "What do you mean, Frank? Oh, for goodness sake! Didn't y'all go to town today? Wasn't she with you?"

"She was, Ma'am. But ... she didn't like ... she didn't sort of come back with us."

"Did she get ill, then? What? Just spit it out, Frank."

"I don't really know, Ma'am. I truly don't. She just kind of went. I don't know where she is. We did try and find out, honest to God, but I'm sorry to say we couldn't find her any place. She's just disappeared. Just clear gone."

"Disappeared? Ridiculous!"

"But that's all there is to it, Ma'am, honest. She's gone. Lordie, I wish I knew where to. I'm right sorry about the roast chicken." Pa, I could sense, was trying not to cry; his face was taut, his teeth clenched. For a moment or two Mrs Brigham stood stock still. Then she turned and strode straight out of the room slamming the door loudly behind her. As Pa led me back home I glimpsed silent tears glistening as they rolled down his cheeks.

Ma didn't return the next day, the next week, the next month. Time seemed to move slowly, or not at all. I stood on watch at the window, waiting to see her walking back up the track. My dreams and nightmares were full of her image. I sometimes awoke thinking her disappearance a dream and then reality would slowly crawl its way back over me. The Brighams, of course, took their revenge. In her place they employed a succession of 'helps'. I was not allowed in the house to do the chores nor go to the back-door. They even begrudged me food. Each evening Pa went up to the kitchens but the amount left for him to scavenge after the 'helps' had had their fill was hardly enough to sustain us. With Ma gone we had to survive on Pa's meagre pay, and as the months dragged by life got harder. Incessant winds screeched like ghouls about us and 'dusters' grey and heavy with grit abraded our strength, in mind as well as body. Our monthly trek into Elkhorn still continued. Vladimare slowly dragged us to town through the miasmas of whirling winds. Pa, I think, still thought, or hoped, that Ma would return. We tarried in the station yard just on the off-chance. I pestered Ruby regularly and asked if she'd heard anything. Blankly she just stared back at me, shrugging her shoulders. She didn't seem in the least bothered. The Sheriff took particulars but knew nothing. He didn't seem to be in the slightest bit perturbed, or show any surprise, either.

The storms grew more ferocious and frequent. They grew dark and grew thick. Every morning the floors were covered in ripples of dust as if the tide had come and gone. It was in the air you breathed. It stuck to your skin. It matted in your hair. When the winds blew hard over the plains your eyes smarted and your nostrils clogged. Plagues of shrill grasshoppers began to gnaw their way through the farmlands eating whatever they could. Through the night you could hear enormous centipedes 'sis-sissing' their presence through the wooden walls. They were large, longer than the hand of a grown man. Ceilings sagged and collapsed under the weight of debris. Tarantulas and Black Widows held sway in rooms where parties once were held, their painful bites a reminder of one's own life blood. Nothing dared grow apart from the Russian Weed which ripped across the wind-torn plains. The skies darkened to vulture-black, and ragged trees and ashen bushes avulsed by their roots were lifted clear out of the lifeless dirt. Flames of static electricity whipped like devils dancing the length of fences, and cars blackened by the inferno lay soulless across the land.

It was at this time that the Brighams decided to move back to the city. They told Pa they were leaving until things had much improved. They closed the big house up and left Pa in charge of the ranch. We had no choice. There was no choice. We had to stay. They didn't offer to take us with them. We grew hungrier. Pa hunted, but there was nothing much left to hunt. We had been 'minding' the provisions stored in the big house but, as time went on, the provisions dwindled. The winter came and went. Vladimare died. Then Pa died.

It was my fault, I s'pose, when Pa died. It was the day the big tornado hit our area.

They called it 'Black Sunday'. It was April 14th, 1935. I was outside sitting on my haunches scratching at the earth with a stick desperately looking for a few left over root-vegetables. It was windy, very windy. I'd covered my mouth and nose with a scarf. Dried-up old branches, wrenched from decaying crotched trees, were hurtling across the ground. I looked up. The sky was a strange mix of grey. A mark appeared. And then I saw the sky split apart. A pus-yellow cone oozed through, its noxious content swirling and spewing and heading towards us. I heard a shout. Pa was stumbling, tumbling, scrambling forward. Yelling silently. I couldn't hear; the boom of the wind was far greater. He kept struggling towards me, pointing, reaching out to the house. At first I didn't know what he was meaning. I stood there staring at his wild gestures. But the wind mounting behind shunted me back towards the building. The door was already blown open and I got thrust inside. I turned to look back for Pa, and just before the door banged closed I saw Pa soar upward like an angel, his arms stretched out like wings. A crashing of windows. A drumming as the corrugate of the roof rapped up and down. A smashing as things juddered off the shelves and the walls started to rise. Then drop.

Silence.

I pulled myself up. Pa was not with me. The door was swinging on one hinge. Through the sinking dust I saw him. Pa was lying crumpled against the stoop. His moaning cut through me.

"Get up, Pa! Get up, get up!" His eyes were open. He was alive. I could hear his rasping breath. I tried to drag him. He was too heavy. I tried to roll him over. He screamed. He grabbed my hand and held it close to him. I lay my head on his chest and for a few moments I could feel his heart still pumping through his clothing. The pumping stopped. His eyes closed.

My hand still clasped in his, I lay my body along his side. Eventually, his hand dropped open from mine. I was truly alone. I was only seven, maybe eight, years old. I draped my arm over his chest and drew in the last bit of warmth from his body. I could smell and feel the blood oozing from his mouth. I licked his chin and tasted the saltiness. And there I fell asleep. Life and death entwined.

It was the cold that woke me. I was shivering. My nose and eyes were thick with gunge. I dragged myself away from him and crawled back inside to what remained of my home. I hunched in a corner, whimpering. I was half-awake. I was half-asleep. There was nothing I could take comfort from. The ceiling was a broken jigsaw.

Night passed and, at dawn, a jagged shaft of light awoke me. It glared harshly through what once was our roof. I stood up. And through the hole of a window I saw Pa. He was lying just as I had left him; a crumpled heap of dust-laden rags and jutting, angular bones. Overhead, birds were circling in a sky soaked with blood-red clouds. They were squawking, shrieking and screaling their gluttonous delight at the feast below.

I looked around the room, my world. My world now smashed. It was in a million pieces. Nothing was as it had been. Everything broken. A floor board had lifted and underneath, unscathed, lay a tin. I opened it and inside was a photograph of I don't know who, some old couple. And a handful of dollars. Pa's life savings. My life savings, now. My life, now. I pocketed the money and walked outside. I stood silently staring at the rags that clothed the body of my pa. A shroud of dust was already settling over him. Separating from him, and separated from myself, I strayed through the yard and drifted, without backward glance, onto the track that led towards the highway.

Debris and decay lined my passage. I reached the main road and stopped. I could go right, or go left. Going right was to Elkhorn. Turning left led to the mountain range and to the other world beyond. I turned left. Trucks passed me by, piled high with chairs, chickens, dogs, people, pianos. Sometimes a mule or pony dragging a laden cart would trot along.

Once a dentist's chair with occupant juddered by. The road ahead was dead straight. I kept on walking. I passed abandoned half-buried cars. I passed dug-outs unrecognisable apart from, maybe, just a chimney pot or a few tiles left sticking out of the dirt. Skewered and shrunken animals were strewn along the edge. I kept on walking. The mountains came no nearer. I kept on walking. From the direction of Elkhorn an open back truck chugged along. I could see it was loaded with odd bits of furniture, boxes, dogs yapping and children staring wide-eyed. A woman sat in a rocking chair on the back, nursing a baby. As it overtook, all the children turned around to gape at me. The woman shouted and the truck stopped. Without invitation I hounded up and leapt up on the running board.

"Where you going, girl?" The woman on the chair looked down at me quizzically, her head tilted slightly to one side. I noticed her chair was tied firmly to the inside of the truck. The children sat gawking, their scabby mouths open.

"My aunt's. She lives just over there." I nodded my head towards the mountains.

"That's some distance for a little girl to be walking on her own. Does your Ma know?"

"Uh-huh. She sure does so, Ma'am."

"Well, you can have a lift if you really want. You'll just have to hold on mighty tight. Give me a shout when you're ready to hop off and I will get my Ron to slow it down for you. What's your name?"

"Ruby." It just came into my head. It was the first name I could think of. I don't know why I said it. "Thanks Ma'am."

About six children were crammed amongst the load, niched into small spaces between the goods. Most were older than I but a couple were a bit younger. The older ones were holding onto the younger ones, stopping them toppling. A girl about five, missing front teeth, smiled. After a while she crawled across to clamber up to me.

"You be careful now, Lucille," the mother shouted.

"You look mighty sad, Ruby," Lucille said. "Do you want to hold my dolly for a bit? Her name's Jacqueline. That's a French name." She thrust the almost hairless and naked doll towards my face. I pushed it away. "Well, if you change your mind, just ask. You can hold her whenever you want." She squeezed herself back into her space. She lay her head against her mother's knee and started to suck her thumb. Her mother stroked her hair fondly. I turned my face away.

The mother was speaking to me. "You know what, Ruby, I think you can swap places with one of my boys for a bit. Give those little arms of yours a break." She knocked on the roof of the cab and the truck came to a halt. "Ron," she called, "get one of the kids out the front to swap places with the little girl. I don't want her falling off the back." There was a commotion inside but eventually a tall gangly lad climbed out and I clambered into his place at the front. There were two more bigger kids in there. Nobody spoke.

I must have fallen asleep because suddenly we were stopped. "This is as far as we're going today," Ron said. "You need to get out now. We'll be stopping the night here. Where is it you're going again?" I pointed across to the mountain range where the sun was setting low over the tops. I got out and saw the family were making up some sort of camp for the night. The boys were scrambling around looking for bits of dried firewood. Again I started walking along the road. The mother shouted after me. "Ruby, if you want to stay over with us tonight, that's okay." I continued walking but the road was debris-strewn with vegetation. I got my ankle caught in some brambles and fell down into a ditch. It felt good lying in the ground. I didn't want to get up again. I stayed still, feeling the earth around me, wondering what it would be like to be buried under the soil. To me, it seemed comforting. I didn't want to move. I heard children's voices in the distance. I pulled myself under the bushes as far as I could so as to be hidden if they happened to come too close. It was of no avail. I could feel myself being dragged out by my ankles.

"Leave me alone," I yelled. I kicked. I lashed out. I punched whoever it was that was pulling me. "Put me down! Put me down!" Then I screamed out all those words that I had learnt from the Brighams back at the big house. But with all my wrestling the children somehow still kept hold of me and carried me, struggling like a snared animal, back to the truck.

Ron sat me down in front of the fire. He held me tightly by the shoulders. "Now, young woman. Sit still! It's mighty dangerous to be out on the road at night. There'll be snakes and all sorts of wild creatures out there. You stay with us 'til morning. Then we'll drive you over to your aunt's. We must be close by now, unless she's living up in those hills? Your ma shouldn't have let you come out so far on your own. I'm surprised she let you. You're not telling us no fibs, are you?"

"My ma don't care where I am," I yelled back.

"Now, I'm sure that's not the honest truth, but your aunt must care a bit otherwise you wouldn't be going up there now, would you? You just sit still. Don't move and I will let go of your arm. If you start wriggling again I will tie you down."

"I don't belong to you," I hollered.

"Be quiet, girl! I may not be your pa but I can still give you a good hiding."

The children were all standing around their ma. I pulled a face at them and stuck out my tongue. I sat there glowering. I was outnumbered; I knew that. They were all watching me. A big cooking pot was fetched out from the back of the truck. The ma threw in some vegetables, beans and some water. The boys went rabbiting but came back empty handed. As it grew dark, dishes were filled from the bubbling pot and passed around the family. The ma came over and gave me a bowl. I shook my head. She put the bowl down by my side.

"Now, you eat that up, Ruby," she said, much to the protestation of the others.

"I'll eat it, Ma." I heard some of the kids cry out.

"She don't want it."

"It's not fair!"

"I'm still hungry."

"She's not even family."

"That's enough, now!" the ma snapped back. "It's her share. Let her be. She may get an appetite later on. Poor kid. She looks more than half-starved. Little mite."

The family huddled down under their coats, hitching bits of ragged blankets over themselves. They crowded around the fire. I watched them until I heard their sounds of sleep then, furtively, I dipped my fingers into the stew and lapped it all up. It tasted good. I licked the bowl clean and, exhausted, fell into deep sleep.

4

It was dawn when I awoke. A blanket was tucked over me. Lucille's doll, corpse-like with eyes rigid and staring, lay by my side. In my fancy of half-sleep, I was back home, curled up in bed with Ma and Pa, their smell mingling warm with mine. A passing moment of bliss ... then the bitter-cold bucket of reality doused me, snatching my breath away. Gasping for air and with heart battering I fought against awakening. Let me sleep for ever. But no, the fantasy was over. I woke to a nightmare world. I pushed myself up onto my elbows and watched as the sun gouged through the trees and scowl of hills behind. And, shoving aside my cover, I quietly pulled myself up. 'Happy Family' were still snoozing. Lucille's doll had fallen face down, her nakedness exposed. I got hold of it by its few remaining strands of hair and let it drop into the smoulder of the dying fire. Its face crumpled in anguish. And with the hurt done I stealthed away through the thick scrub.

Realising that once their belongings were packed up the family would probably try to hunt me down, I decided to hide low. Spotting a thicket of dried-up bushes, I crouched down and peered out through the brush. Sure enough, their truck soon shunted by. I watched it pass. I caught sight of Lucille. She was crying on her mother's lap. What a cry-baby! I felt pleased she could hurt too. I continued darting through the undergrowth. 'Happy Family' didn't reappear, so with an animal-like vigilance I went back trailing the dusty road. I hid whenever I heard the rumble of tyres. I stooped low.

A small side-road forked to the right. It was heading up into the hills. I chose to take the turning. A signpost stood at the junction. I couldn't read it. It didn't matter though. It would have been meaningless. This road was quiet. No traffic disturbed me. I moved along, passing battered shacks and sheds and other 'tumble-downs' still clinging to the earth. A few little farmsteads hung on the side of road, dilapidated and abandoned. Time passed. I felt nothing. I followed the line of the road into the hills. A dribble of water bubbled from a little creek down an embankment. I clambered down through the tangle of undergrowth and squatted down at the water's edge. I wiped my face and hands clean in the cool water and cupped my hands to drink. The water made me hungry. I was hungry.

A barking in the distance. I followed its yapping, drawn instinctively to the sound of the living. A little house came into sight. It had a lean-to at one side and was surrounded by a patch of tended land. On the porch a couple of old folks sat rocking, their chairs squeaking with each lurch. They spied me coming along the road. They were eating some fruit; apples, I think. I was hungry. When I got to the front yard I stopped and hovered outside their gate. The dog kept barking. I stared at their food longingly. I was hungry. They were chewing. I was hungry. I could hear the crunch of the fruit against their teeth and the squelch of juice on their tongues. They rocked backwards and forwards, their chairs creaking and squealing. The man spat a pip out on the dirt. The dog strained at its chain to get at it. The woman reached for some bread and threw it. The mutt caught it, swallowing it in one gulp. I was hungry. They looked at me. They said nothing. I stared at them. They said nothing back. So, jutting my tongue out at them, I continued on my way. Several times I looked back. They were still straining their heads to watch me go. Chewing. Maybe they'd never seen a girl, a hungry girl, walking on her own in the middle of nowhere before.

As I got higher along the road the land appeared less parched. My eyes hurt but I constantly searched for signs of fruit on trees. I didn't bother taking any more turnings to left or right. I just kept on going straight up as if being drawn towards my goal. Somehow I felt the road was leading me to where I needed to be. I didn't know where I was, and I didn't care. My feet and legs were hurting, my head was hurting, my eyes were sore and my stomach ached, but I just kept moving on. Searching for I don't know what. The sun was lowering in the sky and I needed shelter. A derelict hut loomed into view. A shutter was swinging off a window frame. I could see holes in the roof and the yard looked as it had been previously ransacked. I went inside the enclosure and scratched at the dirt. Apart from the dead skin of a rotten-soft carrot there was nothing edible. Its putrid smell put me off even trying its flesh. All I could glean were some roots. I gnawed them. As darkness came I lay down, leaning my head, hesitatingly, against the wall. Like me, the hut was empty, nothing inside. All the furniture and niceties gone. I was out of the wind, that was good. Wind saps your strength. It takes your life away. Throughout that night the shutter creaked and creaked. I could hear bugs moving about me. On me. I was so tired, I didn't care. I disappeared into sleep, hoping not to waken.

The next day the warmth of the sun kissing my face eased my eyes open. I got up and searched the yard. There was nothing. Nothing at all edible. My eyes hurt. My throat hurt. Nobody to care if I lived or if I died. Nobody knew where I was. There was nobody to know! No point whimpering; no one to hear. I walked on. As the morning haze cleared, I saw, spread across the land, signs of human life. Buildings appeared like rips on a greying table cloth. Some had smoke rising from chimneys. A smell of home. I edged along and surveyed their land for food. Apart from the occasional dandelion, there was nothing for the taking. Then on the horizon I noticed tractors and horses moving slowly and deliberately across far fields.

Ding! Ding! Ding! I could hear a bell. I tracked the sound as I moved along. Ding! Ding! It stopped. I stopped. Then, as if summoning me to follow its call, the bell started up again. Clanging on and on. Entranced like a child in the Pied Piper, I was drawn forward. The ringing ceased but, still enlured, I continued. At a crossroads I halted. I turned a corner and saw a car parked outside a small timber building. I walked towards it. All was quiet but the door was open. A path led me up to the entrance. Without thinking twice I peeped inside. Three desks, three deep, stood neatly in rows. Each desk was set out prepared with paper, pencil, an eraser, ruler and book. A dark piano filled one corner of the room, and pictures, maps and a flag were pinned hither and thither across the walls. Behind a table, high on a dais, sat a woman, bespectacled, examining, what I later understood to be, an attendance register. Her chin rested on her folded hands. A floor board creaked beneath me and, startled, she looked up. Soft blue eyes stared at me hovering in the doorway.

"You're very late," she said to me.

"I'm sorry, Ma'am."

"Speak up! What did you say?"

"I'm sorry," I said louder.

"Well, please don't do it again. Punctuality is most important. Now, take your place. Name, please?" I stopped. I couldn't think who I was, or who I was supposed to be, or who I should be.

"Name?" she said again.

"Kit," I answered looking down.

"Kit what?" She gave a deep sigh. "What's your second name? You know, a surname."

I had to think about this. I had never thought about having another name before. Everyone knew me as Kit. Sometimes Pa called me Kitty-Kat. But I didn't think this lady meant that name. My ma's second name was Ellie and Pa's was Frank. Then I remembered that when Ma got mail, the envelope would say 'Ellie Wardle'. I remember tracing her two names with my fingers and asking why she had two. 'We all have two names,' she would say. 'When I married your pa, I took his second name and when you were born you got his second name too. It means you're a family, like the Brighams are a family. It means y'all one family.'

"I think it's Wardle," I said.

Opening a large book in front of her she ran her pencil slowly down the page. "I can't see your name here in the register. Wardle, did you say? ... Are you new here, by any chance?"

"Yes, Ma'am. I think so."

"Well you should have said so earlier. I'm quite new here too so I don't know everyone yet. Now, Kit Wardle, apart from punctuality, I expect honesty from all my pupils. Do you understand?" I nodded. "Good. I have no time for children who say one thing and then do the other. Age?"

"Nine. No seven, I think, or six, no, nine."

"Date of birth then?"

That was one I really had no idea about. Sometimes when I was little Ma or Pa would say, 'I think it's your birthday today, Kitty-Kat. You're four', or, 'you're six', or whatever the age I was that year. And Pa would swing me up in the air and Ma would bring me something from the big house or draw me a picture with coloured pencils. Sometimes she made a chain of cut-out dollies for me. That was fun. But I didn't remember being told it was my birthday of late. I didn't remember being either seven, or eight. Maybe I was still six.

"Don't know, Ma'am."

"Okay then. Parents' names and address?"

"I don't have parents, or an address, Ma'am."

"Everyone has parents at some time. Otherwise you wouldn't be alive. Who do you live with, then?"

I shook my head and suddenly I started to feel dizzy and real sick deep in my stomach. I don't know if it was just hunger, the dusty water, or maybe the roots I'd been chewing, or even trying to answer all the hard questions. I darted outside. Before I could stop myself I vomited in the yard. The woman followed me out. "Oh, dear!" she said.

"I'm really sorry, Ma'am," I said. Then I vomited once more.

Gently, she rested her hand on my shoulder and wiped the hair out of my face. "Better out than in. That's what I say. You better come back inside and lie down for a bit. You'll be all right soon, you'll see." She guided me back between the desks through to another room. It was a small room with flowery wallpaper. Beneath a window a couch was strewn with needle-work cushions. They were covered with pictures of cats and dogs. I caught sight of one, a Scottie dog with snow-topped mountains behind. "You lie down there, now. I'll fetch some water and a cloth and give you a bit of a mop-up," she said. I lay my head down on the Scottie dog cushion and stared around the room. There were a lot of interesting things to be seen. Soon she was back carrying a bowl of warm water. It felt good to have my hands and face washed and wiped dry. I pretended it was the mother Scottie cleaning its puppy with her tongue. She put a towel under my head and a pot by my side. "Use it if you need it," she said. "Now have a sleep. I need to get back to class. We can sort you out later and then we need to get on with lessons."

She padded softly away, shutting the door quietly behind her. The heavy curtains were closed and the room warmly dark. Apart from the couch and an armchair, there was a table crisply clothed in gingham and a place set neatly for one. A kerosene lamp sat on a mantle shelf and a gilt framed mirror hung from the wall. There was a radio-set on a cupboard alongside a gramophone player with two records lying on its lid, and a dresser chock-full of pretty china and ornaments. A pot-bellied stove stood in a corner next to a sink. Framed pictures covered the walls. From my bed I studied the painting of brightly coloured houses overlooking a shimmering lake. I couldn't see any people in the scene. My eyes closed. And in my dream world I crept into the picture and sat dozing by a tethered boat on the empty shore.

First I smelt the soup and then I heard her voice. "Wake up, sleepy-head." She stroked the hair from my face. "You've been asleep now quite some hours. It's time you were on your way but I think you should have some soup before you go home. It'll do you good, particularly if you've not been too well. And I've also got a note written out for you to take back. Give it to your parents ... or whoever it is you're living with." She sat by my bed and she fed me, sip by sip, spoons of the hot broth. I can still savour it now. I opened and closed my mouth like a fledgling. It was so good. I didn't want the bowl to ever empty. Eventually she said, "That's probably enough now. I don't want to make you sick again. Now, let's see you get up. Yes, that's better. You've got some colour back in your cheeks, too. Now, run along and don't forget to take this note back home. I will look forward to seeing you back here tomorrow. Don't be late this time. I like my school in order. Lessons start at nine am ... on the dot! You'll hear the bell. Now, which way do you live?" I pointed left and walked off in that direction. At the crossroads I turned to look back over my shoulder. She was standing there waving at me. I waved back.

5

The school squatted on a small plot near the crossroads. I turned the corner and dawdled past some houses and a store. I was in no hurry to get anywhere. I didn't know where, or why, I was going. I could just about make out the recognisable shape of a gas station so I headed off that way. It was closed down. A dog on a chain strained snarling at me from a shed. A voice yelled out to 'shut it'. A collapse of small dwellings lay about me, scattered and frayed. This town wasn't big like Elkhorn. I passed by a chapel, its doors shuttered. Ahead I could make out skeins of tangled trees and a shatter of shacks silhouetted grey against the skyline. Several cars trundled by, their occupants nosing out at me out from the windows. Nobody stopped. The sun was lowering and I spotted, half-hidden behind some scrub, a dugout. It looked abandoned. I wandered up to the door and pushed it open. A wall of air heavy with the sour stench of rot swung back. A drape of spiders' webs hung like grimed lace across the window opening. I wasn't too bothered. Spiders I quite liked except for when they bit me bad. Rats were what I feared the most, but I couldn't see any signs of their encroachment.

For a while I mooched about the yard seeing what I could see but, just like the night before, there was nothing much to be had. I kept thinking about the soup I'd eaten. I could still smell it on my breath and taste its saltiness on my tongue. I wished I could've eaten more. It was whetting my appetite. I was hungry again. I started to fret. Should I've told the school teacher my real name? Maybe I was now wanted for burning up that stupid doll. I s'posed I could go to jail for that. It was probably a good idea that I didn't say my name was Ruby. A few twigs lay scattered on the ground. I picked one up and started scratching out a picture of the lake I'd seen hanging on the teacher's wall. I crouched back down on the dirt and sketched in a tiny person sitting on the edge of the water. Then slowly, letter by letter, I etched out my name and joined it with an arrow to the teeny figure. Soon, too dark to see, I crawled down inside the dug-out trying not to inhale the stinking air. I slept away the hours of night.

"I thought I'd find you here." A voice broke through my slumber. In the doorway a woman's shape blanketed out the morning light. She came up to me and shuffled down by my side.

"So this is where you live, is it?" She looked around from side to side. "Really? You know, it wasn't too hard to find you, particularly with 'Kit' written in the dirt outside. Good picture, by the way." She held out a tin cup. "Drink up." The coffee was milky and sweet. "Anyhow," she continued, "I reckon if you don't a get a move on, you'll be late for school again. Two days in a row is not good. My pupils get detentions for regular late attendance. Up you get! You're coming along with me." Outside her car was waiting, the engine running. "Hop in, missy," she said. "I think you've got some explaining to do." She handed me a chunk of bread off the back seat. It was ready spread with jam. As we drove along she waved or honked at people. "You see, Kit, there's no hiding places here in Quivering Creek. Everyone knows everyone else. You're easily spotted. That's the first lesson of the day. The second will start at nine am. Then tonight we'll talk about things. I'll tell you about me; and how about you tell me about you? Is that a deal?" My mouth was stuffed full so I just nodded my agreement.

When we got to the school house she led me back into her rooms again. She gave me a towel, a bowl of hot water, soap in a china dish and a comb. "Get yourself nice and clean, now. There's a mirror over there. You can't go to school unwashed. I'll fix you up with some fresh clothes after lessons finish. Make it quick because when you're all cleaned up, the

school bell will need ringing fifty times to let folks
know that school's open for the day." When I was
done she took me outside and showed me how to ring
the bell properly. I rang it fifty times, slowly. I couldn't
count up to fifty but I made a pretty good guess. I
wondered, as I rang, how many children would come
to school that day. I wasn't too happy in case they
were mean like the Brighams. Or worse still, what
if Lucille came in with all her brothers and sisters? I
felt bad about her doll now. Furtively I looked up and
down the street and then darted back inside.

"Sit down, now. There's space at the front, in
the middle please. Sit there so I can keep my eye on
you. No chatting before lessons." She looked up at the
clock. I did too although I didn't know what it said.
Then she stood up, went to the door and yanked the
bell-pull several more times. The wall clock struck
nine. "Good morning." She seemed to be addressing others as well as me. I looked around just in case
somebody had slipped in without me noticing. No,
the room was empty. Just me. "Good morning," she
repeated looking straight at me.

"Good morning," I replied, prompted.

"I would like you now to say 'Good morning,
Mrs Hurtigrutensson.'"

"Good morning, Mrs, er, Hurti...n...ginsham."
My voice trailed off.

"Try again, now. Mrs Hur-tig-rut-ens-son."

"Mrs Hur-ting-rut-gens-son." My voice trailed off again.

"Better. Now say it all again. Good Morning, Mrs Hurtigrutensson."

I then realised how hard school could be. "Good morning, Mrs Hurtingr...ison."

"Hurtig-rut-ens-son."

"Hurting-gen-son."

"Okay," she said, "that'll do well enough for today. Now I'll do the register. When I reach your name put your hand up and say, 'Present, Ma'am.'"

I was so glad I didn't have to repeat her impossible name again. One by one she read out names from the register. Of course, no one answered. But she gave each 'pupil' a moment to reply. At every non-answer she marked a cross in the book.

"Kit Wardle," she called out.

"Present, Ma'am," I shouted, and stuck my hand up. I got a tick by my name, and a smile. I liked that game. I got something right at last. She closed the register, stood up and, addressing the class, she told them to open their reading books. "We will start with Kit as she is new today. Turn to the first page." There were some nice pictures on the first page of a girl and a boy. "Start reading, please." I did. "Can you read it aloud, Kit, please." I looked down. I didn't recognize any of the words on the page so I just made them up. She didn't stop me until I stopped.

"Very good," she said. "You speak very well, and you have a good vocabulary. A little help with the reading, maybe, but you have a fine and clear voice. And an imagination. Excellent!" Looking over her glasses at me, she smiled. I was so pleased with myself.

"Now we'll do some writing and we will see how you get on. First write your name on the paper." That was easy. Than I had to do 'cat', so I drew a cat. Then 'dog'. I drew a dog. Then 'house'... "Well," she said, "you're very good at drawing. You have a fine eye, Kit Wardle. I can see you're a very, very clever girl. As you are so good I am going to show you another way of writing words, which is a little bit tricky, but I know you will be able to manage it." Our schooling began.

✳ ✳ ✳

Delphine put her hand on my shoulder. "She sounded real kindly. Wish my schoolmarm was that nice. You know, if you got anything wrong, or didn't know something, my teacher would soon give you a quick rap across the knuckles. No wonder I often played truant. My momma, bless her soul, was good with me. I remember her saying, 'Now, Delphine, if you don't want to go to school today, that's fine. But, if you're goin't stay home you're goin't work doubly hard. So here you are, take this box of onions, peel them and chop them up fine, then that bucket of potatoes will need scrubbing. Do that, or get back to lessons. Choose now!' As you know, Kitty, I never did get on right well in the kitchen department – hey, I saw that smile! You didn't have to agree so readily! – Anyhow, it made me think twice about missing school.

Talking about chores, though, I better get my running shoes on now. I need to sort that linen. And I got a mile high of ironing to get through. It's good to get things nice and straight for the week. I know, how about I bring the laundry up and whilst I'm slaving away over hot irons you can go on with your story? It'll be nice for both of us then. You'll be all right there, won't you, for an hour or so, while I get it all sorted?

"Sure, I'll be fine. I wasn't thinking of going anywhere!"

❉ ❉ ❉

As the school room clock struck twelve, Mrs Hurtigrutensson picked up her hand-bell. She rang it twice. "Class dismissed!" she announced. "Come along now, Kit. Follow me, it's lunch break. Come on."

Back in her room she turned and once more smiled at me. "You may now call me Stella. In the school room I like you to address me as Mrs Hurtigrutensson, or if you prefer, Ma'am. But outside school hours you may call me Stella. Is that okay with you?"

"Yes, Ma'am, I mean, Stella."

"Good. Now wash your hands over there, that's right, and then we'll share some lunch. After luncheon you may play outside until the school bell rings. When you hear the bell it means it's the start of afternoon lessons and you can proceed, quietly of course, back inside. Can you set table?" I nodded. "Good. Put a plate and a knife for each of us. Fetch a jug of water and some beakers. I'll cut the bread. I have some cheese lurking here. And I've got some tomatoes hiding somewhere. I love tomatoes, don't you?"

"Yes, Ma'am."

"Stella, you mean! Tomatoes are my favourite food, you know. I could eat them all day long. Sometimes I put them up high so I'm not so easily tempted to pick at them. Then, you see, I have to get a chair to reach them and then sometimes I can't find a chair so it slows down my consumption. I do say I'm quite gone on them. We all have our little weaknesses, don't we?" I nodded again. "And a passion for tomatoes is not all that serious and doesn't offend. When I was little I wanted to be a tomato farmer. Isn't that sweet?" I nodded. "Lucky I didn't go down that road because there's not much money in tomatoes. As you can see I've even got some growing right over there." She pointed to the window sill. "I should put them out really but they're so pretty to look at too." I smiled my agreement. "And have you smelt their leaves?" She breathed in deeply. "Absolutely divine!"

"Yes, they're divine."

"Kitty, do you have a favourite food?"

"Ice cream," I said. I didn't have to think about it at all, not even for one second, so I pretty well understood why she was so passionate about tomatoes. I was passionate about ice-cream. "Maybe I could own a soda bar when I grow up 'cos I don't think ice-cream grows so well around here. It's far too warm. I'd mix you some lovely flavours and cover it with loads of sprinkles."

"That's a nice idea," she replied. "I wonder if you can get tomato flavour ice-cream? That should be interesting. I bet you can in Chicago, or in New York. I bet everyone on Broadway eats it. Anyhow, I think that's enough talk now about ice-cream, and about tomatoes ... for the moment, anyway. Let's get that lunch going. Oh, when you finish setting table, can you reach up and get the pickles down from the larder shelf. As it is your first day here, and I hope there will be many more, you can choose whichever one you want as a welcome. The carrot relish is quite good, and I can highly recommend the pickled peach, but choose whatever you wish."

"Thank you."

"My ma makes them all. She thinks I'll starve without them." I stood on a chair in the larder and gravely studied the shelves loaded with jams, relishes, chutneys, catsups, jellies and pickles, vinegars, bottles of sauces and glass jars of plumped-out fruit. There were so many. Of course, I couldn't read the labels so, after some thought, I decided to go for the jar with the cheeriest coloured contents. It was piccalilli; I remember well. Could I forget! Back at the table I spooned a large amount onto my cracker. I thought it would be sweet; but 'wow-wee', what a shock I had when I swallowed. My eyes watered. I sneezed several times. I coughed. I spluttered. Stella passed me some water and I knocked it back as fast as I could, dribbling and spitting. She continued eating, spreading a tiny teaspoon of the mustard-hot piccalilli carefully onto a dainty slice of bread and tomato. I wiped my mouth on my sleeve and crossed my arms, annoyed that I couldn't read the label and annoyed I could have had the sweet-carrot chutney instead. "If you're finished now," Stella said, "you can get down and go and play outside in the yard. Put your dishes in the sink first, and here," she threw me a tomato, "eat this."

I was eager to get back to learning. In the morning we'd done reading, writing and numbers, but in the afternoon the subject to be studied was to be Geography. On the wall a large tube dangled a tail-like string. She gave the cord a jerk and what I know now as a map came juddering down in a fog of dust and a cluster of roaches. We both coughed and flapped at the air. I was astonished. I'd never seen a picture like that before. I was a bit puzzled by the erratic mix of colours. Some were overly pale and others clashed. Moreover, the pattern was imbalanced. I thought I could paint it out much better. With the cloud settled and our sneezing abated, Stella pulled out a cane and asked me to point out the United States of America. I had no idea. I think I pointed to Australia; shape-wise, it looked more interesting. It was nicely coloured in and it was encircled by soft blue. After several prompts I homed in on America. She showed me our state of Colorado and neighbouring Kansas, New Mexico and the jut of Oklahoma. Finally she pointed to a tiny black dot which she assured me was where I was sitting right there and then in a place, she said, called Quivering Creek. I was so impressed with the notion that I was actually on this picture. I studied the dot. I couldn't really make myself out. I needed to improve that situation and re-colour it. I needed to make myself more obvious. Stella continued to point out things on the map: the shady-grey line of mountains, The Rockies; the dark-blue trace of rivers; and the light sky-blue of the oceans. I was quite enthralled. All I had to do now was to climb the next ridge, lean over and see this other world spread out beneath me.

6

"Come along." I tailed behind Stella as she made her way across to the general store. It was just along the highway past the school turning. Lessons were over. "Right," she said decidedly, "let's get you sorted. Hop along with me. You know, you've done really well today. You're a very clever girl. I'm so very pleased. Now we're going to go and pick up some things and get you fitted out properly."

"Well, howdy, Mrs H," a voice greeted us from behind the counter. Why is he calling her Mrs H, I wondered. Maybe Stella has yet another name when getting provisions. How many names could a person have? "Ah," a voice emerged from behind a towering pile of canned beans. A moustachioed face look down at me. "Is this the young lady here? The one you were looking for earlier?" Stella nodded. "Glad you found her. It must make a nice change having a pupil back in class."

"Very grateful for your help, Walter," she said. "She was exactly where you and the others spotted her. I found her straight off. And you were quite right, she is on her own. Anyway," she continued, "she will be staying over for a while so I'll need some things. She doesn't seem to have any belongings. I was wondering, Walter, if you had some clothing that would fit a little girl? Or do I have to send off to Sears, or go into town?"

I didn't know you could just go and get things. I'd never been bought clothes before. I remember flicking through a Sears catalogue in the big house but those posh dresses were never for the likes of me. Ma made all our clothing, that is, apart from her uniform. She sewed them up from cut up flour-mill sacks or from chicken-linens. Oftentimes I'd bear the message '48 lbs net' or 'Buck-eyed Feed Mill'. I didn't think anything of it. Others in Elkhorn wore similar, advertising 'Goch's Cornmeal xxx' or, more amusingly for us children, 'Open other end'. Sure, we made fun of each other but we were all stuck in the same boat so it didn't matter.

"Well, you don't need to go sending off to Sears, for sure, Mrs H," Walter said, sizing me up and down. "I think I can just about manage to fit the little lady out in something wearable; 'long as she's not too fussed about what she wears." He looked at me. "No Paris fashions here, Miss. What d'you say to these bib-overalls and this shirt? Very practical." He held them up to me. I nodded. "Now, go and try them on for size over there behind those drapes. And see, there's a mirror back here in the corner for you to admire yourself." When I came out I went over to the glass. I looked in it, turning vainly from side to side, in the way my ma would have done. The clothes were far too loose but I wasn't bothered. They smelt new and against my sore skin they felt luxuriously smooth.

"She'll grow into them," Walter continued. "She's at that age for sprouting up. 'Fraid I've not got anything smaller in stock, not at the moment. Children grow mighty quickly these days. Anything else you need?"

"Yes, some undergarments. Two sets, please. And her shoes look as if they won't walk one step more. Have you any girls' ones? And also she'll need some night-wear. She may be staying some time. Oh, and let's have a look at the wool you have. She will need a sweater for the fall and I'm not the fastest of knitters. If I start now, I might be finished by the end of this year!"

"You're mighty generous to that child, you know. Is she family of some sort?" I looked up hopefully.

"As you well know, Walter, all children are part of God's family." She turned to me and said, "Let's look at some wool now. I'm thinking I'm going to make you a sweater, or maybe a cardie, for when it's colder. Which do you prefer?

"I don't mind."

"You're an easy young lady to please. I was so very particular when I was your age. It drove my ma to distraction. We better get something thick. It will start getting colder in a couple of months' time, especially at nightfall. What's your favourite colour?" She looked at me. "Is it blue?" I nodded.

"Just like your eyes." How did she know? I liked red and yellow too. And also green. But blue, as I said, was my favourite.

"I don't mind, honestly. Whatever colour is easiest to knit," I replied. "I don't want to cause you more work than necessary, Mrs H."

She laughed. "I like you, Kit. You make me laugh. But remember, I'm Stella to you." She chose some light blue wool for me and picked out ten balls. "This will do. That should be enough. I've got some needles somewhere at home. Walter, if there's too much here can I bring some back?"

"That's fine with me, Mrs H, as long as you don't unravel it. I'm 'fraid I haven't got any bar shoes. Will these 'Busters' do? Both girls and boys are wearing them nowadays. And they don't wear out so quick."

"We'll take them. We can always find something prettier another day, you see. They fit all right, Kit? Don't pinch any place?" I shook my head enthusiastically.

"That was easy as pie!" Walter said, rubbing his hands together. "And here, as you're such a good and easy-going customer, help yourself to a candy and take one for Mrs H, too." He offered us each a 'Mary-Jane'. I unwrapped mine immediately and chewed it greedily.

"Thank you," I said, my mouth full of toffee.

"Thank you, Walter. That reminds me now, I think we better have a toothbrush too. Put it all on account, please." And with my teeth stuck solidly together I collected up the rest of the parcels and gambolled back across the road.

As soon as we got back Stella stoked up the boiler. She passed me milk and a cookie to nibble. I sat there 'happy as Larry' munching and slurping in front of the fire. She clattered a small tin bath across, and several buckets of water later she had filled the bath. "It's a good temperature now. Time to jump in." Shyly I stripped off and slid into the water. I got a thorough good washing. "Eyes shut," she commanded, pouring water over my head, and she soaped my hair like never before. The water smelt clean and sweet and the soap was like lemon cream. "Out now, Kit." She held up a large towel for me to step into and, tightly wrapped, I was sat down by the stove. While I dried she tipped my pile of old clothes into the used water and, on her knees, set to scrubbing and rubbing.

"Not much life left in these," she said. "I think you stopped off here just in time. I can imagine these pants falling apart as you bob along. And those boots of yours, I'm afraid they're too far gone even for mending. We're going to have to throw them." I didn't care. I just agreed. She handed me my nightgown. "You might as well put it on now, that is, as long as you're really dry. Save you doing it later. Here, have a comb. I'll let you comb it through before it tangles. I don't want to pull your tags. That wouldn't do, now, would it? When you're done, come and give me hand. I need to make up your cot." She led me through to a bedroom and then through to another beyond, a tinier one with a high window. The bed was made up with a thick red comforter. She puffed up a pillow and angel-white feathers flew up in the air, and as they floated down they covered me softly with their wings. A rickety chair stood by my bed. Carefully I climbed it and through the window I spied a rough rope of mountains glowing like embers in the setting sun. A tiny spider was hiding up on the sill. I let it crawl on my hand, then I let it go.

That night we feasted on succotash. It was chock full of black beans, tomatoes and corn. I dunked bread in the tomato catsup and wiped the plate dry.

There was a pot of red jelly on the table, so I ate a couple of spoons straight out of the jar.

"That good?" Stella said, enjoying the spectacle. I nodded. "I made that peach jelly myself when I was visiting my folks last summer. Eat as much as you want. You might as well finish the jar, now. I got loads left." I did what I was told and emptied it out. "So, tell me, do you have folks back home?" I shook my head. "Am I going to ask you questions? Or are you going to just tell me things?"

"Like what?" I said.

"Like where you come from? And if you want me to, I'll tell you about my folks and where I come from." I'd never thought that older people might have mothers and fathers. I was silent. "Shall I ask you things, then?" she continued.

"Okay, but I mightn't know all the answers."

"That's okay. Just do your best. Tell me, now ... um ... what shall I ask first? Okay, how did you come by here?" First I told her about walking, and then about sleeping the night through in a shack. Then I told her about the happy family who gave me a lift on the back of their truck and how I slept the night in front of their fire. I didn't tell her about the doll in case she didn't like me anymore. "And where did you start off from?"

"The Brighams."

"The Brighams, oh, where would that be, then?" I shrugged my shoulders.

"A big twister came across," I volunteered, "and blew it right off. Don't know where it got to. Don't know where it all went."

"That was some tornado, wasn't it? We only got the edge of it here but it sure roughed things up for us. Was your place hit really bad?"

"Yes, Ma'am."

"What about the people there? Were they okay?"

"The Brighams left yonks. They just left me and Pa and Vladimare to keep an eye on their place."

"Who's Vladimare?"

"Our pony. We called her Vladi sometimes. She took us to town and to different places. She had a nice mane but then she went and died; dropped down dead, just like a stone, and we couldn't go nowhere no more. Pa said Vladi couldn't find nothing to eat and that's why she dropped dead. No grass left. There was nothing for Vladi to eat no more. Nothing at all."

"And what about your pa?" she asked gently.

"Pa died too."

"And you were there all alone?"

"Uh-huh."

"And your ma. Did she die then too?"

"No!"

"Where did she go?"

"Not too sure. She just kind of disappeared when I was a little shrimp. It was yonks."

"I see," Stella said. "Well, you're not alone any more, Kitty. I'll look after you long as need be."

"Okay, Ma'am."

"Stella, you mean. Remember, I'm Stella except when we're in the school room. Otherwise it will confuse the other pupils." She smiled. "Hey, is it all right if I call you Kitty? That's such a pretty name and it suits you fine." She picked up my hands and squeezed them gently in hers.

"S'pose," I nodded. "Pa used to call me that sometimes."

"Then, you'll be my little Kitty too. Now, you'll be all right, Kitty, believe me. I know these things. Now that was a lot to tell me." She handed me a hanky. "Okay?" I nodded, sniffing. "Sad things do happen in life, and sometimes real bad things, too. It's all part of life. We just have to make the best of what we can. You know, I've had sad things happen to me but I will tell you about that some other time, if you want me to, that is. Do you want to sit up with me awhile or would you rather try out that new bouncy bed and that feathery pillow of yours? I know what, how about I read you a bedtime story? I bet you'd like that."

"Uh-huh."

"I thought so. It's been a long day hasn't it? Lots has happened. I always say you never know what the wind's going to blow in next. I'm so pleased you came by. Come on, Kitty. That's some yawn. Bedtime now. School tomorrow. Say, just thought, would you like to be my school-bell monitor? I could do with that help on a regular basis. Very responsible job, you know. Always has to be right on time."

"Pleased to be of help."

"That's just great. You've got lovely manners, you know. Now pop some salt on your brush and give your teeth a good scrub, then hop into bed. I'll wake you when it's time to get going in the morning. There's a 'gazunder', as my ma called it, under the cot, if you need to use it. Now, do you say prayers?" I shook my head. "That's okay. It's up to you, but how about just saying, 'God Bless Ma and Pa'?" I repeated it and she said, 'amen' afterwards. Having read me a story she tucked me up tight, leant over and whispered, "Night-night, sleep tight, mind the bugs don't bite!"

The bed was cold but I curled up as happy as could be. I worried about the bugs biting but I couldn't feel any. Anyhow, I quite liked bugs. I could still taste the sweet residue of peach jelly on my tongue and my tummy felt filled and round. I snuggled down to my dreams.

The morning came soon enough. I was still slumbering when Stella woke me. "Wake up, sleepy-head. Time to get ready for school." On the end of my bed were my new clothes, freshly pressed and neatly folded. It hadn't been a dream after all. And today I was going to be 'School-Bell Monitor'. I washed, dressed and scooped my breakfast.

"Now," she said, pointing to the clock on the dresser, "as soon as the little hand points to the nine and the big hand of the clock is right close by, you know it is quarter to nine. That is the time for you to ring the school bell. Fifty times, mind: not too fast, not too slow. That's your job. It's important. Watch that clock closely." At the allotted time I raced out and clanged the bell. I scanned the road but happily for me nobody turned up again. Returning to my desk I sat down and crossed my arms. As the big hand on the schoolroom clock touched twelve Stella tinkled the hand bell.

"Good morning, class."

"Good Morning, Mrs Hutig-ges-sen." I couldn't get it quite right yet but she did not seem to notice. She took the register and when she got to my name I yelled, "Present, Ma'am." She ticked the page, smiled and I smiled back.

7

"He died from wounds," she said, sighing. "Mr Hurtigrutensson died from wounds." To me it sounded a pretty serious thing to die from. At the time we were listening to one of Stella's two records; it was the Tosca. Stella was knitting along in time to the call of the aria, her arms and face charged with emotion. Supper cleared away, she and I would often listen to music or tune into a radio station. By the warmth of the stove we'd laugh and light-heart away the hours of night. We'd chat about the shows we'd heard. I liked the funnies best, programmes like 'Fibber McGee', or the 'Jack Benny'. And we'd roll about with laughter and with tears streaming down our cheeks. Stella, however, preferred the dramas, particularly stories of high suspense. If, at the crux of some mystery, the presenter declared, in a solemn tone, 'To be continued next week', Stella would gasp and shriek. Her beguilement in the tale being told was often reflected by the click-click of needles. As the story mounted to a crescendo her speed of knitting would decelerate until it hit the slow-lane. But once the 'gun was fired' or 'swindler exposed' she would race off again only to discover, at the end of a section, the wayward behaviour of her emotionally-charged stitches. As if personally affronted she would, huffing and puffing, disentangle the unruly yarn with much annoyance.

Other times we'd have musical evenings. I didn't enjoy these to the same extent. Sometimes she'd let me wind up the gramophone and we'd listen to one or other of her records. I liked the 'Sally' but Stella preferred the 'Puccini' and her eyes would fill as she soared along with 'Floria'. She encouraged me to join in but I had no voice. It was more akin to the screeching of a crow rather than her song of a nightingale. Similarly, my renditions on the piano were not, to Stella's dismay, impressive. "One of these days," Stella said after I finished a particularly tuneless practice, "I'm going to consult someone about your hearing. It's probably just wax but, on the other hand, it could be your tonsils playing up. I know there's a pretty songbird inside you somewhere. We just need to let it out of its cage."

On other occasions we'd just sit and chat, play cards or flick at tiddlywinks. There were also times when we just slurped our way through bowls of ripe-red tomatoes, adding, for fun, pinches of salt, sugar or other condiments. We'd comment, in superior voices, on the quality of the individual fruit: sweet, juicy, delicate, delicious, delectable, divine, luscious, over-ripe, under-ripe, rotten, dry. We made it into a game. I learnt some good adjectives. It was like painting pictures but instead of a brush of colour we painted with words.

The knitting sessions, unfortunately, were not improving, with, or without, the interference from the radio set. Cursing and sighing concerning the cardigan's unintended shape often accompanied her efforts. Over and over again I had to stretch out my arms or stand up unnaturally straight and forcefully tall while she fussed and measured and re-measured about my body. One of my arms, she argued with all seriousness, must have grown faster than the other. I don't think knitting was a favourite of hers; there were often dramatic unravellings, row after row after row. She could never be appeased; she felt she had to do it right for me. To me, I wasn't bothered one little bit what shape it ended up. What I liked about it was that she was creating something just for me. But whilst she clicked away we chatted.

Stella liked to talk about music. I asked her why she loved the 'Tosca' songs so much more when 'Sally' was the more jaunty. She answered, with a sigh, that the record was a present from her late husband. In hushed tones she divulged that they were only married six months and six days before he was taken from her. "He died from wounds," she reminded me in a wavering voice. At the time I didn't know what that was so my imagination created an illness. I thought it some awful disease like 'tonsils'. I hoped it wasn't catching.

About two months into my stay I gained the confidence to start questioning Stella. Being accustomed to keeping my mouth shut it took me some time to start talking unabashed. Stella seemed happy to answer my questions. I had been chewing something over for quite a time; where were all the other pupils? Not that I wanted them about. It was just that I knew all their names. I even knew their second names. I just wondered where they'd all gone.

"Ah, very good question. I'm sure," she said, offering me a tomato, "pretty soon, my pupils will be coming back. You keep ringing that bell and, before you know it, they'll come marching through the door."

"But, Stella, why did they stop coming?"

"They just did, bit by bit."

"So, did their folks go and die, or get wounds, or something like that?"

"Well, let me see. Yes, some of them got sick with the 'dust'. That's true. Others went off to the big cities looking for work. I don't blame them. There were hardly any jobs around these parts. There's been poor harvest for several years on the trot. So, with no work and no food, people got real hungry."

"Then what?"

"Well, now, many moved off. But don't worry, Kitty, I think the worst has blown over. Let's hope things will pick up."

"Me too. Are they coming back, then?"

"Well, I hope so, but lots of those families just upped sticks and went. They didn't want to chance it. They took everything they could with them: lock, stock and barrel. Some may not come back. Many moved out west."

"I wished Pa had done that."

"I know you do, sweetheart. But, you see, people never know what to do for the best. Some of those people may have chanced it but, I bet you, many of them weren't many beans better off after they moved away."

"That's what Pa said."

"He was probably right. Sometimes it's better to sit tight. The reason I stayed around is because my work was set out here. And your pa's work was set out to look after that ranch. I bet he did it well."

"I think so too."

"I'm glad I stayed here, otherwise I would never have found you! — Here, give me a hug, that's nice — No point, I say, running away for the sake of running away. You know, the grass on the other side is not always greener! But, I think, now things are picking up some of those folks will come back. Some may not, of course. Some won't be coming home no more."

"Like Pa?"

"Uh-huh, sweetheart, but some will, you'll see. They'll be back like new flowers blooming in the desert. I'm keeping the school register open for them. It'll be nice for you to have some play-mates. I was an only child. It can be pretty lonesome."

"I'm just fine," I said. "I like being with you. You're my best friend."

"And I like being with you too! You know, you're the bee's-knees. You so make me laugh. But you also need to play with people of your own age."

I didn't see why. I wasn't sure if I liked the idea of having others about. I wasn't lonely. Moreover, I was rather taken aback when Stella said the grass was not always greener on the other side. I was sure it was. I was sure if you looked hard enough you'd find greener grass. It was just a matter of looking.

Regularly, after school on a Thursday, Stella would scoot off to town. She gave singing lessons to a lady who lived in Silverton. The lesson over, the two women would sit and have a coffee together. One afternoon, Stella came back all excited. Her pupil, Lois Cummings, had sent me over a little wrap of chocolate brownies as a present. Never before had I tasted chocolate in such quantity. It was pure magic to my lips! The only other time I'd tried chocolate it was as 'sprinkles'. Chocolate, I decided, was the best thing in the world ... that is, next to ice-cream! Lois Cummings was the doctor's wife and, according to Stella, had the prettiest house in town. "It has a front yard," she enthused, "bright full of flowers and trees. There's even a swing-seat hanging from a branch. You'll adore it! She's got a daughter, Sybil, who's nearly eleven. Most of the time she's away at school but she'll be back in the summer. Mrs Cummings thinks you both may get along very well together." I wasn't so sure.

One afternoon an excited Stella returned from Silverton. "Guess what?" she said, handing me a tomato. "You've been invited out for tea next Thursday. Sybil will be back home and Mrs Cummings wondered if you two girls would like to enjoy each other's company. Wasn't that kind of her?" I nodded unenthusiastically. "I'm going to give Sybil, as well as Mrs Cummings, music lessons. During the summer break she gets lonely and, like you, she doesn't have brothers or sisters. Nobody at all to play with. So, of course, some of the time she gets a bit moochy about the place. Mrs Cummings and I thought maybe you and Sybil could have some fun together. She's going to bake a cake especially for the occasion. What d'you think?"

I didn't think much about the idea; not one little bit. I wasn't too keen about playing with another child. I'd got used to the company of adults, and anyhow, I wasn't sure how to go about this playing business. It bothered me, in fact, to the extent that, the following Thursday, I feigned a severe tummy ache. Stella, being concerned, allowed me to stay home. Unfortunately, Mrs Cummings re-invited me for the following week. I had already made up my mind that Sybil was not the type of girl I would like as a friend. I pictured her looking somewhat like the Brigham girls. I could see her frou-frou-ing about with long blond sausage-curl ringlets, pink ribbons flying everywhere, and surrounded by a menagerie of ponies, puppies and dolly-prams. Even though Stella assured me that I would find Sybil great company I decided, in my own mind, to dislike her intensely.

The day came and, once more, I tried to make myself seem sick. Stella would have none of it. With a flourish she bundled me into the car. We drove off in silence. Long in face and long in feet I followed her up the path. At the door Sybil and her mother were waiting in welcome. Sybil and I glared at each other. There was no smiling.

"I know," Mrs Cummings suggested, sensing our mutual dislike, "what d'you say we do things the other way about? How about we all go sit down and have a bite to eat now? Get to know each other a bit better. Then when we've all done with chatting we can settle down to our lessons. How's that?"

"Thank you, Lois, that seems a jolly good idea," Stella said over-cheerfully.

"I've been baking something special so I hope you two girls are ravenous." Sybil and I both nodded. At least we agreed over that!

The house smelled of caramel sugar and, just as Stella had described, it was real pretty. In the kitchen, to my delight, I saw a chocolate cake, thick with icing and pecans surrounded by tiny kisses of meringues. I sat down. Stella gave me one of her 'raised eyebrows' as if to say 'wait to be asked'. But Mrs Cummings just smiled. Soon Sybil and I were munching away and eyeing each other across the crisp white of the cloth. We both glowered. I was happy enjoying my feed but felt obliged to maintain a sour demeanour. Sybil, I observed, was small and dressed in checked pants and top. Like me she wore 'Busters'. Her red hair was cut short. It was curly, but not sausage-curly, and a cloud of freckles covered her face. Thick ginger eyelashes fluttered like petals around small brown eyes. I decided she didn't look too bad.

I accepted a second slice of cake. I took a large bite but, without forewarning, I sneezed. Cake and milk everywhere! I spluttered as a crumb got stuck in my throat and my eyes watered and tears trickled down my cheeks and nostrils. A chocolate grin spread itself across Sybil's face as she watched, with enjoyment, my spluttering and coughing. She started to giggle. I wiped my face on my sleeve and, much to Stella's embarrassment, I started hiccuping loudly and uncontrollably. I extended Sybil a toothy grin and Stella, excusing my behaviour to Mrs Cummings, gave me another 'raised brow'. Mrs Cummings, not the slightest perturbed, started to laugh too. Sybil crossed her eyes, bucked her teeth and gurned a face back. I returned by licking the tip of my nose with my chocolate-covered tongue. To my astonishment Mrs Cummings joined in! "My!" she said, "that just takes me right back to when I was a girl. Me and my little sister, Esther, used to play that at table. It made my mom so mad. I can see it now." And with that Mrs Cummings twitched her nose from side to side.

"Well, can either of you two girls do this, then?" Stella added. She gathered back her hair and wriggled first her left ear, then her right and then her left again. Her dexterity of ear was most impressive! We all got the giggles. The proverbial ice was broken, and with much chocolate still stuck around our mouths Sybil and I scampered off into the yard.

Sybil grabbed hold of a rope ladder dangling from a branch and, swinging wildly from side to side like a chipmunk, she disappeared into the leaves. I looked up and she beckoned me from her bower. I saw, to my delight, a little wooden house crotched in the branches. With no further invitation I clambered right after her and we tumbled into a heap of brightly coloured cushions on the floor of her den. When I got myself the right way up I looked around. Old rag rugs and worn blankets covered the boards. Piles of books and comics were scattered everywhere and drawings were nailed haphazardly to the rough old trunk. I was entranced. Sybil watched me as I leafed through the pages of books. At last she spoke. She had a lovely soft voice, almost melodious.

"Would you like me to read you a story?"

"Yes, please," I replied. "Don't mind if you do."

"Not at all, I just love reading stories."

"I love stories, too."

"Who's your favourite?"

"Not quite sure. Who's yours?"

"I just absolutely adore *Anne of Green Gables*. Don't you think she's divine? And so eloquent. I think she's truly rapturous. She suffered so much ... just like me, what with the red hair and all that. Do you mind my hair, Kitty?"

I was surprised. "Why would I mind your hair?" I replied, "It's so very pretty. I wish my hair was like that."

"Oh, thank you so much! It's such a novel experience being complimented for something one thought was so obnoxious."

I wasn't sure what she meant, so I just smiled.

"I think I like you tremendously. You are very understanding," continued Sybil. "Would you like to be my kindred spirit?"

"Okay," I nodded. I wasn't too sure what one was but I was happy to go along with being one.

"That's wonderful, because I've always wanted a kindred spirit of my own. Can I be yours too?"

"Of course," I agreed. She hugged me so I hugged her back.

We lay on our stomachs on the floor of the tree house and she opened up her *Anne of Green Gables*. She read to me and we both empathised greatly with *Anne's* suffering. Me, for being an orphan and Sybil, for having to contend with the hair. Her reading was deep with expression and she delighted in giving voice to the characters. It made me giggle and Sybil, heartened by my response to her rendition, smiled warmly back. I studied her face as she read and decided that, after all, I really did like her. Stella was right.

From the yard below, a voice called up, "Girls! Hello, girls. Are you still up there?" We both closed our mouths tight and tried to suppress a giggle. But like all suppressed giggles laughter eventually spluttered forth. "I know you're up there," shouted Mrs Cummings. "Time for your lesson, dear. Come down. Come on. Good girls." Reluctantly we slid down, knocking off leaves and twigs in the descent.

"Was that fun?" Mrs Cummings asked.

"Oh, yes," Sybil replied, "just rapturous."

"Yes," I agreed, "just rapturous."

"Well, wash your face and hands before you go in, Sybil. It's still covered in chocolate. Maybe, Kitty, it would be a good idea, too, if you do the same."

Washed and sitting in their kitchen I waited while Stella gave Sybil her piano lesson. I stroked their fluffy cat.

"Has your cat got a name, Mrs Cummings?"

"Yes, that's Crumble. She's a nice old thing, isn't she? Rescued her from off the streets. I think she was unloved."

"Oh, how sad! How can you not love her? I'd love her even if she was covered in dust and suffered from wounds."

"Me too."

"Thank you so much for inviting me over, Mrs Cummings. I've had a lovely time. The cake was a delight."

"Well, thank you, my dear. How very polite of you to say so." After that I didn't know what else to say. But Crumble purred happily away on my lap and gave me an occasional lick of affection. Every now and again the doorbell would ring and Mrs Cummings would take off her apron and go answer the call. When she returned she'd whisper to me, "Just a patient to see the doctor, that's all."

The piano lesson finally came to an end and Sybil burst back into the kitchen. She still had some chocolate stuck around her mouth. She put an arm around my shoulder.

"Can Kitty come back soon, Ma, please? She's my bosom friend now."

"Well, of course she can. That is, if she would like to. Would you like to come back, my dear?"

"Yes please, Mrs Cummings. The cake was so *delvine*." I looked up at Stella. "Please can I come back for tea, and to play stories with Sybil?"

"Of course you may," she said. "Are you sure that's okay with you, Lois?"

"Of course it is, Stella. Same time next week?"

"Oh, yes please," I replied. "I do like being a kindred pirate."

"Spirit, you mean, kindred spirit."

"Yes, oh sorry, Sybil, kindred spirit I meant."

✳ ✳ ✳

"Sybil was my first friend ..."

"... But not your last," Delphine interrupted. "You've always been good at making friends, Kitty. Why, you just have to sit in the square and complete strangers walk right up to you and start chattering. Next thing, you've become, more or less, a close family friend of theirs. Then they're sending you birthday cards and photos of their children and popping in as they pass by laden with bunches of flowers just to say hello. Why, you've got so many friends there can't be any people left in the world to make enemies of. A kindred pirate, indeed!"

8

We played away the summer. To Sybil I was a treasured little sister and she treated me with the care and gentleness I so needed. I responded by holding Sybil, and her renditions of *Anne,* in the highest regard. We'd sit, entwined, reading and acting out *Anne.* We produced little plays and performed them with, or without, willing audience. Crumble, her cat, was often included, albeit reluctantly, in our make-believe. We'd gallivant off with her strapped into an old pram or wheelbarrow, dressed up as a baby in bonnet or as an old lady in shawl.

We took to intrepid adventuring and, on occasion, Mrs Cummings would pack us a picnic lunch to sustain us on our way. First we'd corner and capture Crumble, forcing her down into a lidded basket. We'd swing her along yowling until we found a suitable tree to conquer. And for the duration of the day the tree would become our fort and look-out. We'd tie one end of rope to the basket and fling the other end high over a top branch. Great amounts of hissing and spitting could be heard as Crumble was launched through the air into a canopy of leaves. The basket would sway and jerk dreadfully, her futile attempts to disembark mid-flight somewhat precarious. However, Sybil and I hovered patiently at the bottom of the trunk yelling, to our prisoner, words of encouragement and confidence. I don't think Crumble enjoyed her transit as much as we enjoyed tracking her flight. For, as soon as the lid was open, she would spring out and, wriggling, attempt to escape our firm clutch. Frantically she would claw her way back down, mewling and growling as she went. She never enjoyed her dressing-up, either. We didn't worry; she'd always find her way back home and fortunately, for us, Crumble's memory of our exploits appeared short-lived.

While Sybil suffered her piano lesson I would sit in the kitchen reading or drawing. Mrs Cummings would be busying about but would help me write down recipes for cakes she'd made. I often drew little pictures to illustrate the ones I favoured. Mrs Cummings, I liked a lot; Doctor Cummings was a different case. I felt he found me an annoyance. In his presence, I sensed disapproval; maybe it was his brusque manner. Stella, always concerned at my lack of musical talent, got him, on one occasion, to check out my hearing. I studied him as he studied me. I was scrutinized from top to tail, as if I were a broken-down car. His opinion, after great deliberation, was that I wasn't suffering from wax, or tonsils, as Stella had supposed. Instead my problems, he confirmed with strange glee, were congenital; it was something I picked up, back home, off my ma or pa.

It had slipped my memory that, come the fall, Sybil had to go back to school. The day before her return arrived and we both vowed to continue our friendship for eternity. We marked the occasion solemnly. Between eating slices of red-velvet cake we sobbed and wailed. Instead of being sympathetic, Stella and Mrs Cummings seemed to find the pathos of our weeping highly amusing. Much to our disgust they failed in their attempt to stifle their laughter, even from behind the protection of their outsize handkerchiefs and colourful scarves. Sybil and I ignored their heartlessness and continued our outpourings with passion.

The long hot days of summer and their balmy evenings had passed too quickly. During that time I noticed that sometimes Stella appeared slightly distracted: she daydreamed, she sighed, she mumbled to herself. Often, I'd find her sitting in her chair staring at absolutely nothing. Other times she'd rock, side to side or backwards and forwards. Her nails were well nibbled, her lips sorely bitten.

But, apart from that, we had great fun. Hand-in-hand we'd saunter the scrub-covered paths following trails of rabbit, fox or deer. We picnicked on tomatoes, biscuits and boiled eggs and quenched on julep-syruped waters. We searched out warblers, cardinals and meadowlarks and revelled in the butterflies and bats that swooped close at dusk. Much of the time we busied ourselves in the yard behind the school house. Her tomatoes needed frequent watering and the meagre crops of potatoes, squash and onions she had planted earlier demanded our attention. We were never idle. She listened to my reading, checked my writing and, to my dismay, supervised daily piano practice.

Money must have been bothering Stella. During the summer she got me to decorate and copy out several fliers for postings:

Private lady tutor available.
All ages.
Singing and pianoforte.
Reasonable fees.
Reference available.
Other subjects considered.
Contact Hurtigrutensson.
Box 14.

Every few days Stella checked the mail box. Nothing. No replies. Then, one day, to our surprise a letter arrived. Stella ripped it open in excitement. I watched as the joy on her face slipped away.

"Oh, horse-feathers!"

"What?"

"Bother, bother, bother!"

"What's eating you, Stella?"

"Nothing," she replied. I waited and asked her once more. She looked up, and seeing my worry said, "Oh, sorry, Kitty, it's just nothing. Nothing to get upset about. As I said just a load of old applesauce!"

I wasn't convinced. Stella swerved her way home; a boy on a bike was nearly sent flying. I tried to keep her focussed by pointing out things of interest along the way. I homed in on the leaves bronzing on the trees, normally a favourite subject of hers, but nothing seemed to interest her. As afternoon glided into evening she became increasingly disinterested in her surroundings. I insisted she make supper for me and afterwards, when she refused to eat anything herself, I decided it was time to tackle her. "Stella," I said, standing up facing her with arms folded, "you know you said we should be honest about things?" She nodded. "Well, I'll be honest with you." I put my arms down by my side, very straight. "I think you're upset about something I don't know about. I think it was something in that letter you got. I can feel it in my boots, and I think you're sad, and I think you should tell me why. I don't think it's right to keep things hidden from me. I tell you all my worries. So what d'you think about that, then?" I gave her my severest look.

Stella put her hand to her mouth and laughed. "Oh, sorry Kitty-Kat. I didn't mean to laugh. It's just you're such a bright little thing. And I think you're quite right, too. I suspect, there's no hiding anything from you. Okay, then. The letter was nothing. As I said it's all just a load of applesauce. It came from the school board. They're the ones who are in charge and pay me my wages. They're the boss people."

"Yes, and?"

She opened out the letter and, in a high-pitched voice, read, "'It has come to the attention of the committee that pupil attendance at the Quivering Creek elementary school has dropped substantially in the last year'... blah, blah."

"What else?"

"Let me see. Blah, blah-blah, blah. Oh, and they are 'considering the viability of keeping the school open'. Same as always ... money before education."

"What's that mean?"

"It just means that a schools' inspector is paying us a call next week. They want to, I think, discuss my position here as teacher." I was silent for a second. I didn't get it. "What they going to do?"

"Don't really know. But listen here, Kitty, don't you worry, it'll all sort itself out in the end, you'll see. We'll just have to wait patiently. And another thing ..."

"What's that?"

"The only thing you feel in your boots are your feet. If you get an inkling you feel it in your bones ... not your boots."

"Oh, I was sure I felt it in my boots, too."

"Now, how about we put the radio on."

When the inspector drove up, I hid. I pressed my ear hard against the school room door. It wasn't too difficult to hear the conversation as the inspector had a loud squeak of a voice. It was rather fitting as, in appearance, she was rather small and rodent-like. Her brown hat was pinned down tight, over a surfeit of mismatched hairnets and Kirby grips. Her suit plain and flecked grey. Her gloves beige. Her stockings and shoes dark. I expected to see a tail trailing out behind. Stella in comparison was sporting her best summer dress, her hands clasped neatly together. The inspector looked serious, Stella frightened. Nervously she was showing the 'rat-woman' my exercise book and commenting on my drawings on the wall. The woman was nodding but looking the other way. She showed no interest in my display and suddenly, without invitation, nosed her way through the passage of desks to Stella's table. Stella followed and watched as the inspector, bent over the register, started scratching through the pages. Stella was explaining how she was ready prepared for the return of her disbanded pupils when 'rat-woman' suddenly reared up on her hind legs. She twitched as she shook her head. Stella stepped back, a flush of red creeping up her face, but she continued on calmly. "I know the children will return. That's why I keep everything prepared. As soon as things pick up they'll be back alongside their families. Why, only the other ..."

"Now, look here," the inspector interrupted. "Those ex-pupils of yours are highly unlikely to return to your teaching."

"Why ever not?"

"Mrs Hurtisson." I saw Stella wince at the mispronunciation. "Let's not beat about the bush. Other reasons have become apparent. There are specific reasons why Quivering Creek lacks regular pupil attendance.

"What may they be?"

"You know perfectly well that the good parents of our town, including members of our own school board, are not too happy, in fact not happy at all, about aspects of your teaching."

"My teaching?" The flush had reached her forehead; she was looking angry. "Whatever d'you mean?

As you well know, I'm highly qualified. I'm a graduate of Greeley! I've been teaching school without complaint for well over ten years. You must have seen my certificates. You must have seen my reference from Canon City. What do you mean? I've had nothing but praise for the quality of my lessons."

"I think you know perfectly well what we are talking about now, Mrs Hurtigessen."

"No, I don't."

"Very well. It's not the quality of your teaching at question but rather, shall we say, the content. Your lack of self-restraint in professing your own views."

"My own views! I see. And what may they be?"

"Your view, Mrs Harttison, to hit the nail on the head, is concerning, in particular, the Holy Book. The teachings of the Bible. It seems that you profess that man was descended from a lower level of life, beasts! Those beliefs are seen by many good Christian folk in the county, myself included, as a wicked distortion of the words of the Almighty."

"I see."

"Look around the room, Mrs Hurtinson; I see plenty of paintings on display but none of our Lord. Why?"

"No, but that is ..."

"Any of the Saints?"

"No."

"Any lessons from the Scriptures?"

"No, I don't."

"I see. I'm sure there were plenty displayed here before we employed you. Were there not?"

"Yes."

"Everyone is free to hold personal views, of course, however misguided they may be. But you cannot pass those views on to your pupils. Have I made myself clearer now? We are a Christian country and corrupt talk like yours has been upsetting a lot of good folk 'round these parts. They don't like it. People want their children brought up with moral correctness. It's all written down quite clearly in the Bible. The Gospels hold the holy truth, the word of God. Who do you think you are, Mrs Hurtsen, to tell good people's children that the words of the Bible are wrong? You deny the divine creation."

"I don't, actually."

"You have been teaching Darwinism."

"And I have also been instructing them in the stories from the Scriptures. The children in my class get a well-balanced explanation as expected from modern teaching. I thought the 'Scope' trial sorted all this out."

"As may be. — Now, talking about children, I come to my second point. The 'district' has been informed that you are housing, without permission, a child on school property. Quivering Creek Elementary School is not licensed, as you well know, as having a boarding facility. You can't hide the fact that a child is boarding with you."

"I'm not."

"Just a few moments ago you proudly showed me her work. As indicated in the register she is your sole pupil. The school board, remember, is not a charity."

"I know that."

"The child in question should be removed from the school and placed in an orphanage and her education funded by the appropriate department." Stella was shaking her head.

"No? You think not? You think very highly of your own opinion, don't you, Mrs Hurtssen?"

"I hold opinions, yes. And in my opinion I believe the child need not be in an orphanage. I can look after her perfectly well."

"Ah! So is the child part of your own family, then?"

"No, she is not."

"Well, I'll have you know that tongues are wagging in town."

"About?"

"I'll be clear about this matter. Not to put too fine a point on it, is this pupil, this girl, a child of your own making, your own flesh and blood?"

"I beg your pardon!"

"To be blunt, I know that people with opinions like yours are often, shall we say, morally lax."

"Excuse me!"

"Without Christian guidance, women like you are known to be free, shall we say, with their affections. Do you follow my drift?" Stella looked down at her feet. "We cannot have single women with children working as teachers."

"I see."

"To be honest, right from the very beginning, we, the committee, had our doubts about you. We were reluctant, as the responsible body, to employ you."

"I see."

"You are a married woman, albeit widowed. You know full well that married women are discouraged from the professions. We made an exception, in your case, due to your youth. But if you are now admitting you have a child of your own ..."

"I'm not."

"... which you had previously hidden from us, we could not, and I repeat, not, tolerate the situation. It would be beyond the pale."

"I have not hidden her."

"As responsible Christians and teachers we are here to set an example to the community. I'm afraid to say that the board will take a very dim view of this whole matter."

"Will they?"

"Have you anything to say in your defence, Mrs Hersinsin."

There was a pause. Stella looked up. "Yes," she replied slowly, "in future, please address me correctly. My name is Mrs Hurtigrutensson. It is of Scandinavian origin, you know. Good day to you." Stella crossed to the school door and opened it wide.

"Very well. I have to confess I don't like your tone, Mrs Hurt ... whatever," she said pulling on her gloves. "Good day to you, too."

Stella slammed the door. She stood there, her shoulders bent, head hanging, shaking. I heard her crying. My anger unleashed at Stella's hurt, I bolted out the back, scrambled over the wall and darted across the road. I picked up a large pebble and, with all the might I could muster, hurled it hard at the inspector's car as she pulled away from the kerb. I missed. I snarled. And recalling all the bad words I had gleaned over the years from the Brigham kids, I hurled insult after insult. Noticing me following, she attempted to steer and, at the same time, lock the car doors. She swerved across the kerb at the crossroads. I followed, yelling. As she attempted to change gears, I flung handfuls of gravel at the juddering car. I kicked the dirt, I spat, I bashed the air with my fist. It was only when I tumbled headlong over my own laces and crashed, face down, into the road that I conceded my chase. I lay there awhile breathing deeply, whimpering, and wishing the dirt would just gobble me all up. A mongrel padded by and stopped to sniff my bloodied knees. I lashed out at it, howling.

"Hey!" a voice sang out. "What are you doing down there? You okay?" Through my puffy eyelids I could see it was Doctor Cummings calling through his car window. "Jump in and I will give you a lift back home." I shook my head. "What's up?" I shook my head again and gave him a surly look. "Okay, Kitty. It's up to you. But I'm telling you that's not how a young lady behaves around these parts." His car moved off towards Quivering Creek. I bet he's going to tell. I limped off, legs bleeding, back to the dugout where I had slept my first night. My name was still etched on the dry ground. I scribbled it out roughly with my shoe. I thumped the inside walls of the shack; bugs burst out of the woodwork. With arms flailing I swiped out at them, yelling insults.

It wasn't long before I heard the familiar purr of Stella's car. And, as before, she came up to me and squatted down by my side. "Hey," she said. Her eyes were red-rimmed. "I think we've both had a pretty bad day. Make mine a bit better now, and come on home."

"It's not my home!" I yelled. "That woman said I wasn't s'posed to be there!"

"Oh, I know she did but I don't agree with her and we will work something out, you'll see. She doesn't think I'm right; I don't think she's right. She just doesn't like me. Doesn't mean I'm wrong. She just talked apple-sauce like I said she would!" Stella lifted me up. "Any-how, let's go and see if there is any mail whilst we're out and about. Then I think we should go and have some fun. Hey, you know what? I've this idea. I haven't seen my folks for yonks. I'll call them and see if they can put us up for a week or so. Have a little holiday there with them. Wouldn't that be nice? They'd like that, too."

"What if they don't like me?" I sniffed.

"Don't be a silly. Of course they'll like you. Who wouldn't? — And it's real pretty there. We could have picnics, go boating, and my ma is always making great cookies. Oh, and they have an old pussy cat liv-ing there with them. She's called Mordicat, or Mordi for short. She's very friendly. Doesn't scratch, doesn't spit. Really purry, a bit like Sybil's Crumble. Though she's only got half a tail; the top half, before you ask! What d'you say?" I sniffed my nose on the back of my hand and nodded. "Let's go then while the iron's still steaming hot."

We picked up the mail and Stella made the call. She let me dial. "All settled," she smiled. "Ma and Pa are really looking forward to meeting you. We can pack up tomorrow early and drive straight up. It's quite some distance but, if need be, as soon as it gets dark, we'll nap in the car. We could even pack a torch and read stories by flashlight until we both fall fast asleep. Won't that just be fun?" I nodded, more interested. "Then when we wake up we'll hit the road again, bright and early, before it gets too hot. We'll need blankets and cushions and some water. I'll wrap up some tomatoes carefully; we don't want them squashed, do we? And we'll get some apples from Walter. They're always refreshing when travelling out and about. Oh, and what about some Oreos? They'll keep us sweet tempered. What d'you say to that?"

We arrived, eventually, at the Matthews' house in La Junta. Her ma and pa welcomed me with open arms. "I'm Abi-Laura, honey bunch," her ma said giving me a big hug, "you're such a little cutie! And this here is my husband, Christopher. But if you want you can call us Ma and Pa too, go ahead, whatever you prefer. I'll leave that to you. Now, how about some milk and cookies? I bet you're hungry as a caterpillar. You come along with me." That night I snuggled up in Stella's old room. Before I settled I wandered about touching everything, picking things up, opening and closing drawers, and breathing in the lavender smell of polish. I ran my fingers over the cool mahogany box on her dressing table and fingered the lace doilies. There were framed photos on the walls; there was one where she was snuggled between Abi-Laura and Christopher. In another picture she was sitting in a row-boat smiling toothlessly at the camera and holding up a fish to be admired. On her bedside cabinet sat a pretty little sampler mat with 'Stella Matthews aged eight, 1908' tightly stitched out in bright colours. I snuggled down under the comforter and before long Mordi joined me at my feet. From downstairs I could hear Stella and her folks chatting below. I couldn't make out what they were saying. There seemed to be some raised voices but I soon drifted into sleep. To me, it seemed a perfect time, a perfect place to be.

However, a couple of days later I was, unexpectedly, bundled back into the car for our return to Quivering Creek. I was surprised as I was expecting to stay on in La Junta somewhat longer. I'd liked playing with Mordi; I'd even planned to take her for a picnic on the lake. Christopher was going to show me how to fish! The Matthews seemed tearful we were going but Stella seemed agitated. Abi-Laura packed us off with more jars of fruit and pickles. I didn't quite understand why we were leaving so soon but Stella must have had her reasons.

⁂

"Maybe it was better you didn't know," Delphine mused. "Children often get the wrong end of the stick."

"That's true. But doesn't it just burn you up when you really want to know what's going on?"

"I'd say so. It would be real nice to be a fly on the wall sometimes, that is until you get swatted, or get stuck fast on a fly-sheet! So, you only stayed over a couple of nights? Not long for travelling such a way. Do you think Stella just changed her mind?" Delphine said, spooning me another helping of pumpkin ravioli.

"Thanks, Delphine, that's enough ravioli. That's far too much. You want me to get fatter?"

"No, course not. Here, have some parmigiana ... if you don't eat it all up, George will. And I don't want no fatty for any husband of mine."

"Well, Delph darling, I'll just have to go back and look up that fancy Lucia. She don't mind what size man I am. The bigger the better, she says. So, yes please, I will have another spoon. No, make it two."

"Anyhow," Delphine continued, ignoring him, "why do you think that Stella stayed with her parents such a short time? Did they not really get on that well?"

"I remember Christopher saying she had 'ants in her pants' which I thought was a funny thing to say and I laughed. Stella didn't seem to like that though, and she didn't laugh back. I suppose they wanted her back home living with them. That's natural for parents."

"True."

"I've thought a lot about that over the years. You know, I often wonder if the reason we went there, in the first place, was to ask them a favour. Maybe she wanted them to mind me whilst she went out looking for another job, and they may have upset her by saying no."

"Could be."

"The Matthews were getting on, you know; by then must have been in their fifties or sixties. I know that nowadays that's not considered really old ... not old like I am! How old did you say I was again ... a hundred and something? But still, too old to have a little girl round the place. They probably turned her down and she got annoyed."

"Maybe."

"And then, I think there was something else going on. I'd a hunch – you know, one of those famous hunches of mine – that Stella and her parents may

122

have been at loggerheads. You see Stella had pretty outlandish ideas, modern for her times, and they were, what you'd call, more conservative in their ways. Probably they wanted her to come home and marry the boy next door. Oh no, that wouldn't have been Stella's way, oh no, far too feisty to settle for the ordinary.

"Years later I found out more about Stella's husband, Mr Hurtigrutensson. He was a lawyer in Canon City and got killed. Some parts of Colorado, in those early days, were pretty rough and ready. Quite a lot of reactionary types were living out in those backwaters. I'm sure it's much improved now – well, I do hope so. Some of those folk, especially those with nothing better to do, thought that outsiders were harming the 'good old US of A'. If you weren't white protestant, you must be up to no good and you had to be stopped in your tracks."

"Are you talking about the Ku Klux?"

"Yes, indeed I am. They busied themselves around those parts. They were a nasty lot and chock-full of baloney. Well, what happened was Mr Hutigrutensson was attacked for defending a black man. In those times lawyers with liberal ideas had a rough time with some of the locals. It happened more often than not that they got abused themselves. Unfortunately Mr Hurtigrutensson died following the assault. Sometimes, you know, it doesn't take much of a hit."

"Uh-huh. Just like my poor little brother. He'd only been living in London a few weeks when he was cornered by this gang of white boys and they kicked him about. And that was that. Collapsed on the spot and died. What a waste! I'll never stop blaming myself. My fault. We got him over there thinking we could give him a better life."

"I know you did. You did what you thought was right at the time. You *were* right. I remember how excited you were about him coming over."

"Such a bright boy. Not a day goes by without me thinking about him!"

"They never caught any of them, did they?"

"I don't think at the time the police were that bothered. He was just another coloured boy to them. Sorry, Kitty, go on. I didn't intend to butt in like that."

"I know. You're not butting in. That's all right. Talk about it when you want."

"I know I can, but you go on."

"Okay. Well, where was I? Oh, Stella's husband. Now what was his name? Morten, that's right, Morten. Couldn't think of it for a moment! Memory's getting bad."

"No, you've got a great memory."

"Well, the killers were imprisoned but Stella felt obliged to move on. You couldn't live normally with people like that all about. She didn't know who was who in town. Those Klansmen were all so secretive and so protective of one another. Nobody said anything. All hush-hush. Stella and Morten, I think, were quite outspoken, particularly back then, in the twenties. They got involved in all sorts: politics, workers' rights, religion. I s'pose they rubbed folks up the wrong way. I'm not surprised that Stella's parents were anxious about her well-being.

"Anyhow, back to the story, a hand-delivered letter was sitting on the floor when we arrived back at Quivering Creek. Much to my irritation Stella waited until I'd gone off to bed before she'd open the envelope. It sat staring at her from the mantel all evening long. She paced the floor, glowering back at its insolence. To put her out of her misery I took myself off early to bed. The following morning I was greeted with a smile. I asked Stella about the contents of the letter. 'Nothing, really,' she replied very casually. 'Just an invitation to meet the school board. Probably another load of applesauce.' She didn't seem at all bothered, which confused me."

"So what happened in the end, then? Kitty. You're keeping me in suspense. Was she allowed to stay on?"

"Well, I think she must have impressed them with something or other because she came out of that meeting with permission to stay on until the Easter. There were some stipulations which made things awkward. The requirement was that she had to follow an approved curriculum. That was okay but the second thing was somewhat more tricky; she had to find alternative accommodation for me. I was, however, permitted to attend class."

"So how'd she get out of it?"

"Let's have a little more wine, Delphine."

"Good idea."

9

"Butterfingers!" A tomato splattered at my feet. "Here, have another, catch!" Stella said, biting hers in half. "Guess what? I put my thinking cap on this morning. I've an idea."

"What's that, then?"

"Well, now Sybil's back at school there's a spare room going at the Cummings. How about I ask Lois whether you can stay in Sybil's room?" Stella looked so pleased with herself. "Now Sybil's away, I can't think the number of times I've heard Lois Cummings bemoan the fact that she gets lonesome. She's on her own so much, what with the doctor off seeing to his patients, and the meetings he attends all over the state. Much too quiet for her. I'd say she'd probably jump at the opportunity to have some company. Aren't those thinking caps just great? I don't know why I didn't put mine on earlier." She shrugged her shoulders and giggled at my attempt to wipe up the squashed tomato from between the floorboards. "At night you could sleep in Sybil's room, and the days you could spend across here with me. I could drop you off at Lois's, no problem, and pick you up, come morning, ready for school. What d'you reckon?"

"No thank you," I replied. She didn't seem to hear.

"Well, what d'you think then?" Her face rosy with enthusiasm.

"No thank you. I'd rather stay here with you. It will be lonely there."

"Oh! Kitty, I am surprised. I'd have thought you'd love being there. I don't think you'd be lonely."

"Yes, I would."

"There's Crumble. I'm sure she wouldn't mind you having Crumble in the room with you." I pouted my lower lip and frowned. "Well, maybe, then, Mrs Cummings can think of someone else you can lodge with, just while things are sorted." I shook my head.

"Maybe someone with other youngsters about?"

"No!"

"Then you wouldn't get lonely. Now, if I'm right I believe she's part of some ladies' discussion group … oh, fiddlesticks! What's it called now? She's always talking about them. They sound a pretty nice lot of ladies and may only be too happy to have you lodge with them."

"No! I'm staying with you."

Stella knelt down and wrapped her arms around me. "Oh, Kitty, I'm just thinking what's best for you.

It's only for a short while. I'm not trying to get rid of you, Kitty-Kat. You'll see, honeypot. It'll be all right. I'll just go and talk it over with Lois. That won't do no harm, will it? She'll know what to do for the best. She's that type of lady."

As usual, on Thursday, we drove over to Silverton. I was still having a grump about the whole business. Stella seemed flustered. And, as we tootled along the highway, I spotted her talking to herself.

"What you saying?"

"Oh, sorry, nothing important."

"Why are you chattering to yourself, then? I'm not going to live with them, you know."

"I know, sweetheart.

"I don't want to go there."

"I know you don't. But it won't be for that long, Kitty-Kat. Just 'til things are sorted. You'll see, it'll be all right."

"But I'll miss you, Stella."

"I'll miss you too."

"I'll miss you the most."

I sulked in the car kicking my feet up and down against the upholstery whilst Stella went in to see Mrs Cummings. She wanted to speak to her in private, she said, and without interruption. As if I would interrupt! When Stella re-emerged she was carrying a bundle of newspapers and a few other bits and bobs. She got in the car and handed me a bag of clothes.

"For the coming colder months," Stella announced. "Sybil's outgrown them." With all the food I was consuming I was also growing fast. And the cardie that Stella was knitting me had not yet materialised into a recognisable shape. I pressed the parcel up to my nose and breathed in the smell of rose-scented soap. It reminded me of Sybil. Stella smiled at me and started up the engine.

"You going to tell me what Mrs Cummings said, then?" I asked impatiently.

"Well, she didn't say that much."

"Well, she must have said something or other!"

"She was good and listened to what I had to say."

"What'd she say about me staying over there?"

"She said there were possibilities; she'd have to think about it."

"Does that mean no?" I asked hopefully.

"No, it does not! It's just she couldn't commit. She couldn't say yes, or say no, without raising the subject first with Dr Cummings. It wouldn't be polite, of course, to make such a decision, there and then, without consulting him. She'll get back to us pretty soon."

"Why'd she give you all those papers?"

"She's a very thoughtful lady. Very kind of her. She just thought the *Denver Post* or *The Herald* may have some useful advertisements for teaching posts."

A few days later I was in the schoolroom when I noticed an envelope lying on the mat. It was addressed to Stella. She opened it and read, '*Dear Stella, the doctor and I would like to meet to discuss the situation concerning Kitty's position. Today, at 4.15pm would be most convenient. Lois.*'

"Strange Lois didn't knock," Stella said. "She must have been hurrying some place or other." We drove over that afternoon; Stella looked excited. I sat gloomily. "It'll be all right," she reassured. I wasn't feeling so positive. As the days were getting shorter the wind of the coming fall was bringing a chill to the evening air. I felt shivery. Glowering through the window I watched as Mrs Cummings opened, and slowly closed, the door after Stella.

I was just starting to get bored with scratching the leather on the seats with my finger nail when the front door of the Cummings house was flung open. Stella raged down the path. Her manner startled me. My heart started pounding and instinctively I squirmed down low trying to make myself insignificant. Memories of my ma's raging came flooding back. Stella hurled herself into the driving seat and crashed the door closed. Something fell off with a crack as she shot off down the road. Damning and muttering under her breath she lurched our way home, crunching the gears, raging her horn and swerving around dogs and other cars in her path. Back at Quivering Creek, I lagged behind her into the school house. Scared, I crawled under the table and made myself as small as possible.

Stella thundered about the room until eventually she stormed into her bedroom, slamming the door behind her. The picture of the boat on the lake shook and crashed to the floor into a myriad of glass splinters. I heard cursing and the thud and thump of kicking and things thrown hither and thither. Suddenly, all stopped, the room quietened. The only sounds I could just make out were muffled nose-blowing and the occasional sniff. The storm had passed. I crept out and, gathering a bowl of tomatoes, I knocked gently on her door. "Stella! Stella!" No reply. I lay the dish down on the floor and backed away. Back in my hide I drew a picture of bright rosy tomatoes. Carefully I posted it through the gap underneath the door. *'Sorry your sad.'* I wrote on the note, *'Love from Kitty-Kat Wardle.'* It was in my very best writing with swirls, and little pictures of cats adorned the page. Soon a note came sliding back out. *'It's not your fault Kitty. It never has been. Love Stella. PS. Mrs Cummings sent you some cookies. They are in my bag. Help yourself to milk too. I'll be out later when*

I'm feeling more myself. PPS. 'Your' should be spelt, 'you're'. I found the cookies and tuned into the radio station. I picked up the friendly-dog-face cushion and, hugging it, munched the night away.

By morning the cookie bag was empty. Even the last crumb had not evaded my attack. Several jars of jam, peanut butter and sweetcorn pickle lay open and abandoned on the shelves. Bowls of Krispie-Weets marooned in pools of milk and half submerged spoons covered the table cloth. It was light when Stella reappeared. From behind the safety of the cushion, and still in my hide, I watched her move steadily around the room, picking things up as she went. She lit the stove and fixed some coffee. She spied me watching her over the dog-face cushion, and smiled back. At this prompt I pulled myself up and ran to hug her around her waist.

"Did Mrs Cummings say no, then?" I whispered, still hopeful, looking up at her face.

"Yes, too right, she did." Taking a sip of coffee she slumped down on the couch listening to my cheers. She let out a long sigh. Once again silence took hold. I folded my arms and sat next to her leaning on her shoulder.

"What we gonna do, then?" I stared up into her face. She didn't look at me. I moved her chin around to face me. "What ... we ... going ... to ... do, then?"

We were so close we couldn't focus on each other, our noses were almost touching. I sniffed loudly. She smiled and twitched her nostrils back, twice. I sneezed and she giggled.

"Well, what's so funny?" I was still a bit wary.

"I don't quite know, Kitty. I just don't know. Don't fret. We'll find a way out of this mess, just you see."

✳ ✳ ✳

"So, I wonder what on earth had gone on at the Cummings?" Delphine asked. "Did you ever find out? Did the doctor husband put his foot down and cause trouble?"

"In my experience it's normally the wife who makes trouble."

"Ha-ha, George!"

"Yes, that's right, Delphine. That Doc Cummings definitely stirred things up. However, it must have been donkey's ears before I found out what the problem was."

"D'you mean 'donkey's years', Kitty."

"Do I? I like the sound of 'donkey's ears' better. Their ears are as long as years."

"I s'pose that's true. Anyhow, go on. I'm dying to know now."

"Where was I, then?"

"Not finding out what happened between Stella and Doc Cummings until 'donks' later."

"Yes, kids don't often want to know why things happen. They just want those things to be put right."

"Uh-huh."

"Anyhow, I probably wouldn't have understood what they were talking about. At the time I was far too young to know about that type of thing."

"What type of thing?"

"Would you mind getting me a drink? I'm awful dry."

"Would you like coffee, or a tea?"

"No George. I meant a drink-drink."

"Oh, excuse me! Would Madam like pink, white or red?"

"I was thinking more of a Whisky Mac."

"Sorry, Ma'am, we're right out of Whisky Macs."

"I'm going to have to move to a better supplied establishment!"

"Well, we're coming with you wherever you go."

"Okay then, a cup of tea will have to suffice."

"At your service, Ma'am but just wait on 'til I'm back. My ears are wagging now."

"Yes, I can feel the draught. I'll wait. Don't worry. If I can wait for donkey's ears, you know, I can wait for yours to return."

"Would you like another cup, Kitty?"

"Yes, I would, George, just half a cup. I'll get on with that story now."

"You sure you want to go on? You've been chatting quite a while today."

"Thanks, Delphine, but I'm fine. I want my story told."

"Okay, are we all sitting comfortably? Anything anyone wants before we get back to those good old days?"

"No thanks, George. — Well, have you heard of eugenics? It was a movement fashionable back in the twenties and thirties. It started across here in Europe. Lots of people believed in eugenics. It was considered a valid science."

"Still is by some weak in the head," George added. "The Ku Klux also got that notion of eugenics into their head. Head, I said, by the way — I don't think they had a brain!"

"But," Kitty nodded, "other seemingly normal, 'nice' people believed in it too. It sold itself as being scientific. The idea was that social ills could be eradicated by breeding out human flaws."

"So, I suppose that all depended on what people considered a flaw?"

"Exactly, Delphine. That was the danger. It's astonishing that people actually believed social ills, like poverty and stealing, could be passed down through families by the flow of 'bad' blood."

"That idea is still going around some places."

"True. They said the only way these 'human flaws' could be culled was by preventing people from breeding and passing on undesirables. That way, the eugenicists could engineer the human race. Anything considered degenerate was to be 'bred out' by the use of forced sterilisation and abortion. Blacks, of course in those days, were seen as inferior so they were targeted as well."

"Same as ever."

"Even people marrying outside their own race was considered criminal."

"It's still frowned upon! People haven't changed that much yet."

"But how did all that affect you, Kitty?"

"Well, George, you see Stella knew all about that type of thing. She was a thinking person; she wasn't the type to just go along with common thought. Although, personally, sometimes, I think, she disagreed for the sake of being contrary."

"Oh, is that where you caught it, Kitty?"

"George, mind your manners!"

"He's only fooling, Delphine. I can still take a joke even though I'm a hundred and something! – You know, Stella was the type of person who made up her own mind about things. Unusually, independent in her thinking. Anyhow, she was adamant I was not going to be carted off. Not only didn't she approve of me going to an orphanage, per se, but she knew what would probably happen once I got there."

"What would happen?"

"Well, in those days, some institutions forced sterilisation on their inmates. Can you imagine it! It was compulsory: jails, mental hospitals, orphanages, homes for the feeble-minded or itinerants ... all sorts of places."

"So are you saying this forced sterilisation went on in Colorado?"

"Yes, it sure did ... but other states were worse. Later on I found out how harshly they treated unfortunate young women like me. In California, you know, they had a directive insisting that all 'undesirables' were to be sterilised; California had one of the toughest sterilisation policies going. However, in the long run, it didn't seem to up the stakes of their local intellect!"

"Now, Kitty, that's a naughty thing to say."

"Sorry, Delphine, it just slipped out. But it also happened close-by to us in Kansas, too; they were really over zealous in the carrying out of their mission. Everything depended on the personal decision of whoever was the chief medical officer in the area."

"I see, so you were had for if the big boss man believed in eugenics?"

"Exactly, and not just boss men; there were boss women too."

"I know a boss woman."

"George! It's not funny!"

"Yes, boss."

"Well, to go on, it so happened that Dr Cummings was a leading member of the 'Fitter Families' organisation and obviously pro-sterilization. Loose morals, miscreant behaviour and poverty were all, according to him, inbred defects. He was the president of the 'Colorado Medical Society' and wrote articles for the 'Eugenics Journal' which had a worldwide readership. It was an important publication."

"No wonder he made you feel bad."

"Indeed he did. So when Stella went around that day he told her, in no uncertain terms, that I should be institutionalised. She, of course, would not stand for that."

"Good for her."

"There's still more to tell! Doctor Cummings had also been investigating my personal background. He had tried to find out if my parents were still living ... that was fair enough. But, he used me like a guinea pig. I was an example for his statistical evidence. He'd got word that my Pa's family came from generations of 'no-hopers', and my ma's morals were, as he put it, 'not intact'."

"Not a nice thing to say."

"He raged on and on and told Stella that my inherited weaknesses were apparent to all. Not only was my hearing poor, but I suffered rages, I absconded, I was backward in my learning, I was underdeveloped for my age, and so forth. The indication of my inbred poverty was as obvious, to him, as 'pork is to pig'."

"Nice expression!"

"No way would I've been allowed to stay with them. He was a doctor of medicine, so of course, he couldn't have had contaminated goods on his premises. No lowlife! The only place suitable for a girl like me was the orphanage; a place where they were equipped to deal with people of my type."

"Your type!"

"He didn't stop there! Playtime with Sybil was to finish forthwith. Sybil, he declared, was a sensitive girl and, being at a tender age, could be easily influenced by my presence."

"So Stella blew her top?"

"Not surprisingly! She was not expecting or prepared for his rant. She was so ruffled about it. I don't think she had an inkling that he was going to say those things."

* * *

The new school year was supposed to start up the Monday after. I was pleased I still held position of the school-bell monitor. Again nobody turned up. The register was taken. Stella, or rather Mrs Hurtigrutensson, acted as if it was just any ordinary school day. We went through the lessons as normal. She was totally focused. However, every time I heard a sound from outside, I jumped. Leaves rustled around the school yard in the gusting fall wind.

The weeks passed and I was just starting to relax when a school inspector came by. Stella showed him the register and he asked if I was the only pupil in attendance. I couldn't say a word. I was mute with terror. Reassuringly, Stella told me to answer all the school inspector's questions "loud, clear and with honesty." I was awful worried that the inspector might know about the doll, too. It was still preying on my mind and, more often than not, it crept into my nightmares. Stella still wasn't aware of my crime. I stood up and admitted that I was the only pupil in school. I admitted I had no parents. I admitted I lived with Mrs Hurtigrutensson. He didn't mention anything about the doll but I was ready to confess. I felt bad about burning the doll.

The inspector thanked and smiled at me. Then, with a serious face, he turned to Stella. He opened his briefcase and handed her an official looking envelope.

"You give us no alternative," he said to her gently. "I'm awful sorry, Ma'am. Some of us understand what you are trying to do here but, unfortunately, there are some on the board who have more power than others over the situation. I — we — tried our best, believe me. The vote was not unanimous. The best we could achieve is to allow you to live in the school house for a temporary period until you find other accommodation. The school is now officially closed. I'm afraid your contract is now terminated and salary stopped."

"I see."

"If we don't find someone else, as substitute, you can stay here until Easter. Then, sorry to say, you'll have to go, whatever the situation. I'm so sorry. It wasn't my decision. I want you to know we're not all like that." He gave Stella a little bow and strode out.

"Well, not as bad as I thought!" Stella winked at me. "I bet something will turn up. It'll be all right, you'll see. Now, let's get back to lessons. Where were we ...? Ah yes, division ..."

10

My blue cardigan didn't shape up. The only things knitted, that fall, were Stella's brows! I watched with interest as furrows, deep as a wheat field's, opened and closed across her forehead. Night after night she fumbled angrily and muttered, in annoyance, when the wool did not present itself as she would have wished it presented. She dropped stitches and, piqued, regularly ranted at their insolence. Finally the creation was cast aside. She was unable to focus on her work in hand as more pressing demands exacted her attention. I suppose, by that time we were probably living on a pittance and mounting credit extended to us by the enterprising Walter in the store.

The wind blew colder and hoar-frosts appeared along the branches of leafless trees. Only the pines stood tall and unwavering in their fine greenery. We moved lessons from the school room to the main house where the warmth emitted from the kerosene stove improved our mood. Hour after hour we sat close to the heater, writing and reading. Stella scoured the newspapers. Every day letters of introduction and application were composed. Each one displaying an enthusiasm for the position advertised. The carefully written advertisement offering piano tuition had not attracted any takers. No response whatsoever. And the Thursday music lessons were no longer happening. Occasionally Stella received a polite reply to her application for a teaching position; each one, prior to the opening of the envelope, raising her hopes. As she read I watched her face. And always felt its fall. My fault.

The monotony of disillusionment was broken, one afternoon, by a knock at the house door. This was an unusual event. Normally we didn't have unexpected visitors. In fact, we had none at all. We looked at each other. I mirrored her quizzical look and, scared as a rabbit, I closed my eyes and burrowed myself behind the sofa.

"What are you doing, Kitty?" I heard her whisper. Ice-cold air whipped through the room as the door opened. I curled myself smaller. "Oh!" I heard Stella's surprise. "I wasn't expecting to see you again."

"Please, I'm really sorry, Stella. Please understand."

"No, Lois, I don't understand. Not one little bit."

"Can I come in?"

"If you must, but I am busy. You see, I've got to find a new home for me and Kitty in addition to finding some income. Unlike you, I haven't got a husband to support me." Stella sounded unusually abrupt. I didn't like to hear her voice like that. It made me tremble all the more.

"I know. I'm really so sorry."

"Sure you are!" There was a moment of silence. "Do you want me to say that it's all right, then? Is that why you're here?"

"No. Are you alone?"

"Well, I wasn't," Stella said, looking across to my burrow. Blushing, I squeezed out of my hole.

"Hello, Mrs Cummings." I said glumly.

"Hello, Kitty." She smiled down at me and handed me over a basket. "Here, take this. There's some little goodies tucked down inside, specially made for you." I reached out gratefully but Stella snapped, "No thank you, Lois." I pulled my hand back and tucked it hard down into my pocket. I could feel tears prickling in my eyes and I was trying hard not to cry. I chewed at my lip.

"Oh! I see. I'm sorry, Stella. I should have asked first. Well, can Kitty just have this please, Stella." She pulled a little pink envelope out of the basket. "There's a letter here. It's from Sybil to Kitty. Is that okay? Can she have it?"

"As it's from Sybil, yes she may," Stella replied. "Kitty, I want a quiet word with Mrs Cummings. Can you go and sit in the schoolroom for a bit. She won't be long. You can take your letter with you and read it. Pop on your coat. It's pretty cold out there now. I will call you back as soon as we're finished."

I shut the door and pressed my ear hard against the hole in the timber.

"Please, Stella, please hear me out. I've come to apologize. The doctor does not know I'm here. He's out on call somewhere. You see, my life, with the doctor, is exceedingly difficult." She paused and drew a deep breath. "I've never spoken to anyone about this before now. My life's not difficult in the ways your life is; you've had to cope with lots and lots of things ..."

"Always had to cope," Stella butted in, "always had to struggle. Yet here's one more thing again I have to face! Let down, once more, by people I thought I could put my trust in."

"Stella, I'm sorry. I know life's been harsh to you. I really don't know how you manage to cope. I think it's unbelievable what you've achieved. I so admire your strength of character. You're a wonderful woman. But please, you have to understand something. I am the doctor's wife. I have to conform to what is expected of me. Everyone knows who I am in town. I'm being observed and judged continually. Lionel sets me rigid standards which I have to follow."

"Why?"

"I don't have a choice, that's why."

"We all have choices in life."

"But I can't just go away and leave him. He has my money, and worse ... he has final authority over Sybil. If I went he wouldn't let me see Sybil. I know that for sure. He's said as much. I have nothing without his say-so. You've heard his ranting. I hear it every single day of my life. If I step outside the line I'd be homeless and without Sybil.

"Do you think I wanted to send Sybil away to school when she was just seven? Oh no! No way! Of course I didn't want to. She was everything to me. I didn't have a job to fill in that gap. The doctor wouldn't permit it. I wanted to be a news correspondent when I was younger. My parents paid for me to go to college for that. But then, as these things go, I met Lionel and he just seemed so impressed with me. I was overwhelmed. We married. And from that day on he wouldn't hear of me working outside the home. You know, well enough, what it's like once women become wives. Everything changes. All dreams shattered.

"I'd so rather be back in New York now but, of course, Lionel wouldn't allow it. He won't move. He rules his little kingdom right here and it suits him just fine. I have no say but to go along with all his wishes. I'm roped down. Please understand, Stella. I desperately need your friendship.

"I really didn't know Lionel would object to Kitty coming over when I first befriended you. I thought he'd approve of Sybil having a companion. I knew he didn't like me making acquaintances without his say-so but I didn't think that extended to Sybil. And honestly, I was pleasantly surprised that both girls got on so well together. As you know, Sybil is generally very shy and retiring. Normally she doesn't make friends too well. I was so taken with the girls getting on like a house on fire." Stella snorted.

"Please listen, Stella. You want to know how restricted my life is? Lionel even has to approve my reading matter! He gives me journals, with articles encircled in red ink, to study. Some of the articles are written, by so-called well-respected men and women, on subjects that he thinks as the doctor's wife I should be knowledgeable. He wants to make sure I don't show him up when we meet with others in town or at his clubs. He tutors me on eugenics and any other current obsession, so that I can be supportive to him. You know how he thinks!

"He expects me to read these articles and then, like a school pupil, he tests me. It's like being at school. He insisted, last summer, that I write an article for 'The Colorado Women's Journal' on the subject. He corrected my work as if I were a child. I'm a trained journalist! I only go along with it, Stella, to shut him up. I don't want Sybil to hear us arguing. I want her happy.

"You know I don't believe in the rubbish I write. I know I'm wrong. I know, I know. I'm weak, believe me! It's pathetic. But there's no way I can give up my daughter, not for anything in the world. Even if you can't forgive me, Stella, please please understand I really regret my actions. I will do what I can, in any way possible, to make amends."

"If you say so. So what are you going to do then to make these amends?"

"First of all, Stella. Have a look at this. I've got something for you here. I took it off the doctor's desk. I was in his office dusting." She started to whisper.

Even with my good ear pressed really hard I couldn't hear any more. I felt pretty sorry for Mrs Cummings. She seemed genuinely apologetic. Another draft of cold air whooshed through the school house. The front door clicked shut and I ran across to sit down at my desk. Stella called me back through. By then I was feeling pretty cold but I soon warmed when I saw, still sitting atop the table, the basket covered in a strawberry-patterned tea cloth. I peeked inside at the hidden delectables and pawed at the contents. Stella didn't stop me. She was totally absorbed in reading a letter.

"Is it okay if I eat some, now Mrs Cummings has gone?" Stella didn't look up. "Stella," I shouted, "can I eat some now, please?"

"Oh, what? Yes, eat it!"

"All of it?"

"Yes. Eat whatever you want. Shush! Let me read."

She went into her bedroom closing the door firmly behind her. I lay down on the couch, a peach cream muffin in one hand and the first letter I'd ever received in my life clasped in the other. It felt good. By the time Stella came back in, I was curled up dozing. My stomach felt happily heavy with my coveted letter tightly clutched to my chest and crumbs spread widely.

"So, you won't be wanting any lunch, then?" Stella said, seeing the emptied basket. "None left for me? Not even a tiny bite?"

"Sorry," I said, "I really thought you didn't want any."

"It seems a lot of people have been saying their sorries to me today!" she said looking over her glasses.

"I'm sure we all are," I replied. "Isn't that good?"

❇ ❇ ❇

"What was in the letter Stella got? Was it good news?" George was serving me some crisply fried and vanilla sprinkled tiny doughnuts. I nodded my contentment. "My momma used to make these for us when I was a sprog," he continued. "She would feed all; not just the family, anyone passing, anyone, that is, she could get to open their mouth long enough. You know, the kitchen took over most of our place. My world was a bubbling, steamy, noisy world. Everyone was in there. All chopping, whisking, frying. That was some spicy kitchen! Always smelt good. Made you hungry just passing through. And my momma always there, always right in the centre, always cooking away."

"And now you brought part of her spirit over to cook for us."

"I did indeed. She set me up well."

"I'm so pleased she did."

"So, Stella, what about the letter? Did you find out anything?"

"Well, probably not for forty odd years."

"Forty years? What! That's time enough to cook a heck of a lot of chicken!"

"It sure is, George. But you know, even now, after all those years I still find the letter difficult to talk about. I'll tell you in a bit."

"Oh my darling, excuse me." George squatted down and held my hands. "I didn't mean to pry. I'm truly sorry if I upset you."

"George Horus Hale," Delphine said, "sometimes you don't know when to keep that big mouth of yours shut."

"No, Delphine, he didn't upset me by asking, not one little bit. Get up, George! It's just me being a silly old thing, not you!"

"Are you sure?"

"Yes. I will tell you but not 'til I'm right ready to tell. Stop apologizing! Delphine, let him be. It's okay! I want to tell you both, but just not tonight. Everything in its own time. Hey, that sounds as if I'm making it all sound mysterious. No, it's not. The only reason that I can't tell you now is that I can't talk with my mouth full of these little doughnuts. They're good. I hope they're not too fattening! Anyhow, they're too good to savour over sad stories."

"Like another?"

"If you insist. You know, I never got my hand around baking and things. I wish I had. I should have met you earlier, George. You could have taught me how to cook."

"So," Delphine said, "wasn't Stella nifty in the kitchen?"

"No. She wasn't really domesticated ... except for her bizarre craze about tomatoes. She was always bottling them in different ways. But cooking wasn't really her thing. To me, though, everything she made tasted just like nectar."

"Food always tastes good made by someone you love."

"But you know, her cooking was just like her knitting. To me, yes, it was wondrous, but shall we say, it wouldn't have won any competitions."

"Just like someone else I know." George waved a finger at Delphine.

"Are you saying you don't like my cooking!"

"No, Delph, like you, it's perfect."

"Lucky you said that, dear."

✳ ✳ ✳

Even as a little child I could sense Stella's discomfort. It would start with a look of bewilderment as if she couldn't focus attention on her surroundings. I'd be having a lesson when, all a sudden, she'd stand up and aimlessly wander the room. Occasionally, she'd hover at a window, pleating the curtains between her fingers. Sometimes she'd murmur to herself. I'd carefully watch her staring into nothingness. At first I was frightened by her look but I learnt, over the weeks, that these occasions were harmless and would pass. Rising quietly from my chair I'd pad cross the floor to her side. Her arm would gently alight upon my shoulder like a butterfly landing on a flower. And, in response, my head would come to nestle against her warmth, my arms in a love-lock around her waist, and in reverie we'd sway, cradled together. At those special times there was no call for hurry.

It just so happened that we were entwined when Mrs Cummings's car pulled up outside. It broke the spell.

"Oh, look! See what the wind has blown in," Stella said sarcastically. I felt sorry for Mrs Cummings. "I s'pose we'd better let her in, then." Before Stella had moved I had sprung across the floor to open the door for her.

"Hello, my dear. Is Stella about?"

"Yes, Lois, I'm over here by the window. Step in. Close the door quickly before we all freeze to our deaths. Put the kettle on for us, Kitty, please. Have you time for some coffee?"

"Thanks, Stella. Yes, I have. That's most kind of you. I've got some fresh gingerbread in here, somewhere."

"You know, Lois, there's no need to bring us things to eat. We manage." I looked aghast. Whose side was Stella on! I thought bringing baking was a fine way of making amends for all the upset caused.

"I know, dear. But it gives me pleasure to cook for Kitty now Sybil's back at school, and, for sure, Kitty does have a sweet tooth just like my Sybil." I nodded enthusiastically and showed her my teeth. Mrs Cummings smiled back at me. Stella looked rather askance at my pert manner and arched a brow.

"Well, okay then, thank you, Lois. As you can see Kitty obviously appreciates your gesture."

I was allowed to make them coffee. Stella opened the cake tin and arranged the slices neatly across the plate.

"To what do we owe the pleasure of this visit, Lois?"

"Actually, I may have some good news. I'm not sure if I can talk freely. Can I?" She looked across at me and back across at Stella. Stella looked at my expectant face.

"It's okay. Speak your mind, Lois. I will leave you to decide upon the discretion. It's a far too cold to hang about in the schoolroom now. Although, I suppose, Kitty, you could go and read in your bed-room under the covers," she said looking at me.

"No! I'm happy here. Please can I stay. I won't listen. Look." I put my hands over my ears and started humming.

Both women smiled. "You don't have to cover up your ears," Stella said.

"And I'd rather you didn't hum," Mrs Cummings added, laughing. "There's one thing I need to ask you, Stella. Please, please don't mention this meeting to Lionel."

"I don't think that's likely, do you, Lois?" Stella shook her head.

"No, I suppose not."

"And, I wouldn't dream of it, either," I added, crossing my heart. "I swear on my life."

"You don't need to swear on your life, Kitty, but thanks anyhow. Well, you may recall I have a married sister living near New York city. Esther's her name. Lionel has never got on too well with her husband. Her husband's English, you know. He doesn't think much to his ideas and he doesn't like the British, anyway."

"Not surprised he doesn't."

"So, because of Lionel, Esther and I don't meet up that often. I haven't seen her for years and years. Sadly, I've never ever seen my nieces and nephew. She's got three now. Lionel always argues it's too far to visit. But, I know, of course, there's more to it than just the distance. I've even tried suggesting to Lionel that Esther could travel here for a couple of weeks during the summer. We've got the room for them. But, of course, there's always the excuse, patients come first. He can't be disturbed. You know what he's like.

There's no point in trying to dissuade him. It would make things worse.

"No, I s'pose there wouldn't be."

"Personally I always liked Henry, that's Esther's husband. But you know Lionel, if he takes a dislike to you, that's that!" We both nodded our understanding. "Anyhow, Esther and I keep in touch. We get on just fine, always have done. They have two girls, twins, and a boy about five. The twins must be coming up thirteen, I think. Time flies.

"Esther and Henry said they'd like the girls to be schooled over in England. They're not too happy about them growing up in New York for some reason or other. Well, that's their choice. Henry, of course, still has his own family living over there. There's the girls' grandmother and he has an older brother. Henry's mother has never set eyes on her grandchildren. Kind of sad for her as well as for the children not knowing their grandmother. Both mother and son live near a town called Cambridge which is, I've heard, a really nice place to live."

"I've heard that too. It's a big university town."

"Esther's always been saying that, one day, Henry would like to go back to England to live. Now that day has nearly come. Both our parents have passed away so there's no valid reason for Esther not to go anymore. Esther's never been afraid of making changes, you know. She likes the idea of seeing different places. But, of course, Henry first needs to set himself up in Cambridge with a job. He doesn't want to move overseas until it's all properly organised. So, first of all they'll get the girls off to boarding school in Cambridge. Then, hopefully, something will turn up for Henry and they can move back to England and set up house. It seems an okay plan to me and it won't interrupt the children's education as much. It's silly but I'll miss Esther dreadfully when she's gone. It's not as if we ever see each other anymore, but still."

"No, that doesn't sound silly; England's another world."

"And, on the other hand, it will be nice for the old grandmother to have the girls about, get to know them properly. I've been told Henry's brother has plenty of space in his house. It's the old family home. Henry's father has passed on now but his mother's still about. It would be nice for Esther to have more family around her. I wish I could go with them."

"Hmm," said Stella, "that's all very interesting. But, Lois, how does that affect me? Where's all this leading?"

Mrs Cummings leant forward. "I've just got a letter from Esther. She was saying that she would feel happier if she knew the actual person who was going to accompany her girls on the sea voyage. There's an agency that does that type of thing but, of course, she would prefer to know whoever it was by personal recommendation. She needs someone to take them over and settle them safe and sound. I thought of you, Stella."

"What!"

"I know it's not a long-term job, but I just thought it might suit you in your present situation. I hope you're not offended by my suggestion."

"Offended, no: astonished, yes. I appreciate you thinking of me, Lois. But, honestly, it's a big undertaking. That's a bit more than I can manage. I've never travelled anywhere much before, apart from Colorado. Across to Kansas once but that was with my Morten. I couldn't travel all that way to England, Lois, not on my own. That's a world away. But thanks for thinking about it."

"I'd be with you, Stella," I piped up. "You wouldn't be alone. I'll look after you."

"You're not s'posed to be listening."

"Sorry, I forgot."

Stella paced the room. She clucked her tongue several times. Hovering at the window she stared into the nothing. Mrs Cummings and I smiled at each other and sat quietly picking sugar crystals off the top of the gingerbread. Eventually Stella settled herself back down like a chicken ruffling out its feathers. "Lois, have you mentioned me to your sister yet?"

"No, not even suggested it."

"Good."

"But if you wanted me to, I could do when I write back. I'm one hundred percent sure that she'd employ you simply on my say-so. If you do go to England things may have gotten better by the time you return home. And, moreover, you'd then have a good reference. There could even be some more work going for you out east. Esther is sure to have some contacts. She used to teach school before she had the children."

"True," Stella nodded. "Not having a reference is my downfall." She tapped her fingers on the table. "I've the heebie-jeebies now, Lois. Don't know what I should do for the best!" I held her hand. "It would be an experience, that's for sure. But I'll have to think about it. Yes, go on, write to her. I'll wait and see what she says. Then I can chew it over."

Mrs Cummings stood up and went across to Stella and hugged her. "It'll be just fine. Don't you worry. And I won't mention the Lionel incident. Esther already senses that things aren't right between Lionel and I, and I don't want her fretting even more about me."

"That suits us both, then. Thanks, Lois."

"I better be going now and get that letter written up fast."

"Don't forget your bag," I said, handing her the empty basket. "Nice to see you again, Mrs Cummings. Come back soon."

I watched from the window and waved her good-bye. She waved back, smiling. Shame about her husband, I thought.

"What have I done!" I turned around. Stella was sitting at the table, shaking her head from side to side. "Well," she sighed, "I do get myself into some situations! What a pickle! England, indeed. Probably Timbuktu, or Samarkand, next week. Anyhow we'll just wait and see. Nothing may come of it, of course. But on the other hand beggars can't be choosers."

"You'll see," I said. "It'll be all right!"

II

"It's blueberry shortcake," Mrs Cummings mouthed to me as she stepped up the path. Silently, I nodded back enthusiastically. A week or two had passed by since Stella had been introduced to the idea of overseas travel. I swung open the front door as soon as I heard the click of the gate and the tap of Mrs Cummings shoes along the hard ground "Hi, Mrs Cummings, great to see you again. Can I help you off with your coat?" She was hardly over the threshold before I started tugging at it. A round tin emerged from her bag. Mmm! Blueberry shortcake sounded good to me.

"Thank you so much, Mrs Cummings," I said clutching the tin to my body. I didn't give Stella a moment's eye contact chance she objected. The horrible thought of Stella spurning edible offerings traumatised me. "How very kind of you," I continued. "I hope it gives you as much pleasure to give, as it is for me to receive. I'm so heartened to think I remind you of Sybil's teeth." I gave her another toothy grin. "And how are you today, Mrs Cummings? And Doctor Cummings? Good. Raptured to hear it. Do take a seat."

"Thank you, Kitty. That's quite enough, now. Let Mrs Cummings and I have a chat."

An explosion of sweet-scented blueberries burst out of the tin. I inhaled deeply. "It smells absolutely *dovine*. Thank you, thank you so dreadfully much, Mrs Cummings. I really adore it. It looks so desirable with all that golden and purple ... stuff everywhere."

❋ ❋ ❋

"You know, Delphine, I can smell that pie right now. It's as if it is actually right here with me, right under my very nose. My goodness, how that smell transports me back a good few years. Mmm, delicious!"

"Oh, that's probably just my fancy new cologne you can smell," George responded.

"George!" Delphine smiled. "I must say, Kitty, my stomach seems to totally agree with yours. That blueberry shortcake sounds quite something."

"You know what?" George continued. "As I love both you ladies so very much, how about I go and cook you up one of those pies? It shouldn't be too taxing. I can't guarantee it will taste as good as Mrs Cummings's but I'll give it my best. Are your lips actually drooling, Kitty?"

"Sure are. You're such a love, Mr George Horus Hale. You know how to keep an old lady happy. If only I was thirty years younger I'd run off with you today. Wouldn't think twice here about Delphine. Or that Lucia."

"Hey, Kitty! I'm here in this very room listening to you two old love birds!" responded Delphine hands on hips.

"Sorry, Delphine. But you know me, my stomach comes long before loyalty. Always has done. George, sweetheart, I'd really love you to make that blueberry shortcake pie for us. I could eat it right up this very second. Maybe a spoon, or two, of that nice Chantilly on top wouldn't go amiss either. What'd you say to that, now, Delphine?"

"I'd say that pie sounds right down my street!"

"Okay, ladies. Blueberry Shortcake pie it is. Give me an hour or so. I'll see you later my favourite alligators."

"In a while, dearest crocodile." The door shut, then re-opened. "One problem, ladies – I'm missing an essential ingredient."

"What's that, then?"

"Blueberries! I have this suspicion that blueberry pie may be quite tricky to make without having blueberries as an ingredient. I don't think I've even seen them around these parts. Say, would raspberries do instead, Kitty, or cherries, maybe? I think I've still got some of our own bottled left over from summer."

"Either way. Both sound just great."

"Hey, but wait on, Kitty. I want to hear what happens next. So if I make you a raspberry shortcake, with crumbles, and vanilla sugar, will you promise not to go on with the story until I get back?"

"As long as there's a spoon, or two, of Chantilly cream? No, make that three."

"Chantilly it is."

"Okay, I promise," I said, raising my palm. "I'll restart after dessert. I think I'll have that little nap now."

❈ ❈ ❈

"I've had a letter back from Esther." Mrs Cummings smiled. "She thinks you'd be an absolutely perfect companion for her girls. I knew she would! She's pretty worried about them making that Atlantic crossing with strangers. Of course, she'd do it herself, but with little Clive charging about it would be nigh impossible. I believe he's quite a handful. She'd probably spend all day chasing him around the deck and most likely end up fishing him out of the sea!"

"Better not to, then."

"And from what I can remember, going back all those years, Esther's no sailor either. You know, we used to have a little row-boat, and even paddling out on the lake she'd turn a shade greener. Anyhow, Esther asked me to let you know the basics. Then, if you're interested and want to go ahead, she will write you some more. Are you happy with that, Stella? I don't want to push you into anything you don't want to do."

Stella nodded. "Suppose as sure as I'll ever be. Nothing to lose, hey?" She stood up. For a moment she looked as if she was about to say something. I held her hand. I could feel the tremble. She smiled down at me, mouthing, but speechless.

"We thank you so much for all your help, Mrs Cummings," I said. "You've been most *considerative*." Stella nodded her approval. Mrs Cummings laughed and gave my cheek a gentle pinch. I've never quite understood why adults think that children like their faces pinched but I knew it was supposed to be a sign of affection. Stella seemed to be rocking slightly on her feet so I gave her hand an extra squeeze. Eventually she spoke.

"That's truly wonderful, Lois. You're a good, good woman. I'm so sorry about my manner and snapping before. I was just ... bothered. But, tell me, Esther does know about little Kitty-Kat here? I just couldn't go anywhere without her." She gave my hand a gentle squeeze back.

"Yes, I hope you didn't mind me mentioning it. I said you would have your foster daughter travelling along. Is that okay? She didn't mind at all. There's two bunks in each of the cabins so it's all the same to her. The twins will share and there should be plenty of space around the ship where you can have lessons and not be disturbed by the other passengers."

"That sounds just great."

"From my understanding she'd like to meet up with you in New York. Probably for the month before you set sail. It'll give you a chance to meet them all and get to know the girls better. Esther and Henry have a loft room, over the garage, which they'll make comfortable for you and Kitty. Oh, I do wish I was coming too. Will you write me and let me know everything?"

"I'll try my best."

"Me, too." I replied.

"I know you'll become friends with Esther. She would really like that. And you'll like Henry too. The family are just lovely. I do miss them. I do wish I could go."

"I know you do, Lois. – Tell me, what's happening when we get to England?"

"Well, she said you'd be taking a train up to Cambridge. You have to go through London first. Esther would like you to stay with them until they're settled in. I think you'll most likely be gone several months. You'll be a bit like their nanny. The girls will probably need a lot of help getting ready for their new school and buying things like uniform, hockey sticks, tennis rackets, books, painting sets and other bits and bobs. I found out Grandmother is pretty old so she probably won't be able to help out too much. Then when everything's sorted you can come sailing back home."

"So when do the girls start at school?"

"End of April, sometime."

"April. That's still quite a while off."

"It'll be here before you know it," continued Mrs Cummings. "Then it's just wait and see. It'll be such an exciting adventure for both of you. Afraid I don't know any more details. You'll have to discuss the rest with her. Look, I've got her address written down for you and a number here if you prefer the telephone. She said to make a collect call whenever you want."

"This all sounds too good to be true. I think our luck has changed, Kitty. You know, Lois, you have been a good friend to us. I'm really sorry about, you know, my poor behaviour towards you. I was really rude. I was just feeling so upset about 'you know what'. I know it wasn't your fault."

I didn't really know what 'you know what' was but, wholeheartedly, I agreed with her. I was so pleased that, once more, we were all good friends. I wasn't too sure, however, about this England place. I'd asked Stella where England was. She showed me on the school map. "It's where the princesses live. You know, Princess Elizabeth and the little Princess Margaret. Their grandpa's King of England. They live in a palace in a big, big city called London. That's in England. England's in Europe. It's far away, on the other side of the world, on the far far side of the ocean. It's called the Atlantic."

"In the Old World?"

"Uh-ha."

"Will we have to cross mountains and things? Will we see dragons breathing fire in England?" I asked with all seriousness.

"Yes, to the first question and, sorry, no to the second. All dragons gone now. I think the knights of old 'got em all' going back quite some time now." I was quite relieved. I'd heard dragons could be quite temperamental. You can never be too sure with a dragon. "But for sure, Kitty," Stella continued on excitedly, "there'll be mountains to cross and hills wide and rolling in mauve heather. I've seen pictures in calendars. We'll be passing through pretty little villages with cottages roofed in golden straw and there'll be white ducks with yellow beaks quacking about in ponds everywhere. And there'll be castles of old and waterfalls and gardens spilling over with the most beautiful flowers you've ever seen. It's so pretty there. You'll love it."

"So how do we get across the big sea?"

"Well, there'll be an enormous ship. The sea will be jam-packed with fish, you know, and there'll be dolphins leaping giant silvery waves. I've seen photographs of them, too. And when we get to England, there will be little creeks with stepping stones across them and huge forests ripe-green with trees. I've seen that at the movies. We're going to love it, I know we are. Just you see."

"Will they have a cat in England?"

"Yes. I'm sure. Remember that girl 'Alice' in the book? She lived in England with a Cheshire cat."

"I thought that was in 'Wonderland'."

"I think it could be the same place."

Letters came and letters went. The mail-box was never lonely. Stella rehearsed our travel itinerary over and over again. We chorused it without script. We drew maps and coloured in pictures of England. We listened to the wireless keen to hear news from 'The Palace'. I wondered if the king and the princesses knew we were coming and should I write to them? Stella, with great sentiment and in forced English accent, read me poetry from Elizabeth Barrett Browning. I clapped gleefully at her renditions.

Esther's final letter arrived containing our travel arrangements to New York. Cramming our heads together we scanned it excitedly. Everything had been set out precisely for us: the agreed date, the time of arrival in New York confirmed, the meeting point highlighted, the fares to be forwarded. "Henry will meet us at New York Central Terminal," Stella read. "He's going to greet us by the central information point which is under a tall clock with four opal faces." It sounded like being in an adventure story. "Henry," she continued, "is going to drive us back to Upper West Side ... that sounds so grand a place ... where we'll meet Esther, and her twins, Margaret and Marion. Oh! ... and they've already got the tickets for the crossing!" she squealed, her voice rising in excitement. "Oooh! That's getting my heart going thump-a-thump. And the liner is ... the SS Brittic! Look, she's enclosed a picture of it for you. How kind!" I stared at it with amazement. "That's so posh!" she continued. "It's even got a swimming pool. We'll have to buy bathing costumes. I'll put that on my list. I wonder if Walter sells swim suits." I shook my head. "No, you're right, I don't s'pose he does. Oh, Kitty, I'm all a-flutter, now."

"Me too," I said, bouncing up and down. "I'm going to England, I'm going to England!"

"I'm going too, I'm going too!" she echoed, dancing me around and around the room. "It's like being a movie star! We're going on a liner to England.

So posh!" Grabbing my hand she polkaed me across to the piano where she started to bang out tune after merry tune.

So, straightforward? — No. Getting to New York was not as simple as Stella first thought. And I didn't help matters. It was all very confusing. Stella had sought timetables off different railroad companies and wrote to travel agents for advice on mapping out our journey. There were differing and contradictory responses. She studied the logistics for hours, and her itinerary would be more or less sorted out when I'd hear a cry of, "Oh, bother!" Or, "Oh, applesauce! That train does not connect with this train." Or, "This train does not connect with the Santa Fe, bother, bother, bother!" And, "There's no sleeping car on that service, so we'll have to sit up the night, oh fiddlesticks!" Eventually satisfied, she let out a deep sigh of relief. "All done now," she said rubbing her hands together. "All done and dusted. I'll let Esther know tomorrow and she can wire the fare. Then we're ready to roll." We whooped around and around the room.

Our excitement didn't last long. That evening, I traced the red artery of rail track. I scrutinised the black dot of every station, and town, en route. Suddenly my finger came to a halt. It stopped. It seemed powerless to move on. I stared at the dot beneath and made out the name: 'Elkhorn'. The name I knew so well. The high place, and low, of my earlier existence. I shuddered. With the chill draft that ran through the room the gas-light flickered about me and macabre shadows danced the walls. I quavered; an intrusion of unwanted thought misted through me. Ma still missing. Ma still missed. Missing my ma. My finger still wouldn't move. Ensnared. I couldn't move. I couldn't call for Stella. About me a whisper of voices: Elkhorn, Elkhorn, Elkhorn. My eyes scan the room for Stella. She is reading to herself. I shout for her but my voice has been ripped away. The black dot suddenly looms large. No, I'm shaking my head. No, no, no! It swells like the stomach of a long dead cow. And bursts, mouldering to a morass. A morass of dust, of bones, of death. Images of Ma's raging envelopes me. Her face menaces. Her mouth opens as if to speak. She encircles me, both our mouths gaping but without sound. Suddenly she chokes herself back into a vortex of swirling greyness ... she is gone. I eye the dot closely but she is gone. She's gone again. Gone again. Gone. Pawing the map, I try to claw back her image. This time I will hold her down. I won't let her go.

She didn't return. She was a ghost. Gone from me for ever.

"Whatever is the matter, honeypot?" Stella put her arm around me. I was rubbing my eyes.

"Kitty-Kins? Tell me. What has upset you, sweetheart?" Stella was rocking me.

"I saw Ma. She was there," I pointed to Elkhorn on the map, "and then she disappeared. She disappeared again."

"Oh, I'm so sorry, sweetheart. I never thought."

"Do you think my ma's dead, Stella?"

"Oh, darling, I don't know."

"I think she is. She's gone and died on me."

"Oh, if only I could I'd make things better for you I would, my darling. But you can't turn the clock back. The past has gone for all of us." She hugged me in her arms. "Tell me, why do you think she's dead?"

I told Stella what I'd just seen. Stella was adamant that ghosts did 'not' exist. "They do not exist! There is nothing to be frightened of." It was just my imagination, she maintained, but I wouldn't be reassured.

"I can't go, Stella," I continued. "I just can't. I don't want to go back there ever ever."

"But we're not changing trains in Elkhorn, or even getting off to walk about. I'll tell you what I'll do; I'll pull the blinds down before we get to the station so we can't see out. You won't even know you're there. You've just got a touch of the heebie-jeebies."

"No, no! It's more than the heebie-jeebies! What if she gets on? Or if she's on already? I want my ma. I want my pa. I want Pa back. Why'd he go and die?

"I don't know that, sweetheart."

"What am I gonna do if I see them? I want my mama."

"They won't be there anymore."

"They are there! You don't understand."

"I think I do."

"No you don't. I'm never going there. I hate it."

"But, Kitty. We have to go through Elkhorn if we're going to New York. It's where the line goes through from around here. We can't leave here without going through there unless we're going to build our own rail line!" She wiped my nose for me. I smiled too at the thought of putting down the tracks. She gave me some hot nutmeg milk and tuned into 'Jack Benny'. And sitting on her knee, sucking my thumb, I listened to a song about not having any bananas.

However, in the dark of my bedroom that night, my imagination once more ran wild. I started whimpering. Stella must have heard because she came and sat down on my bed. I told her the rest of the story. I told her about the tornado and leaving Pa to the savagery of the birds. And then I told about Ma. I told her how Ma had gone crazy and then, one day, how she just vanished into the dust. Stella stroked my temple and nodded. She held me close to her, rocking. I fell asleep in her arms but nightmares continued to harangue me. In my sleep ghosts of Ma and Pa flew along the rail tracks. Ma's face caught again in an open-mouthed scream and Pa with eyes hollowed. I saw dolls' faces dripping melted wax onto my burning hands and black-feathered vultures screeched and pecked at my skin. Bones jerked out of the dust and woke me several times from my sleep. Stella was always there sitting on my bed, her eyes fixed on me. I clambered for her hand and she held mine, tight.

Next morning my heart was thumping when I awoke. I could not go back to Elkhorn, not as long as I lived. I needed to find a way out, or a feasible excuse. I considered feigning a serious and mysterious sickness on the day of departure, but then that wouldn't tarry the train journey for ever. I thought about running away into the forests, but then what if I wasn't found? A bear may hunt me out. Sybil, I knew, would know what to do. 'Look, Kitty,' she'd say, 'see what *Anne of Green Gables* would say.' *Anne,* we knew, had suffered every trauma of life. She, through the power of verbal persuasion, however, could solve all. If only, I thought, if only I could render Anne in the manner of Sybil. Only then might I have a hope of convincing Stella. Surely, then, only the most heartless soul could turn me down. I practised the words in my head, over and over again, and prepared to deliver a stirring plea at breakfast.

"I'd rather die a *violet* death," I wept to Stella at the table. I placed one hand against my temple. "A maiden, such as I, can stand only so much anguish. I am but a mere little rosebud in a sea of thistles. If I return to that place yonder then my heart will wither and I shall be no more. Your golden ..."

"Okay, Miss Anne of Green Gables, I don't want no withering around here so we'll have to see what can be done. All night long I've been thinking about our problem. I put on my thinking cap and I thought we could check whether there are other routes to New York. Maybe we could go via the North Pole? Is that all right, Miss Anne? We could see polar bears and sleep in an igloo. That'd be fun ... but cold." I nodded. My face flushed; I'd been foiled.

We got the map back down. Geography had never been such fun. But even I could see we were kind of stuck with going through Elkhorn.

"I could walk," I proffered.

"It's miles. It would take you months, honeypot," she laughed.

"I've walked before."

"I know you have, but that was before you met me. I won't let you walk. You're too precious. And I can't walk that far, anyhow."

The middle of the following night she woke me from sleep. "I've an idea," she whispered. I sat up, eyes wide as vowels. "Why don't we drive as far as we can, sell the old car and get ourselves a train at the nearest railroad station? Now, isn't that's a capital idea, even though I say so myself?" I hugged and hugged her. I was so relieved. "Actually, now I've got my thinking cap really tightly screwed down, I've got an even better idea. Here's what we'll do. How about we drive up to La Junta, get Pa to sell the car, and then take the train from there! That's nowhere near Elkhorn and we'll be well on the way. Now, why didn't I think about that before? Good thinking, Stella."

I'd noticed several things had started to go missing. I think Stella was bartering with Walter in return for provisions. The precious gramophone and the 'Sally' HMV had gone, although the 'Tosca' still held pride of place on the dresser. The gilt mirror had disappeared and the tapestry, too. Probably there were other household luxuries which had also been carted away without my knowing. Mrs Cummings kept up her visiting. Sometimes she brought us a cheese, sometimes a fresh loaf. Once she brought a bean stew. She explained her generosity as being only fair play as she was always drinking up our coffee ... although, more often than not, she brought us over the coffee beans.

It was just before Christmas when Mrs Cummings arrived carrying a gift from Sybil. It was a book, *Little Women.* Sybil couldn't visit. She'd returned early from school suffering from serious influenza.

And, of course, she was forbidden to play with me. Instead, we sent each other little notes and colourful drawings. I missed Sybil and she missed me. Every night Stella read me a chapter. I didn't enjoy the story very much.

Fortunately Sybil got over the worst of her illness. Doctor Cummings, however, decided to send her off to a sanatorium. Sybil, of course, wanted to recuperate at home with her mother. Mrs Cummings begged her husband to let Sybil be nursed at home. But it was to no avail. Before any further protest, he whisked Sybil off to some place in New Mexico where she could fully regain her strength. We never said good-bye to each other.

A week or two before our departure another letter arrived for Stella. By then it must have been coming up late January. Mrs Cummings turned up in a blizzard. She passed the envelope to Stella without saying a word. I had hardly drawn off her coat when I was shuffled over to the couch and she engaged me in some chit-chat. From her bag she took a book and started to read me the story. It was about a princess who lived in a far-away tower and who fell in love with a fierce dragon, who turned out in the end to be a prince. I wasn't that impressed. Dragons were never reliable and you would have thought the princess would have known that right from the beginning. You never knew

where you were with them. But I was looking forward
to meeting these princesses. They always seemed to get
into such scrapes. I was most disappointed to think
that dragons were no more although I understood
there were still Cheshire cats grinning in England. But
one or two dragons would also have been nice to see,
that is, at a distance. What if one of the dragons was
a prince in disguise? It was one thing to hunt fierce
dragons but another to hunt handsome princes. I was
wondering if I would meet a handsome prince but,
I thought, unlikely as I did not possess the required
long, flowing, golden-blond sausage-curls. The story
came to an end and Stella got up from the table and
said quietly, "Thanks Lois for bringing this over, and
thanks for reading Kitty a story."

"Would you like me to read her another story
while you have a think ... about ... things?" Mrs Cummings asked Stella in a strangely stilted voice.

"No, um, that's okay. I think I know what I'm
going to do, if I can, that is."

"What are you thinking then, Stella?"

"Well, Lois, I need to do what's right. I think
I may just have to add another stop to our journey."

"Where to?" I said, confused by their curious
conversation.

"I forgot, Kitty," Mrs Cummings butted in,
"how about you trying one of these honey-walnut

buns for me? I've not baked this recipe before. I could really do with your opinion on the mix." I purred approval. "Good?"

"Uh-ha!" I nodded, my mouth crammed full with crumbs.

"Well, I'll be off now, then. Glad you're enjoying them, Kitty."

"I'll see you to the car, Lois." I heard Stella say. "You stay there in the warm now, Kitty. Eat the buns. I'll be straight back."

"See you soon, sweetheart. You may keep the book, Kitty. I don't think Sybil reads it any longer." I wasn't surprised as it wasn't the type of book either Sybil, or I, would have chosen.

Whilst munching, I watched Stella and Mrs Cummings talking at the gate. It was bitter cold outside and Stella was holding her arms tightly across her body. Mrs Cummings drove off and yet Stella still stayed outside, arms folded and her hair flying loose in all directions. Eventually she came back in shutting the cold out after her. She pulled the heavy curtain across the door. Ice was definitely in the air and we both shivered. In silence she stoked up the old pot-bellied stove. I watched her thinking. I didn't dare to interrupt. I collected up some buns in a dish and buried myself on the couch under the comfort of a blanket. Once the fire was burning comfortably Stella sat down and once more opened the finger-worn map book. In the flickering light of the kerosene lamp she carefully unfolded the pages. Yet again I saw her trace the line of track. Still she hadn't said a word to me. I couldn't bear the suspense any longer.

"Are we going somewhere else, now?" my voice said.

"Maybe."

"As well as ... or instead of?"

"Oh, as well as."

"Do your pa and ma not want us to go to their place no more? Is that it?"

Her smile returned. "Of course they do, Kitty. Don't you fret! All that's settled." She breathed out a deep sigh. "I just thought that, on the way, it may be nice to go and see another place; maybe look up an old family friend. I may not get the chance to come back round these parts again."

"That's okay. I like seeing new places."

"Good. Me too."

I went to bed but I didn't sleep too well. From under the door I could see low light emerging from the main room. It was glowing well into the night. I felt something was amiss. But, I was happy to acquiesce. I knew it would be all right. Stella said it would.

PART TWO

12

"Damn!" Stella kicked the car. She had over-estimated her car's capacity. We packed, we unpacked, we repacked and we re-unpacked. Stella shoved and pushed, her face red and hair dishevelled with effort. She yelled at the car for being so inadequate. She insulted the boxes when they allowed their contents to overspill. She whipped string under the hood to tie down some baggage which then immediately snapped apart. Gathering up a box of items she couldn't manage to ram into the trunk, she hurtled to the store with the hope that Walter would make a purchase. Within minutes she stumbled back still carrying the same things. Some books flopped onto the sodden ground, their covers splitting open amongst the slush. "Damnation! That idiot in the store won't take anything off me; not at any price. Damn! He could sell them on, no problem. Damn, damn, damn!" She kicked the car tyres and hopped away in pain. Astonished at her cursing I became silent and, making myself as small as possible, I snaked into the car. Parcels landed on top of me, piled high. Eventually I couldn't see out the front. I don't think Stella could see out that well either! The door was tied shut. I was hidden within the myriad of sharp cornered packages and soggy papers. Stella slammed the door of the school house with an almighty bang as if, in some way, it had wronged her. She forced her way into the car and chugged off without saying a word. I turned in my seat, as best as I could, and waved it a sad little good-bye. There was nobody to see us off.

When we got to Silverton Stella stopped outside the surgery, and having extracted herself marched up the path tripping over her own feet. Agitated, she clanged the bell rope too hard and it came away in her hand after the third pull. Mrs Cummings answered and both women hugged and rocked each other from side to side. Mrs Cummings poked Stella's hair back into place and refastened the buttons on her coat to a correct matching order. Being wedged in my seat I couldn't get out so Mrs Cummings padded out to me, leant across the driver's seat and placed a vanilla-scented kiss on my cheek. Tears, I noticed, were pooling in her eyes.

The trip to La Junta was not fun. The road was icy in places and it was very cold. We skidded along much of the way. When darkness fell, Stella stopped. I needed to use the toilet and I had to be unpacked from the front seat in a blizzard of snow. We ate some bread and cheese and fell uncomfortably asleep.

We were moving again when I awoke. We slid into La Junta. Abi-Laura and Christopher were waiting at the window and were overjoyed to see us arrive safely. Immediately, I was deposited in large tub of steamy hot water and I swam about for a bit. Then, washed and fed, I was put to bed even though it was only afternoon. I was so tired I didn't mind. Mordi came and joined me on the comforter and together we purred ourselves to sleep.

Next day the car was unpacked and apart from our two suitcases everything else was stored in their loft. Christopher drove us to the railroad station. Nobody spoke. We collected the tickets and Stella and Abi-Laura clung to each other. When they separated Christopher pushed a wad of notes into Stella's hand. She looked down at it. "No, Pa," she said, "that's not necessary. I'll be getting paid soon."

"I know," he said, "but just in case."

"I will pay you back one day. Just you see." She hugged him.

"I know you will. You're a good girl. Ma and I will be off now. We don't want to watch you go if that's all right with you. Take care. Write as soon as you can. Bye, daughter." He turned to me and ruffled my hair and said, giving me a wink, "Look after her for us, Kitty."

"I promise."

"Pa!"

Stella and I watched them walking slowly away, arm in arm. They turned at the station entrance and waved a swift good-bye. I don't know if Stella ever saw her parents again.

"Up you jump," Stella said on finding our correct carriage number. "Careful how you go, now. You first. Hold on to the handle. Good girl. I will hand the cases up to you. Hold them tight as I lift them." I'd never been inside a train before. It was very exciting. Stella let me sit by the window. She crammed our suitcases into the golden luggage rack, with bars shining out like sunrays above our seats. The whistle blared and, with a hiccough, the train juddered off. I surveyed the car. By my side a little table was folded flat against the wall. It reminded me of a bird and I flapped its wings up and down. It was quite simple to manage and after half a dozen attempts I could fly the bird easily, although its 'tweet' was somewhat loud at every movement. A woman opposite kept sighing every time my 'bird' sang. I thought, maybe, she had a headache, so I stopped. Above my head I noticed a tiny light. I switched it on, and off. The light could be made bright, brighter or dim, or off altogether. I tried them all. I liked it best when it went from one to another rapidly but then Stella said it may break so it would be better to leave the light be, for a while, or we may be asked to pay for the damage. I remembered her pa giving her some bucks at the station, maybe that's what the money was for. I spied a mirror stuck to the wall but, without bouncing up and down on the seats, it was far too high for me to see my reflection. Stella didn't think I should bounce too frequently as some of our fellow travellers, she explained, may be put out by my attempts. None of the other passengers disagreed with her. I wouldn't have minded someone bouncing. It wasn't as if the train wasn't rocking in its own right!

I scooted down the carriage to see if there was anyone who wanted to chatter. Most people fell asleep whenever I attempted some conversation. They must have been real tired. Some even started to snore. It was such a pity to miss the journey by sleeping. There were so many things to do on a train. Advertising posters and notices were dotted along the walls of the carriages. I studied them all. There were many, many places to visit! There were pictures of skyscrapers in New York and paintings of mountains in Oregon covered in masses of flowers and thronging with birds and butterflies. There was land to be had for a pittance in Arkansas where fair-haired families could grow up tall, safe and strong; and rivers full of jumping fish just for the taking in the state of Maine. Best of all was a notice showing big white-teethed people joyously biting into pies whilst sitting on a train. Underneath, a slogan announced 'Harvey Meals All The Way'. It all looked delicious. Back at my seat I found a curtain cord. I pulled it open and closed several times. I couldn't decide if the windows looked prettier with the curtain half-drawn or fully open. I tried it all ways. Stella suggested it would be a shame to miss the scenery whilst there was still some daylight. I agreed and left them open so I could look out at the passing countryside. The trouble was that it all looked the same. There was nothing out there: no houses, no people, no animals, just miles of empty flat lands.

I walked the length of the train backwards and forwards. I bumped into a bored looking man dressed smartly. He was pushing a trolley punctiliously along the swaying corridor. He was serving cold drinks and hot drinks and other snacks to the passengers. He was very slow and scratched his head a lot. I followed him along asking questions about his work until he told me in a loud whisper to 'scram!' I thought that was unnecessarily sharp as I was only trying to help him. I skulked away. I was opening the pull-down window on one of the doors to get some fresh air when another smartly dressed man in a white jacket ringing a bell shouted that dinner was now being served in the dining car. He wasn't scratching so much. I offered to help him ring his bell. I told him that I was a bell-monitor at school and knew exactly how to ring a bell properly. He declined, but at least he was polite about the business. Knowing what was on offer and that my services were not required I raced back to tell Stella the news that we could eat hot meals all the way on the train. I felt quite cheated when she refused my request to go and eat pie.

"No, Kitty. Ma's packed us a picnic supper. It's a surprise. I don't know what we've got." She handed me a starched white cloth to put across my lap. Carefully she unpacked our picnic with cooing sounds of 'ooh!', and 'yummy!' and 'lov-er-ly!' Out of the basket emerged a quantity of wax paper bags full of crustless little sandwiches sliced into fours. There were polished fruit, and rosy plump tomatoes. She immediately bit into one. Glasses of ready-made 'Jell-Os' in red and orange, and paper bags bulging with tiny golden muffins and crisp cookies were carefully packaged so as not to break. Abi-Laura had even remembered the paper plates and brightly coloured plastic spoons. I flapped open the bird table as quietly as I could and decided to play at being a posh lady in a restaurant. I politely offered food and titbits to Stella. She was impressed with me and graciously received my offerings. I drank my juice with one finger sticking out like I'd seen princesses do in story books. I even tried eating my jelly and peanut butter sandwich with a plastic spoon until it went wrong. I didn't mean it to happen, of course, but unintentionally a piece of peanut flew out of my sandwich into the air and landed down the neckline of one of the other lady passengers. She was snoozing at the time and it made her 'start'. She leapt up and shouted that a roach had fallen from the ceiling and gone down her front. Stella and I really tried to stifle our giggles but without success and with the result that Stella ended up spluttering her corn muffin all over the place.

At the bottom of the basket we found some cherry flavour 'Life-Savers'. I offered the 'bugged' lady one to make up for my peanut misdemeanour. She refused my offer and glared at me in a most unpleasant way. I wasn't too sure about people on trains. They weren't the friendliest lot but I didn't mind her not sharing our 'Life-Savers'. We sucked them and tried to balance the hole on the tip of our tongues. Sometimes they slipped out of our mouths onto the floor before I could chance to catch them. Night seemed to fall quite quickly and Stella and I took advantage of the lighting. We pulled silly faces at each other and seeing their distortion reflected in the window glass made Stella and me just howl with laughter. The train kept stopping and starting and bumping along. Pretending we couldn't sit up straight we swayed our bodies in time to the train's erratic movements. Our compartment emptied bit by bit. I wasn't sure if people were disembarking or just moving off to other cars where the entertainment was less disturbing.

I found a little packet of Abi-Laura's peanut cookies which she had packed especially for me. They were in a little tin with a painting of a white kitten on the front. I chewed on one and soon fell asleep, my head lolling backwards and forwards, dribbling against Stella's shoulder. Every now and again we were jolted awake by the juddering of the train. Early in the morning we rolled into Dodge City. I'd fallen asleep munching on one the peanut cookies, and sticky crumbs clung to my jumper as well as all down the front of Stella's coat. We had to get off at Dodge to wait for the connection to Grand Bend. A 'Harvey Roadhouse' stood by the station and we used the facilities to clean ourselves up as good as possible. Stella thought we'd better buy a drink there as it wasn't seen as polite, she said, "to just use their bathroom. Otherwise, people might think we're a couple of hobos." I drank the hot milk she ordered and she let me have a slice of pie. The waitresses in the roadhouse wore the cutest uniforms with bows in their hair. They spoke nicely to me, nothing like the unfriendly folks on the train. I thought it was wonderful at the 'Harvey's' and I announced my intention that I'd get a job there when I grew up. The waitress said, "You bet!" and laughed.

On the way to Grand Bend the land seemed to flatten out. I stared out of the train window as endless prairie passed us by. The horizon never moved. The land looked dead. There were no cows nor horses nor houses nor people. It was a sad place to see. A few brightly painted farmsteads began to appear, and then a few more. The train slowed to a halt. "I think this is where we get off now," Stella said. She was looking pretty tired and had stopped chatting a while back. We stood on the platform and gave the town a once over. "First of all we need to find a motel or some place to stay," she said eyeing the street.

"Are we here, then? Is this New York?"

"No, Kitty! Of course we're not. We're just going to spend the night here. Have a break. Freshen ourselves up. You know, get ourselves together for the next bit. Get some food in. The picnic's all done now."

A boarding house sat across the road opposite the station. Stella looked it up and down, nodded her approval. By then it was late afternoon but hardly a soul anywhere about. I could see a few shops, a roadside eating house, a couple of drug stores, a barber, a gas station. I spotted a picture house decorated with posters of movie stars. The more I looked around the more exciting the town seemed to appear. Stella, surprisingly, didn't seem very interested. Particularly surprising, as this was the town she so wanted to visit. We were shown our rooms and immediately Stella lay down on the bed and fell into a deep sleep. I pottered about: picking things up, turning the taps and flicking the light switches.

As evening fell the town seemed to liven. Cars parked along the kerbside and shop windows brightened. Neon lights flashed on and off advertising 'Burgers' or 'Fries' or 'Chophouse'. A few people were hanging about on street corners. I watched them closely. They were mainly young men, laughing, squabbling, smoking, whilst others seemed deep in conversation with their heads close together. Occasionally a squabble or some punching would start up amongst them but, just as quickly, quieten down. Some of the boys were playing card games or dice on the pavement, and giggling girls strolled by, arm-in-arm. Carefully they tip-toed a path through the cards. The boys watched them as they went by and an occasional wolf whistle would ring out followed by a titter of girly laughter. If a girl turned her head the boys would shout, "Not you, the pretty one in front!" I knew they were teasing. I liked the night, bursting with colour and movement. I needed to go to the bathroom and switched the main light on. Stella woke up, startled. "Goodness, what's the time? Oh my! I hope I haven't overslept. Quick, let's go and eat." She briskly wiped my face as if cleaning a window, smoothed my hair and wiped my clothes down with the same cloth. Then she tended to herself, looking in the mirror; she pouted her lips and smeared on some lipstick. She sighed at her reflection. I had never seen her put on lipstick before and watched her with interest. It made her look glamorous.

"Are we going to see your friend now?" I was impressed she had a friend in such a fine town. "Well, we'll have to see if she turns up or not. Let's get going," Stella replied. She was jittery.

"Well, I'm as ready as ready can be."

Stella seemed to know where she was off to. She was hurtling along the main drag. I jogged to keep up. "Have you been here before, then?"

"No. Why?"

"Just wondered."

At the end of the town's main stroll was a sign flashing 'Burt's Burgers'. Stella hesitated then pulled me through the door holding my hand tightly. We went in and a server showed us to a banquette. She poured us water and asked us how we were doing.

"Just fine," I replied.

"Why, you're a little cutie-pie!" she smiled back. "My name's Dominique. What can I get you, ladies?"

"A menu wouldn't go amiss," Stella replied.

"Okey-dokey! I'll be back in two ticks."

"What's a menu?" I whispered to Stella. I was disappointed. I imagined it as a kind of bean stew. I still wanted more pie.

"Oh, it's just a list of different things to eat. You choose what you want to eat from it and they bring it to you."

"Oh boy!" I said. "What, anything?" I couldn't believe my luck.

"Well, anything written down in the menu as long as they still have some cooking in the kitchen." Stella read out the menu slowly. At each dish named she stopped, awaiting my reaction. My eyes widened as she read out the desserts. "Is there something there that tickles your fancy, then?"

"Yeah, strawberry ice-cream pie."

"Okay, you can have that. But you need something else first."

"Something else?" I loved this town. "Chocolate ice-cream, then." Stella laughed.

"Something sensible, you know, savoury not sugary, I meant. Let's see, how about chicken burger with fries? Then you can have your ice-cream pie but only if you eat up the first course." I had no problem eating things up, ever. I don't know why she said that.

❊ ❊ ❊

Delphine smiled. "I think that ability of yours has lasted to this very day."

"That's true," I said. "Apart from that time when I was ill, I've always managed to enjoy my food." The three of us were scraping our plates clean with our forks.

"We won't need to wash them at this rate."

"But I may need to paint the pattern back on!" The raspberry cream shortcake was good. There were sugary crumbs everywhere. "Thank you, George," I said. "You've made an old woman very happy."

"You're not that old," he replied. "My cooking keeps you young. I dare say you look younger now then when we first met you."

"You old flatterer," I replied. "I don't know what I would do without you two."

I thought back all those years to when I first met George and Delphine. A shy little couple, both bone-thin with a frightened, shivery look about them. I could still picture them sitting at Archway station huddled together on a wooden bench. Delphine, with a scarf tied tightly around her head and a handbag clutched firmly on her lap, and George staring straight ahead with his spectacles askew and his cap pulled well down. They sat day after day, squashed up close.

It looked like as if they were holding each other up; keeping each other warm, probably. Even though it was winter, neither was adequately dressed. I suppose it was the warmest place for them to sit. I passed them every morning on my way to the studio. They were never there when I returned later in the day. This particular day, I remember, it was raining heavily. I got to the shelter of the station and shook out my umbrella. There was a bit of a hullabaloo. A station official was shouting at them. He wanted them to move off.

"Do you think you can come and sit around 'ere? These seats are for us English, not for you coloured lot. They're not for nig-nogs like you! Why don't you bugger off and go back to the jungle where you monkeys belong?" Delphine looked like a frightened kitten. I stopped and watched from the shelter.

"Excuse me, Sir," George interrupted. "We were told to wait here. We're expecting somebody to meet us soon. We can stand if you don't want us to sit down. We don't want to stop other people resting their legs."

"You're all the same. You bloody wogs! You're just a whining pack of thieves and liars. I know your game. Get a move on or I'll call the coppers. This 'ere is private property and you're loitering."

"But Sir," George pleaded, "we're not loitering, we've got jobs and we're being picked up from here."

"Oh, 'ave you now? Blimey! You've got some cheek coming over 'ere and stealing our jobs? We didn't fight the war to let the likes of you lot in. Fan-bloody-tastic! Go back to your jungle branch, monkey boy. You coloureds ain't wanted round 'ere. Get out!" George looked defeated. "Go on, 'op it, before I get you thrown out. And take the ugly chimp with you. Get!"

Delphine, I could see, was twisting the handle of her bag and shaking. George took hold of her hand. They gathered themselves together and limped towards the exit. I noticed that the heel of one of Delphine's shoes was missing. They left the station and disappeared into the rain.

Next morning I purposely looked out for them; I'd been really disturbed about what I'd seen and I didn't get much sleep. The couple weren't on the bench as normal or anywhere else I could see inside the station. I glanced out onto the street and, just by chance, I spotted the pair sheltering from the rain inside a 'phone box. I watched George put his arm around Delphine protecting her when forced out into the wet by someone needing to make a call. They didn't have umbrellas but he held a dripping newspaper over their heads. People on their way to work scowled as they bumped into them. Nobody smiled.

"Excuse me," I said. They looked around in surprise. Delphine tightened her grip on George's arm.

"I hope I'm not offending you but I need some help." Immediately, George responded.

"How can we be of help, Ma'am? Are you lost?"

"No, I meant, proper help. You know, someone to help me with a job today. Paid work."

"Oh, you're from the company?"

"No. It's just me. No company."

"Oh."

"Please, I hope I haven't hurt your feelings, but yesterday morning I overheard your conversation with 'Mr Nasty-Works' over there. I heard you were waiting for work. I wondered if it had arrived? Because, if not, I can pay you for doing some odd jobs for me."

"Oh, sorry, but we're not allowed to work for anyone else, but thank you for your kindness, Ma'am. You see, it's part of our agreement with the company. We have to wait in case they need a person to do deliveries." They both looked at each other and then back at me.

"Did you get any work yesterday, then?" George shook his head. "The day before?"

"No."

"So how do you eat? Where do you sleep?"

"Whatever and wherever we can, Ma'am."

There was a pause. The rain slid down our faces. Delphine wiped her nose on the back of her hand. She looked down at the grime-slimed pavement slabs.

"Do you have work to go to, today?"

"We can never tell," George replied. I held my umbrella further over them. Water was splashing down into my shoes. Delphine nodded her thanks. "Sometimes, they bring us work," she said, "posting leaflets through doors mainly, but at other times they don't show up. We just wait and see if they come, or not. They haven't been around for over a week now. Not good news for us."

"I'm Kitty Wardle," I said. "Can you give me a hand at work today? I'm in an awful mess at the studio and I could do with an extra pair of hands to help me clear up the place. I've got a show coming up this weekend and I need help to set it up."

"Like to help out, Ma'am, but I don't know, we could get into awful trouble from the boss."

"George," Delphine said quietly, "what have we got to lose?" George looked down at Delphine. There was a pause. "Okay, honey. If that's what you want. Let's go and help out this lady. We can always say we got sick if they ask." They both turned to me and smiled, grinning from ear to ear. "Sure, we'd be happy to oblige." I extended my hand to George. "George Hale at your service, and this here is my wife, Mrs Delphine Hale." We shook hands.

"Come on," I said, "it'll be all right, you'll see. But one thing, please call me Kitty, not Ma'am. First I'd better get you some train tickets, or 'Mr Nasty-Works' here will be back on you. Stay close to me."

At the gate 'Nasty-Works' clipped the tickets. "They work for me," I snarled. "And don't you forget it, boy."

❊ ❊ ❊

Stella and I sat looking around. I fiddled with things on the table. A big noisy coffee machine sat on the counter. It made wonderful gurgling sounds. I tried to copy its 'glug-glug-glugel', much to the amusement of the servers and other customers at 'Burt's Burgers'. Dominique came back carrying bright red plastic place mats and knives and forks wrapped up in a red paper serviettes. Another server brought us mugs and brim filled them with coffee. Squatting on the table was a giant plastic tomato. Somebody had coloured in two eyes on its rosy face. I couldn't wait to squeeze it. Next to it was a little pot crammed full of toothpicks. I tried playing 'pick-up sticks' with them. But I was most distracted by the glass sugar-pourer. Stella showed me how to use it properly and I dispensed several quantities of sugar into my mug and then, by mistake, all over the table. "Hey, steady on now!" Stella said. "We don't want to be thrown out in the snow before we get fed." I don't think she minded that much. She seemed more preoccupied with twisting around and watching other people in the diner. There was so much to do and see. It was really a very interesting place. Neon lights flashed on and off and the walls were plastered with giant photographs of famous stars smiling or winking at us. I didn't know who the stars were but Stella seemed to know all their names. Staff kept brushing passed us, refilling our mugs and checking to see if we were okay.

I still needed to use the bathroom and Stella pointed out the door to me. Over the wash basin there was a swing soap dispenser and I swung it over and over several times. As I came running out to tell Stella about the wonderful contraption I bumped into a blond server balancing a large tray on one hand. She nearly toppled.

"Sorry!"

"Watch it, kiddo," she snapped. She rebalanced the tray and then stopped. She looked back at me.

"Sorry, Ma'am," I said again.

"That's okay," she replied more gently. "Where you sitting?" she asked. I pointed to Stella. "Okay, take care now. I'll be over in a bit." As I got back to Stella our food was being placed on the table by Dominique. She gave me a big wink. "See if you can eat all that, young lady". Of course I could and to prove it to her I started digging into my burger immediately, chewing ravenously. "You bet!" I said.

I was on my ice-cream pie when the server I nearly knocked over came strolling over. I noticed while I'd been eating she'd been staring at me from across the floor.

"Is everything all right here?" Stella nodded. "Would you like some extra sprinkles on your ice-cream, little lady? On the house, like." She winked at Stella.

"Oh, yes please," I replied grinning.

"Well, if you come back up over to the counter with your ice I will give you a few spoons extra, and some more topping if you give me a big, big smile." She bent down, put her face right close to me and stroked my hair. "Gee whiz, you got pretty hair." I was about to jump up and follow her when Stella put her hand firmly down on my arm.

"No, Kitty. I think you've had enough."

"So you're called Kitty, then. How nice. Just a few, Ma'am." She drawled slowly as she spoke.

"No, thank you. We're going now. So I just need the check."

"Oh, so soon?" The server looked genuinely downcast. "Just a quick visit this time, then?"

"That's right," said Stella sharply.

"You coming back?"

"But …" I was about to remonstrate when another voice joined in. "Hey Liza!" It was Dominique. "Are you trying to steal my customers? This isn't your table, is it now? Or have things changed without me knowing?"

"Just helping the little lady enjoy her ice-cream."

"Why, that's my job. Funny, after all this time, you don't know that yet. See to your own tables."

Stella stood up. I couldn't understand why she wouldn't let me have more sprinkles when she knew I liked them so. Holding my hand tightly Stella followed Dominique across to the cash till, tugging me behind her. I noticed the blond woman watching us through the hatch from the kitchen. She looked sad. I was sorry I nearly knocked her over and I didn't like the way Dominique had spoken to her. She was only trying to be nice to me. I waved. As she waved back Stella shuffled me outside into the cold night. I turned as we walked down the street. Through the diner window the woman stood watching us go. Her hand raised and pressed against the glass. "Why's that lady still watching us, Stella?" I asked. "I think that Dominique was mean to snap at her so. She was only being nice."

"Probably she was after her tip. She looked a bit crazed to me. Come on. Let's hurry. My feet are cold. And stop staring back, now. Don't turn around again!"

"Are you feeling sad, Stella?" I asked as she pushed me through the boarding house door.

"No, why do you think that? I'm just tired." She gave my hand a little squeeze. "Sorry, Kitty. I'll feel fine once I've had a sleep."

"That's okay. It's just your friend never turned up, did she?"

"Never mind," she said, "I didn't really expect her to. It's time for bed anyhow. We've got another big, long day tomorrow. Come on. Let's get you into your pyjamas."

❅ ❅ ❅

"Why do you think that friend of hers never turned up?" Delphine asked.

"I never found the answer to that for a long time."

"So were you right after all? Was Stella really upset about something?"

"She sure was," I replied, "I could always tell. We couldn't hide anything from each other. She knew what I was feeling and I knew what she was feeling. There was no privacy of thought."

"So, did you stay another night there or did you just keep on going?"

"No, we were out like a shot first thing next day. Stella didn't want to see her friend any more. In fact, she didn't want to stay a moment longer then we had to. There were still several more changes to make on the train before we hit New York. It was a long way and Stella wanted to get the journey over with as soon as possible. I can understand that now but, to me, it was a bit of fun and she was spoiling it. Steam engines were slow, stopping and starting all the time. And so filthy with all that coal dust, no diesel then. And come to think about it, it was freezing cold inside those cars and so very bumpy. It couldn't have been right comfy for her or anybody. But, when you're a child you don't notice those little things as much. If I'm remembering correctly the journey must have dragged on about three, or so, days. Things became crazier when we arrived in Chicago. There was a bad snowstorm and we had to change trains as well as stations. Stella had never been anywhere so hectic. She was terrified I'd get stolen, lost or run-over. I thought she was a real spoil-sport. She flinched at every car hooting, and, for safety, she tied me securely to her arm with a long woollen scarf. As we boarded a bus to cross town I dropped a suitcase. It burst open spilling the contents down the wet steps. She was so embarrassed that she let some things roll away down the gutter. Nobody helped us. The driver snarled. Stella couldn't find her purse to pay the fare. Then she found it. Then she lost her glasses. Then she found them. Then she lost her gloves. What a to-do! Was that some noisy town! But we survived, and we arrived, more or less in one piece into the terminal at the Grand Central."

13

A voice boomed out: "Hi! You the Colorado folks? Come to work for the Richardsons?"

Stella and I had been standing underneath the opal clock for well over an hour. We'd heard it strike three. People of all shapes and sizes and colours and ages had bustled past. Apart from the skulk of shifty looking characters hugging the walls everyone else seemed to be hurrying. I heard people talking in odd accents I found hard to follow and others hollering to each other in even stranger languages which were totally incomprehensible to my 'southern' ear. Children squabbled, lovers kissed fond farewells, and old folks with open arms embraced long lost friends. Fur-wrapped dogs, tiny as cats, yapped in the arms of their owners. August ladies with faces painted like clowns puffed magical circles of smoke from cigarettes held in holders of daintiest silver. Smells I did not recognize eddied around, my nose a-twitch with interest.

The height of the station dome and its enormity was a wonderment in itself. My neck ached from following birds swooping above. I watched the faces of the clocks, their hands jigging together. The clock struck three-thirty. The clock struck three-forty-five, then four. We were tired and dusty. The last nine hundred-odd miles had not been easy going. A blizzard of snow from Chicago had laced the soot-laden windows of the train and I couldn't see out. As four-fifteen struck I heard Stella sigh. I wanted to move around the station and look at things but Stella told me to just stay put where I was. I needed the bathroom but she told me to hold on. People around kept yelling and pushing by without apology. I rested my head against Stella's side and snoozed. I think she snoozed too because all of a sudden she gasped and, startled, we both stood up straight again and replaced our smiles.

"Excuse me! Excuse me Ma'am but are you the folks come to work for the Richardsons?"

"Yes. Sorry, that's us, indeed." Stella looked so relieved. "I'm Stella Hurtigrutensson. How do you do." They shook hands firmly.

"And you, young lady, must be Kitty." He shook my hand heartily. "Howdy!"

"Just doing fine, Sir," I replied. I liked the look of this man.

"Well, sorry to disappoint you, ladies, but I'm not Mr Henry Richardson. I'm a neighbour of his. I'm awfully sorry I'm late. My name's Alan Ericsson. Pleased to meet you both. Henry's given me strict instructions to offer you ladies some refreshment before we hit the road. Here, let me take your bags. Goodness, you travel light! Mrs Ericsson, my wife that is, well, she needs about ten times as many cases when she goes on vacation. In fact she takes more suitcases with her than I knew we even had!" I tried to imagine this concept.

"Let's see, now; we'll go across to that place, right over there, by the exit sign. Mrs Ericsson was going to come to meet you too, but then we didn't know how much space you needed with your bags and things. So she didn't, more's the pity. You'd like her, nice gal, but you'll see her around in the next few days, that's for sure. You're probably desperate for your beds but a warm drink before we get rolling again will do you no end of good. I know what these trains are like. Used to travel a lot on them myself. Great way of seeing the country but all so uncomfortable at times. Some of them nowadays don't even stop for water so you can't get out to have a stretch of your old bones or get a good lungful of fresh air. Not that you would want to at this time of year, not with all this snow about. They say Chicago has been hit bad with snow this year. Did you see much on the way? I think aeroplanes are the way forward now. You know you can fly from Chicago to New York in one day? Extraordinary. The world is shrinking."

I think my ears nearly fell off trying to catch what Mr Ericsson was saying. He spoke so rapidly. I had to really concentrate. I'd never heard a New Yorker speak before then.

"Anyhow you ladies, what can I get you now. Coffee? Coke? A soda? What do you fancy, Kitty? And what would you say to some waffles or a dough-nut?"

"I'd say yes please."

"Which?" He smiled at me.

"Waffles and doughnuts, please." I'd never heard of waffles before but they sounded good. Sybil had talked about doughnuts so I knew them to be good.

"With syrup?" he continued before Stella could speak.

"Kitty! Hold on. That's rather too much sugar. You will have a sugar shock one of these days. Choose one or the other, not both." I began to remonstrate but, to my joy, Mr Ericsson was already ordering.

"We can always share. Now for you, may I call you Stella, if that's not too presumptuous?" Stella nodded. "What can I get for you?"

"Just a coffee, please."

"Nothing to eat, then? What about a Danish? Yes! Please an old fellow and have a Danish."

"Okay," said Stella, smiling. "Thank you kindly. I haven't had a Danish for quite a few years since."

Mr Ericsson finished placing the order. He turned back to us, looking more serious. "There is another reason," he said slowly, "why Henry thought it may be a good idea for us to have a little break before we drive across. Henry wanted you to have some update about how things are with the family."

"Oh no!" Stella exclaimed, putting both hands to her head. "Have plans changed? It is still on?" I sensed Stella tense.

"No, nothing like that. Sorry. Gee whiz, I hope I didn't cause you any panic. I knew Mrs Ericsson could do this better than I could. Us men are always putting our big feet in things." I looked under the table at his feet. They were quite large. "Henry has asked me to ... how can I say this ..." He stirred his coffee rapidly. "I don't know where to start, really." We both looked at him expectantly.

"Well, you know what they say," I contributed helpfully. "Start at the beginning." He smiled.

"Okay, then, I'll kick off at the start-line. I know your friend Lois is Esther's older sister. What Lois hasn't been told is that Esther, unfortunately, is not a very well lady. To be honest, Stella, she's pretty sick. Esther doesn't want Lois to know this. She knows that if Lois knew about it she would be really upset and, of course, very worried. It's not being dishonest. That wasn't the intention. Esther just wanted to protect her sister from harsh reality. She knows Lois has a lot of problems of her own. Excuse me mentioning that, Ma'am. She didn't want her to have more worry on top of everything else."

"Oh, I understand."

"That's great, but, you see, Stella, that's not all of it. There's more. This is the hard bit. Esther is also being protected from the reality. Esther does not know she's not expected to get any better."

"Oh!"

"These things happen, I know! Not fair is it? Such a nice lady, too! God certainly works in some mysterious ways."

"I see. How very sad."

"So you may have guessed, by now, that the reason Margaret and Marion are going to school in England is to shield them from seeing their mother's demise. And, of course, there's Henry's family over in England who will look after them ... just in case, or should I say when, the inevitable happens. I hope it hasn't caused you too much upset. Henry thought it was better to explain before we got over there. Give you a little extra time to mull things over. Telling you now is also less awkward. You see, Esther was hoping to be able to greet you tonight but, I think, it may be tomorrow now. But I'm telling you she's so delighted with your coming across. Her girls are so precious to her. Esther said your friend, Lois, has been writing such great things about you. You're quite some lady."

"I wouldn't say that, exactly, but that's most kind of her."

"Esther doesn't say much, you know, but you can tell she's real worried about their future. Who wouldn't be in her situation? You coming has been some reassurance for her and, of course, Henry as well. Henry was going to come and tell you all this himself but, unfortunately, Esther took a bad turn a couple of days back and Henry didn't want to leave her side for the moment. That's why I was late. Hope you understand. Sorry. Until the very last moment Henry was going to come and collect you. If you ask me, I think it is better this way anyhow."

"Well, I'm really sorry to hear all that. It's really all very sad." Stella sipped her coffee, her face grave. "Of course, I will respect Esther's wishes not to tell Lois about the illness, but it makes it kind of difficult for me, you know, having to pretend, possibly lie, to a good friend."

"I can see your dilemma," Mr Ericsson replied. "It's mighty awkward."

"Yet another difficulty to add to my list. But I'll cope. It'll be all right. You'll see." She glanced across at me reassuringly. I was cutting up my waffles trying to block out what I was hearing. I felt for Margaret and Marion. It wasn't nice having a sick ma.

This time Stella was right. I couldn't eat both doughnuts and waffles. I felt a bit heavy. I stopped mid-mouthful. "Sorry, Mr Ericsson," I said, "I can't eat no more. But, gee whiz, they were real nice. Thank you kindly."

"That's okay. My fault in encouraging you. You call me Alan from now on. Don't worry about the mister bit. Anyway," he said glancing at his watch, "we'd better skidoo!"

New York, gaudy with bright coloured lights, honking cars, people rushing here and racing there. Neons flashing on and flashing off, policemen big in coats blowing whistles. Buildings soaring sky-high and vaporising into the white of the night. An hour or so must have passed as we crossed out of the city. I didn't mind. It was all so interesting to see.

A little white cat was scratching at the door as we drove up, her eyes gleaming amber in the headlights. A building large and rambling came into sight. Encased by maples and vines, it was half-timbered and painted a soft hue of blue. Tall windows welcomed us with warm eyes of light shining through. From a large snow-frosted tree a two-seater swing was swaying, and a diamond layer of snow sparkled across the ground. Every lamp in the house seemed to be twinkling. It was as pretty as any painting. "How very beautiful," Stella said, entranced. A dog, massive and furry, bounded down the path and barked a greeting. I patted him and he lolled his tongue and wagged his tail in response. A tall man opened the door and hurried down the steps of the porch. He was smiling. He gave a little nod to Mr Ericsson and extended his hand out to Stella. "Welcome," he said, warmly shaking both our hands, "so pleased to meet you. Come in, come in. Don't stand on ceremony. You must be frozen. Let me take your coats."

As Henry Richardson hung up our coats my eyes immediately fixed upon a wooden curl of a staircase. Pictures of all sizes and all shapes adorned the walls, some gilt framed, others silver. From the ceiling a grand chandelier tinkled a tune. It glistened and gleamed in the glow of the evening light, and hidden in the gloom of the landing I could hear 'tick-tick' from a grandfather clock. Through a gap at the top of the balustrade a wriggle of a little body caught my eye. I waved, and from between the spindles appeared a child's hand waggling back with enthusiasm. Mr Richardson glanced upwards. "Back to bed! Straight away, Clive," he said in a loud whisper. "You can meet our new friends in the morning but now it's sleepy-bye time. Night-night!" There was a scamper-ing, a giggle and a thud.

"Well, that was Clive. Quite a scamp as you can see."

"Is he your little boy?" I asked. "He's a cutie-pie." The cat was rubbing against my leg. "What's your cat called?"

"Oh, that's Little. She's such a tiny cat, isn't she? But fully grown, can you believe it? We called her 'Little', short for Little Cat, of course."

"What about your dog?"

"Well, there again, believe it or not, we called him 'Big'. Bet you can guess why!"

"'Cos he's big? Is he fully grown?"

"Sure is."

"That's enough now, Kitty. Give Mr Richard-son a break or he'll be sending us back on the next train heading west!"

"No!" I squealed, "I'll be quiet now. But, Mr Richardson, I am really sorry to hear about Mrs Richardson being sick. You know, it's awfully nice here, apart from that."

"Thank you, glad you think so. Anyway, come along into the drawing room and take a seat. There's a fire going. In a moment Amy will bring you through a supper tray. We can have a good chat tomorrow. It's a bit late for us now. Obviously, Alan has got you up to date with the situation with Esther. And I truly apologize if it's made you feel uncomfortable, and I do hope it hasn't made you change your mind about things. Anyhow, I will leave you alone now to eat and rest. Amy will show you your room. She's our help, by the way; well, our Godsend, to be truthful. I hope you find the room comfortable. Just say, if you're cold. She can get you more blankets. Ask her for anything you need. She knows what's what. She's the boss, really. Been here now a good few years. Speak of the devil, or should I say, angel! Here she comes. I will leave you in her capable hands and I wish you both a good night's sleep. Shall we meet at about ten tomorrow morning? Sleep well, ladies."

✳ ✳ ✳

"Talking about being tired." Delphine jumped up. "Have you seen the time? We're a couple of night owls. I will make you up your Lemon Verbena and honey now. Or would you prefer a Chamomile?"

"You know what I fancy, Delphine?"

"No. What would that be? A Whisky Mac?"

"No, just a nice cup of English tea, brewed in a pot and served in a nice English china cup and saucer."

"Do you want an English silver spoon, too?"

"Of course. And sugar lumps served with those silver claw tongs. And the silver tea strainer."

"No tea bags?"

"No."

"The whole hog then?"

"No, keep the hog!"

"Thank goodness for that. I hope the tea won't keep you awake. And, I s'pose, a slice of cinnamon toast to keep you sweet?"

"It wouldn't go amiss."

"Ah-ha, I thought so. You know, I think I may as well join you. Can't have you carousing the night away on your own."

✳ ✳ ✳

A nice cup of English tea. That thought took me back. It was at the Richardson's where I first sampled a cup of proper English tea. We were curled up in armchairs or lounging on the sofas in front of the glowing log fire, chatting. I think it was, probably, the first afternoon after our arrival and we were having – or rather, as Henry called it, 'taking' – afternoon tea. We were all sat there, Stella, Henry of course, even Esther. It was the one and only time I ever saw her out of bed. Margaret and Marion were squashed together in one chair, and little Clive was driving a toy train around the edge of the rug. Big was slumped on the floor giving his tail an occasional flick. Outside it was snowing heavily. Amy carried in a tea tray. I admired the china tea-set decorated with yellow and orange flowers.

"They're called daffodils," Esther said gently when she saw me studying the pattern. "You'll see a lot of those in England. They're the flower of spring-time." She sighed, "I wish I was going with you. I'd love to see those daffodils once again. Over there in Cambridge they grow wild all over, just everywhere. I particularly love seeing them dancing along the banks of the River Cam."

"One day, dear," Henry replied.

"I know," she said, clasping his hand.

"And I will paint you a picture of them and send it to you as soon as I get there," I added.

"Thank you, Kitty. That would be a lovely thing to do."

Amy carefully poured the tea through a strainer into each cup. It was shiny and amber coloured, and then she added a little drop of milk. "It's an art, you know, this tea serving business," Henry said through sips. "Some people, back home, say put the milk in first. Causes controversy. Light hearted controversy, of course. Same with scones. Some say 'scones' rhyming with 'dons' and some say 'scones' rhyming with 'tones'. I say the former. Then to complicate it even more, some British put the cream on their scones first, others the jam. I go for the 'cream first' version." I didn't quite follow what he was talking about, but I agreed with him and decided I would do the same from now on. Not that I even knew what a scone was in those days.

The girls and Clive had glasses of milk to drink but I wanted to try the golden tea. I placed two sugar lumps in the cup, and secreted another two in my mouth; then, following Esther and Henry's example, I sipped the tea with aplomb. I couldn't see what the fuss was all about and wished I'd chosen milk instead. Thick chunks of Amy's 'lemon juggle cake' were passed around. I helped myself to the largest piece I could see. I'd never tasted anything so good since Mrs Cummings's blueberry shortcake. Esther didn't seem to eat much. She was just sitting in the armchair supported by cushions, a blanket draped over her knees. Her cheekbones stuck out and she looked like a bird, her eyes deeply set and watery. She didn't really look like Lois at all, or the photograph she showed us of the two of them together from when they were youngsters. It was my pa's face that came to mind when I looked into her face. I thought it a selfless thing of Esther not to tell Lois about the illness. It was the type of magnanimous thing *Anne of*

Green Gables would have done. I would do the same, I thought, if something similar happened to me and I'd had a sister.

Esther said I would enjoy my time in England. "Especially," I agreed, "if I could eat 'lemon juggle cake' every day." She smiled. Stella and Esther chatted away quietly to each other while the rest of us watched the flickering of the fire and the soft fluttering of the snowflakes falling.

"Hey, girls," Henry said, "how about a game of Monopoly?"

"Only if you play too, Daddy," the twins replied.

"As long as you let me win! Have you played before, Kitty?"

I shook my head. "But Stella says I'm a quick little learner. So show me and I'm sure to get to know how to play as quick as a fish." Apart from little Clive we all joined in. Clive insisted on hitting the board with his tiny hands and yelling 'Snap'. I let him throw the die for me but soon, fed up, he turned back to being a steam engine. I scribbled him a little picture of a train. He liked that. I added a little figure sat on the engine and I said it was him driving. He drove it noisily around the room. By this stage in play I, too, had lost interest in the Monopoly. But to this day I can still recall the pleasure of sitting amongst the Richardsons in that beautiful room the likes of which I'd never encountered before. To me it was a palace. The sound and scent of wood crackling in the fire and the deep rich aroma of the wax polish arising off the oak furniture still lingers in my memory, the good part of my memory. For once I felt as if I belonged. It was a wondrous thing being part of a family. I was content watching their fun and it didn't matter, one hoot, whether I lost or won.

The next few weeks skimmed along. I pottered about. I chatted to Amy. I'd pull up a chair alongside her kitchen table. Cuddling Little Cat on my lap, I'd sit, contentedly, whiling away the hours soothed by the sound and feel of her rolling purrs. Other times I coloured picture after picture. Or with enthusiasm wrote down with great flourish recipes which Amy slowly dictated to me. What patience! If the day wasn't too cold I'd go out into the snow and throw balls and sticks for Big to catch. Stella spent her time sitting with Esther. I never saw much of her. At other times Stella would try and give Margaret and Marion their lessons but, understandably, they weren't in the mood to concentrate. The kitchen, I found, was the best place to be as I was out of everyone's way. Amy would tie a big apron around my waist and I'd help her with the whisking of eggs, the coring of apples and peeling piles of potatoes. She'd allow me to lick out bowls of creamy cake and sticky pudding mixtures and suck on the peel of juiced oranges. We'd laugh a lot and together we'd croaked songs remembered from her younger days, homed in the deep south.

The day of departure came. Farewells were being said. Clutching their father and sobbing into his shoulder, Margaret and Marion came shuffling down the stairs. Holding hands they descended slowly, step by step, away from their mother. They had said their good-byes to her. Outside they looked back up to the first floor; Esther was standing against the bedroom window with her palms pressed against the panes. By her side, Amy stood holding Clive who was sucking his thumb. As we got into Henry's car they turned and waved one last time. Henry started the motor and, with the girls sobbing in the back seat next to me, he drove away.

✳ ✳ ✳

"You know, Delphine, I think I may need another cup of tea. That was a pretty sad day for all of us. We were all so upset. Poor Henry, little did he know what was going to happen. Of course, I was really too little to fully comprehend what was happening. But on the back seat of the car, tightly wedged between the girls, I reached out and held their hands all the way to the docks. The skin around their finger nails looked sore and bitten-torn. I tried to say comforting things to them but I don't think it helped much. I offered them my hankie when theirs was too wet for further use. They refused and said it unhygienic; I just thought that was what you did."

"You were a nice little girl, you know," Delphine murmured. "I'll get that tea straight away." She blew her nose. "Then it's off to bed definitely for both of us. There's another day tomorrow."

"Sure is. Oh, sorry, Delphine. Didn't mean to keep you up, and have I upset you? I'm a silly old thing. I shouldn't be telling you sad stories at night. You've had enough sadness in your very own life."

"No, no. It's right to share memories. There's never a wrong time. Share it all: good and the bad. But tell me, before I hit the pillow, did the girls ever see their ma again?"

"No, I'm sorry to say, they did not. Esther died; actually, not long after we arrived in England. They had just started at that new school. At least Esther knew, at the end, that her daughters were settled, and were safe and sound with Stella."

✳ ✳ ✳

Henry stood on the dockside as the ship moved out of port, a little black figure alone amongst hundreds of others. We waved from the deck to no one in particular. Some people threw streamers overboard. Others sang. As the ship moved away Stella tried to distract the girls by pointing out objects of interest along the shoreline. Eventually she gave in to their silence and bundled us all inside. We were on the SS Brittic. I think it was about March, 1936. We had two little cabins next to each other and we shared a little wash area through a connecting door. Stella let me have the top bunk. It was such fun! The day's trauma soon passed me by. I was too busy pressing buttons, opening and shutting curtains, switching lights on and off and adjusting the dimmer backwards and forward. That evening we ate in the ship's dining room. Conversation was stilted. Apart from me, nobody had much of an appetite. Stella tried again to engage the girls in some comforting talk but I don't think they were up to it. For most of the meal they sat with their heads leaning against their arms staring down at the uneaten food on their plates.

Eventually Margaret asked if they may be excused from the table to go back to the cabin. We all got up and I, disappointed, had to settle down for the night. But I really loved it in my little bunk. I drew my blue pleated curtain across and pretended I was in a stable. I fell asleep on the 'straw' and came to dream that I was hanging onto a galloping pony. Even when I woke up, the bucking to-and-fro was still continuing on and on. I got on all fours and bounced away with the movements of the ship, 'whoaing', 'giddy-upping' and 'whinnying' away. I clung desperately on to the safety rail as if it were the saddle, kicking my legs up 'bronco' style. Sometimes I was the pony, other times the rider.

Stella suddenly emerged from her bunk and fell into the wash room. I heard her vomiting. "What's up, Stella?" I asked, shocked, when she returned. She fell back into her berth. "Just feel a bit sea-sick. Could you, would you, just check if the girls are okay," she whispered. "Of course, pleased to help." I leapt on my pony and trotted next door. The girls were being miserably sick too. I couldn't see Marion's pillow but there was a lot of vomit all over Margaret's. I got them a damp washer and wiped their faces. Then I got them towels and put them over their pillow. They stank real bad. "Would you like to play ponies with me?"

"Go away," they both whined.

"Okay!" I whinnied, and galloped back to my stable.

The next day Stella looked dishevelled. She was trying to dress. The cabin was still moving backwards and forwards. "Can you check on the girls again, for me? I still don't feel too good." She flunked back on her bunk and then, with a moan, lay down quickly. I went into the girls' cabin. They were also lying in their berths moaning. "Sorry you're so sick," I said. "Stella is too. She's been throwing up awful bad all night long. I'll get a cloth and wipe your hands and faces if you like."

"Okay," they whimpered, "and bring some water." I brought them some to sip and gave their faces a wipe over again.

"Do you want anything to eat now? I think they've got hotcakes with syrup for breakfast. I can smell it in the corridor. I could get you some if you don't want to get up."

"No," they groaned. "Go away now, Kitty, just go away!"

I went back to my cabin and got myself dressed. Stella was still lying there. She didn't want anything to eat either. She just wanted water to drink. Mumbling, she told me to go and find someone dressed in uniform. "Tell them that we are all ill in our cabins and ask them if they could fix you up some breakfast as you are on your own. And don't go outside on deck! Don't forget that," she added as I cantered out. Trotting up and down the deck I eventually found a nice man in a white jacket with golden things on his shoulders. I explained what Stella had said to me ... apart from the bit about not going outside on deck.

"Rightee-o, young lady. My name's Gilbert. Stay right there and I'll send a stewardess down to your cabins. Then we'll get you going with some breakfast. He was back shortly with the maid. I pointed out our cabin to her and Gilbert, taking me firmly by the hand, led me into the Royal Dining Room for my breakfast. It was nearly empty of customers.

"A window seat, Madame," he smiled with a tilt of his head.

"Oh boy! This is nice."

He popped a large velvet cushion onto one of the grand, gold painted chairs and lifted me up on to the seat.

"Now, what can I offer you then, Madam?" he asked me with great solemnity. I giggled.

"Do you do ice-cream," I asked.

"We do, Madame, but never before luncheon."

"Do you do menus?" I was enjoying myself.

"May I suggest, Madame, some apple pancakes with cinnamon cream, and a side order of strawberries. Maybe a freshly squeezed orange juice?"

"Delightful!" I replied mimicking Henry's accent. "And some English tea, please," I emphasised. I watched the sea come up and splash across the windows. I imagined myself galloping across the white frothy waves on my dappled-grey sea pony. My food arrived: two big thick pancakes smothered with cream and strawberries and other fruit I didn't recognise. Things kept sliding across the table and I had to grab them before they crashed into each other, or flipped off the edge. So much fun! Lots of other people in uniform came by and greeted me. Sometimes I replied courteously, but much of the time my mouth was just too full of food and I couldn't answer them without spitting, so I just nodded. I'd just finished my feed when Gilbert came back. "Your family are just fine now. Don't you worry. The doctor has given them a draft to help them settle. They will probably sleep for a bit, so they won't want disturbing. If you're finished your repast, Madame, I will take you along to the nursery." I couldn't believe my good fortune. A nursery on board as well as a restaurant! I was really in luck. A woman dressed in uniform took over from Gilbert. There were only a few toddlers playing disinterestedly with the toys plus a couple of snoozing babies in cradles. I painted a picture of the sea with ponies leaping over the waves in all direction. My painting was pinned on the wall and the nanny-in-charge commented upon my artistic ability.

"I know," I replied. "Others have told me the very same thing. I may be an artist when I grow up, or a server at 'Harvey's'. I've not quite decided yet but Stella says I've still got plenty of time to make my mind up." There was ice-cream for dessert that lunchtime. Gilbert was right.

Stella, Margaret and Marion were still cocooned in their bunks when I got back. They appeared slightly less sick than before but their appetites had not returned. They wished to be alone so I made my way back, on my own, to 'The Royal' and, without invitation, took my seat as before. For the next few gluttonous days the waiters served me as if I were a hungry princess. And dining in the resplendence of 'The Royal', with its gilt chairs, its crisp linens, its fine gold-leafed china and ornate glassware, I munched my way happily across the Atlantic. The grandeur of the dining hall was not wasted on me. I admired my glittering surroundings. In the centre of the hall white mermaids made of marble reclined in the vast wave of a sea shell. I examined their tails and then their nakedness with great interest. Live goldfish swished about the pool beneath and a fall of water spewed intermittently from the open mouth of a dolphin above. I let the water trickle my fingers and tried, in vain, to cradle the fish against the sway. The ship heaved its way on and the pearl-drop pendants from extravagant chandeliers danced and chinkled to the roll of the sea. A handful of musicians were attempting to balance on a pitching platform. I admired their endeavour to keep themselves and their instruments upright. And on noticing the rapid disappearance of the pianist from the stage I offered to play in his place instead. Politely they thanked me but declined my offer.

On the final day of the voyage all ship board glamour came to a sudden end. From her bunk, Stella proclaimed, "I'm never ever going on a ship again. Don't let me forget that, Kitty." She was holding her head up by leaning on one shaky hand. Through the porthole I could make out the grey coastline of the British Isles. I shouted with excitement and pointed as the rainy land approached but neither the twins nor Stella appeared interested. The stewardess brought them toast and tea to nibble, and slowly recovering they crawled from their berths. The fresh salt breeze on deck awakened them slightly and soon they were willing, at my insistence, to try a little food. Confidently I led them to 'The Royal' but Stella insisted we dined in the worn-out looking second class diner. Its inferior standard of food and lax service disappointed me. The twins, however, didn't seem to care what or how they ate. Stella picked at the tomato on her plate as if it were tasteless. But, once docked in Southampton, the three of them, with new found vigour, disembarked with speed. They hurtled down the gangplank as if chased by a bear and, on reaching the hotel, Stella and the girls collapsed gratefully and heavily onto their beds for the night. Apart from a few snores the room was silent. England, to me, was far too quiet and far too still.

14

The following day the pitter-patter of rain on the grey windows of the journey up to Cambridge seemed to subdue our little group. The girls were scowling and weary, Stella apprehensive and even more distracted than usual. I tried to enliven them with songs and tales of my previous travels by train but none of them appeared in the slightest bit curious. The train eventually chugged into Cambridge and, as it slowed, I noticed Stella was becoming more agitated. I picked her gloves up off the floor twice, I spit-licked a fleck of soot off her cheek and I twisted her hat so it faced forward. She couldn't find the tickets. She tripped over another traveller's bags and laddered her stocking. A button fell off her coat. Her handbag flopped open dispensing her powder and comb to the floor. As the porter lifted our baggage down I spotted a tall man waiting on the station. He was stood unusually close to a tiny white-haired woman sporting a wide-brimmed hat adorned with rather squashed silk roses. I recognized them and jumping up and down I waved and started hoo-haaing with excitement. Stella, bright red, attempted to calm my shouts. The man turned his head when he saw our dishevelled party. Beaming, and with hand extended, he bound towards us taking great strides. Peter shook our hands vigorously and we turned to greet the grandmother. She wasn't next to him, or behind. Looking about we saw, to our surprise, that she hadn't moved one inch from her original position on the platform. She appeared welded to one spot and in some sort of reverie. The girls went and dutifully kissed her. She did not kiss or hug them back but, from under the crush of petals and creased brim, a dainty little face crinkled itself into a toothy smile. Her shining eyes, however, were focussed not upon her grand-daughters but on a place far beyond.

Luckily Peter Richardson drove a large saloon. We all squashed in the back. The luggage was strapped to the roof with bits of rope and bags crammed into the trunk. Grandmother, rigid in body and move-ment, sat smiling at the front, her hat obscuring any hope of view. Peter heaped several things on her lap and about her feet. She didn't seem to notice one little bit. Layering Grandmother with baggage seemed to be a good move because rounding a bend in the road her door juddered wide open; if it hadn't been for her packaging she could have easily toppled out. She did not appear in the slightest bit perturbed. She adjusted her hat and continued to smile as Peter re-parcelled her. It all seemed as if it was quite a normal happening for her. The four of us, however, squashed on the back bench, were quite shaken by the occurrence. As Peter drove on we looked at each other, not sure whether to laugh or not.

"We've still got lots to learn about this England," I whispered to the others.

"Shhh! It's rude to whisper," Stella mouthed back. We all giggled.

"There it is," Peter hollered, his hands waving and raised off the steering wheel. "There it is. There's the house. That's Polstead. That's where you're going to be living. Rather handsome place, wouldn't you say?" I peered through the window to see. Several trees sprinkled in pink and creamy-white blossom lined the drive and dots of little spring flowers flecked the lawn. Through the long grass a cat was hunting mice, and apples, half-nibbled and rosy, lay untouched where they had fallen drunkenly to the earth.

"Welcome home," he said, ushering us into a broad entrance hall. Astonished, we all stopped. We stared in amazement. There were things cast everywhere: books scattered across the floor, paper scrolling off the walls, curtains half off and half on their rails, a tray of uneaten dinner balanced precariously on a stair tread, and a giant of a stuffed bear heavy in dust and spider web stood, claws asunder, in a dark corner.

"Oh, that's just Canute," Peter responded when he saw our surprise. "Don't worry. No, no. He's quite friendly. Never bitten anyone yet! Just joking, just joking. Came back with Great-Grandfather from Canada many, many, many moons ago. Say hello to everyone, Canute. See, he's even too shy to speak, let alone bite. Very bashful, yes. Goodness, now! Oh, where's Mother? Oh I say! I've left her sitting in the car. Better get her out otherwise she will stay there until she starves."

"Oh boy!" I said when he'd left.

"We can't stay here." Margaret whined.

"Don't you like bears, then?" I whispered back.

"It's like a crazy house, they're all crackers in England," Marion added in horror.

"Now, that's just applesauce!" Stella said clasping her hands firmly together. "It'll be all right. Don't you fret. This is your family home. Your pa and ma wouldn't have sent you here if it wasn't okay. You're too precious to them. They love you too much to do anything that wouldn't be just right for you. I'm here now to look after you so don't worry about a thing. Everything will be all right. They're good people, they're not crazy. They're just English, they can't help that. They're just a bit odd in their ways. You'll see!"

❋ ❋ ❋

Delphine laughed. "Well, can I assume there were no women living in that house apart from the old lady? I'd say you can always tell whether a woman lives somewhere, or not. In my opinion it's the woman who makes the house a home."

I smiled. "Don't let your George hear that. We don't want him to give up the apron quite yet! He may take offence and hand you back the housework, lock, stock and barrel."

"Point taken. I'll keep my big mouth closed, then. So tell me, did Stella stay?"

"Of course, yes. She had no choice. Stella never ran away from any challenge. But standing in that hodge-podge of an entrance I don't think any of us really felt like remaining there. However, Stella said it would be all right and so, when Stella said that, I knew it would be."

"What happened next?"

❉ ❉ ❉

Peter walked back into the hall steering Grandma past us. "Sorry, sorry about that. Follow me, ladies." He beckoned us through a doorway, his mother lolling on his arm. We followed him through into a large kitchen.

"Sit down, sit down, make yourself comfy. I will get some tea on the boil, or do you prefer coffee, being Americans?" he asked quizzically, one eyebrow raised.

244

"Tea will be just fine," Stella said, "and the girls will have milk, if that's okay." We took off our coats and hung them on the backs of our chairs. I noticed there was a large cherry cake on the table in an alcove by the window. I sat close by.

"Thank you," Stella said. "That tea's good and hot. May I ask you something? Is it just you and your mother living here?"

"No, no, no. I have a nice couple staying here, very nice, but they're rather old, you know. They like to have a little snooze come the afternoon. Lovely people, yes, absolutely lovely. But getting on a bit, nearly as old as Mother. Can't do much but it's very nice to have them around. David and Hala, yes, David and Hala. They keep Mother company when I'm at work. And they keep the kitchen going for me. Good job too! Do the shopping and the cooking, not much else. No, no. Do their best, yes, their best, but not much else. No. You will meet them tonight and we can have a bit of a chat. David and Hala. We all eat together, you know, in here a' night time. That is, when I'm not elsewhere, or not dining in college. Have to eat there sometimes. Stuffy old place, you know, yes. Food not good generally but one of the university rules, one of many, one of many. Too many, I say. But have to conform. Get my wrists slapped otherwise! Oh I say, forgot to say Hala made that cake for you. Help yourself.

Help yourself. Go on. Don't know where the plates are kept. New here too. Ha-ha! Just joking. Been here generations." He opened a cupboard door. "Plates are in here. No! This one then. See, right second time around. Help yourself, now. Make yourself at home. It's your home as well as mine. You're not guests, you know, you're family. My family. Most welcome, most welcome."

He was a real nice man and we later found out a real good man. He was always taking in life's waifs and strays, not just us. Munching into Hala's cherry cheesecake I could see that Stella was right; it was going to be fine. She said so and she was always right about everything. The girls looked a bit taken aback but that was understandable. In fact, they mostly looked like that wherever we were. Grandmother just sat in her chair and smiled sweetly at something outside the window.

"Excuse me, Mr Richardson. Sorry to trouble you but may we be shown to our rooms so we can clean up?" Stella inquired, interrupting the silence.

"Oh I say, I am so frightfully sorry. I should have done that long before. How remiss of me, how very remiss. Frightful memory. — Come on Mother. Let's go for a little walk. — Follow me, ladies. Up the stairs we go. Careful there, a bit of loose carpet. Tripped over that several times myself. Must get David to mend that. Can't have you tumbling head over heels down the stairs, now. No, no. That wouldn't help anyone. Now I've put you two girls together in here. Your parents said you would prefer that. Now Kitty, I've got you in this little room, the old nursery. Hope you don't mind. I used to sleep there when I was just a nipper myself. Rather nice, I'd say. Rather nice. Nice room, nice and sunny. And Mrs Hurtigrutensson, I've given you the room next door to Kitty. The bathrooms are over here. Plenty of towels in the drawers. See? Have a rest now, freshen up, do whatever you want. If you want to have a nap, nap. Hala will ring the bell when supper's ready so no need to be on tenterhooks wondering. We will wake you. Won't let you starve. No, no starving here. Normally supper's about seven pm. Can be eight, or later, normally around seven, though. Or eight. Otherwise come back down whenever you feel like it or if you are just in need of something or other. Mother always likes to have company. Normally we sit in the kitchen in winter. Nice and warm. Oh, and in case you were wondering we don't dress for dinner in this house. No, no." He led grandmother back down the stairs. "Special occasions, yes; normally no. Only special occasions. Have a bit of a brush-up then. Christmas, birthdays and all that. Come on, Mother."

We explored our rooms. They were surprisingly nice and clean. The sheets freshly ironed and we all had a bowl of flowers by our bedside. Children's books lined my shelf and a fireplace was laid ready for lighting. Swirls of little black and white swans were printed on the curtains which were crisply hanging from a wooden pole. There were large cakes of soap smelling of roses in the bathroom and a bath tub that was as deep as I had ever seen. I could imagine swimming in it, up and down. Hazarding our way back downstairs we removed our luggage from the car and bumped it back up to our rooms trying not to trip over bits and bobs. We unpacked and waited patiently for the supper bell to gong.

We heard it about eight-thirty. By then I was ravenous but we proceeded down the stairs in twos carefully minding the tray of uneaten food. I wanted to slide down the bannister but on the other hand I didn't want to crash into dust-ridden Canute. Hala and David were in the kitchen. Hala raised up her arms in greeting and kissed us warmly on both cheeks. Grandmother was already sitting at the table, grinning. David shook all our hands with great gusto and, with a show of flamboyance, he directed us like a maître d' across to our seats. Peter sat in the centre and told us to help ourselves to the contents of a big stew pot and to steaming bowls of potatoes and caraway buttered cabbage. "Hope you don't mind, ladies," Peter announced, "but I don't eat meat. Hope you don't take offence. You're most welcome to eat meat but Hala just cooks vegetarian food at Polstead. No meat, no meat for me. Better for you and for the cows. Ha-ha! They like it too. I asked them. Ha-ha!" Hala opened her hands, her face smiling, but shaking her head from side to side as if to say, what can I do?

"Theosophist, I am," he continued. Don't eat meat, don't fight wars, don't do church. No offence to you. Feel free to think and eat whatever. But no meat in this house, please. Live and let live. That's my motto. Yes, live and let live."

"You sound like a bit of a philosopher, Mr Richardson. Are you?" Stella asked as we chewed away.

"No, not really, no no. Like philosophy and psychology, you know, but not really a philosopher. Care about what we think and why, but no, not a professional philosopher. Liked to have been, but, you know, not trained. Left it too late now. Historian I am for my sins. Teach history to the 'bright young things'. Modern stuff, nothing too distant. Father was too. Same as me. In the blood, historically speaking. Ha-ha!"

"So are you a don then? Should I address you as plain Mr, or Dr, or is it Professor?"

"I say! No, not Professor, not yet, anyhow. No. Unlikely ever! I go a bit against the grain, you see. Rub the 'Old School' up the wrong way some of the time. Much of the time, to be honest. Speak my mind, you know. Bit of a rebel. Father a professor, good man, and, David here, he was also a professor. In Vienna, you know. He's a medical man, specialised in the mind as opposed to the brain. Very interesting, very interesting. But anyhow, to answer your question, please call me Peter, plain Peter. Not Doctor, no! Not Doctor. Not in the classroom now. May I call you Stella, if that is not too presumptuous?"

"Of course you may, with pleasure, Peter. I don't like stuffy, either. And Margaret and Marion, what shall they call you? Is Uncle Peter fine? And your mother? How should we address her?"

"Mother," he turned to the old lady sitting bemused. She was eating slowly encouraged by Hala. "What would you like your granddaughters to call you?" There was silence. "Sounds like no strong feeling either way. How about Grandmother? Okay with you, girls? Good." They nodded shyly and smiled at Grandmother.

"What shall I call everyone?" I piped up.

"Well, if you like, you can call me Uncle Peter too. I don't mind as long as you don't mind calling me Uncle."

"Not at all," I replied. "That would be delightful. I've never had an uncle so it will be," I hesitated, "absolutely ripping."

"Rather!" Everyone laughed. I had found the expression 'absolutely ripping' in a book upstairs about a boy called William. Stella had been reading it to me.

"And what about Grandmother? May I call her Grandmother too? I've not had one of those, either."

"I think that it would be 'absolutely ripping' if you did," Uncle Peter replied amongst laughter. Even Grandmother was grinning alongside us.

✳ ✳ ✳

"So tell me," George said, "why was a medical man and his wife living and working in Peter's house? It seems kind of a strange thing for a doctor to be doing."

"Well, that story came out over the next few days. David and Hala were from Vienna. They were of the Jewish faith. In those years, as you well know, things were getting pretty hectic over there. The Nazi party were taking over. Increasingly, ordinary people were behaving badly towards the Jews. They attacked them both physically and mentally. Jewish books publicly burnt. David being an academic had no chance. Their positions became untenable."

"So they left Vienna?"

"Yes, Peter had a friend from Cambridge who was a colleague of Professor Lasnovsky, David that is. He could see what was happening in Vienna and asked Peter if he could help find some university work in Cambridge for the Professor. You see, the government would only allow the Jews visas to enter Britain if they had some employment, pre-arranged and verified."

"Like the recruitment drives in the West Indies."

"Similar. But, you know, without official papers they couldn't legally leave their own country. Peter tried to no avail to get David some work as a researcher. Everyone wanted jobs. It was the 1930s. Many Jews were desperate to leave their own home countries before things worsened. Some of them, of course, wanted to stay and fight. But others, maybe those with a bit more imagination, fortune or knowledge, tried to escape as soon as they possibly could. They were the lucky ones."

"Sure were."

"Anyhow, David and his wife needed to leave Vienna. His brother had been carted off by soldiers. He was never seen again. He left a family. Somehow David secured them all a passage to Palestine but in the end, due to British quotas, David and Hala weren't allowed to join them. To cut a long story short, Peter in the meantime offered them a home. In return, Hala offered to cook for Peter, and David offered his help around the house and garden."

"So that's why they were there. Bit like George and me! – And what about Peter's mother?"

"Oh, the old lady. She was a dear old thing. A few years earlier she'd suffered a stroke, 'hardening of the arteries', they called it. She just needed supervising ... but on a full time basis! Harmless old thing ... and not really that old! She was never a problem. Lived in a world of her own. Sad, I s'pose, for Margaret and Marion. They could have done with a closer relationship with her, particularly after the death of their mother. In her final years Grandmother couldn't have been surrounded by a family of more caring people. We all loved her."

"So how long did you all stay at Polstead House?"

***

Stella, as usual, took everything in hand. Even Canute got a dusting. By the end of the week she had the household re-organised. A woman from the village was employed to help with the housework and a man came to help David with the gardening and repairs. Peter was only too happy to go along with her improvements. And Stella took to driving. However, her capabilities behind the steering wheel were not commendable. Stella, you see, could never quite get the idea of right and left; she always confused which was which. Having to steer the car with the wheel on the opposite side to what she was normally accustomed was a rather thrilling experience for her passengers. Regularly she bumped the car off the cobbles and sometimes drove straight into the water-filled channels which ran alongside the main road in Cambridge. Much to my embarrassment passers-by were obliged to help us girls heave the car back out. But to give her due I don't think she ever had an accident ... but I do believe she may have caused quite a few. She would laugh it off. And when irate drivers met her with complaint, she would shrug and credit their annoyance as a whole load of applesauce. In the same fashion when the girls screamed in fear she'd just twist around in the driving seat and yell 'fiddlesticks!' I didn't mind her colourful driving. I knew I was perfectly safe with Stella whatever she did. To me she was invincible.

Shopping days were generally fun for me. There was a time, however, when we drove off into town to buy Margaret and Marion their new school uniforms. I thought they looked pretty all dressed up and sporting straw boaters but they, being teenagers, thought that they looked stupid, and, moreover they thought I was stupid to think they looked nice. There was an argument in the centre of the store much to the amusement of the other customers unaccustomed to American ways. Understandably the girls were unhappy about the prospect of being boarders at their new school and I think that possibly, for some unexplained reason, they were jealous of me.

It must have been April, just before the start of the new term, when Peter came bobbing into the kitchen. The girls were sulking elsewhere. "I say!" he boomed, "I've had a rather jolly good idea, even if I say so myself; jolly good, I'd say. What do you think to this, Stella. Instead of you tootling back to New York, how about you stay on here with us, here at Polstead? What d'you think? I know the original agreement was just for you to settle Margaret and Marion here and then whoosh off back, but I was having a little think. Yes, I was thinking that maybe you and Kitty could stay on here until the girls complete their schooling. You could have the old gardener's cottage as your own place. Yes, your very own. Make it nice. Nobody uses it any more. It's empty, as you know. That is, of course, if you wanted somewhere with your own things. I could get the place done up and made habitable for you; make it nice and cosy with your own saucepans and cushions and other things you ladies like. But if you're happier here in the house you could stay on here in the house. Yes yes. Live on in the main house with the rest of us. Happy families and all that. What d'you say?"

"Oh!" Stella looked astonished at the suggestion. She went over to the fruit bowl and popped a whole tomato into her mouth and chewed it over slowly. She'd swallowed it in a gulp and turned back to Peter. "Well, I don't know what to say. I'm rather taken aback. Let me think this through. Are you saying to me that you want me to stay on here whilst the girls are at school? But what would I do with myself when Margaret and Marion are away? It won't take all my time just seeing to the housekeeping."

"Well, Stella my dear, that's part and parcel of the plan; that's the other splendid bit. The girls, as you know, are not too keen about the boarding bit, not too keen at all. Don't blame them. I didn't like it either when I was a youngster. No, I didn't. But if you stayed on here, Stella, it would mean that they could be weekly boarders instead, home every week-end and at other times during the week, too. You could be like their governess. Be in charge outside school hours and during the 'hols'. Keep a home going for them, and me too, of course," he laughed. "I'm not sure if an old fellow like me could keep two young ladies entertained for long. Probably get bored pretty quickly, bored as a plank of wood. Ha-ha. I'd like them to have a jolly good time whilst they're over here. I promised Esther I'd do my best for them. Don't want to let her down. She's a good woman, very good sort. It's all too bad!

"If you stayed you could accompany them on trips and holidays; do a bit of a European tour with them if you wanted. Go to see the pyramids. See the sands of the Sahara. Ride a camel. Go to the seaside, lots of sand there too, beaches and deckchairs, donkeys, swimming, whatever girls like these days. Make sure they're safe and well cared for. I'd be far less worried if you were around. I couldn't think of a more splendid person to ask than you."

"Thank you for considering me, Peter, that's very kind, but I also have Kitty to think about."

"No problem; thought of that too. She's included in the package, part of the family now, anyhow. You know, there's a frightfully good school down in the village. And when Kitty's older there's the 'Cambridge Girls'. I'm afraid I don't do private schools; don't believe in private education. No no. So not offering that. Not right, no. 'The Girls' is a grammar, yes, grammar school. She will do fine there, absolutely. Excellent education, excellent. I know the head teacher. Fine woman, good principles. Good principal with good principles. Ha-ha! And most important, Kitty will have a home here. A child needs a good solid base. What do you say? Jolly good idea, if you ask me. I know that Henry and Esther will be more than happy to go along with it. They'd back me one hundred percent, yes, one hundred percent."

"Well, I'm not sure, Peter. It's a very big decision."

"Quite understand, quite understand. Take your time."

Stella looked down at me. I looked up at her. "Well, Peter, you've definitely taken me by surprise. I need to have a little think and talk it over with Kitty, here."

I was nodding eagerly. "I think it's a wonderful idea. I like it here and I really like donkeys."

"I don't know, sweetheart. It's kind of a big decision to make." She looked back at Peter. "You know, I still have my own folks back home, Peter. It's a bit like crossing the Rubicon for me. Once crossed it might be pretty hard to return to a life in the States."

"Understandable, understandable," Peter agreed. "Big, big decision. Generally I don't like to talk money but, of course, I'll pay you well so you could go back whenever you wanted. You can have holidays, plenty of free time, plenty. Bring your parents across. There's plenty of room for all. But you must do what you think's best. Anyhow, offer's down on the table now. Think about it and let me know. Take your time, take your time. No hurry. Don't want to harass. Your decision. Won't harass."

Over the next few hours Stella paced the kitchen. I followed with my eyes. She kept chewing the corner of her lip. She stopped at the window and stared out. I crossed to her. The golden heads of daffodils were pushing their way through the grass."

"Isn't it pretty, Stella," I said with my arm around her waist. "I like daffodils. They're so very, very ... yellow."

"Yes, they are. Kitty, what do you really think of Peter's idea?"

"I think it's a jolly good idea. I like it here, and, I really like Uncle Peter."

"Uh-ha. He's a very nice man."

"And, Stella?"

"What sweetheart?"

"Do you remember what you said when we sailed over? You said you were never ever ever getting on a ship ever, ever again. Remember now? And I don't ever ever want to leave here either ever although I did like the ship. They made me lovely pancakes."

"I sure did," she laughed. "Okay, Kitty-Kat, you're right. What's there to lose? Let's round the cattle up. You go tell the girls to come down straight away. I'll fetch Peter back in."

We all congregated around the table and Stella explained Uncle Peter's proposal to the girls. They smiled and hugged each other. The first time I'd seen them happy in weeks.

"Well, let's shake hands. That's a deal," Stella said. The girls cheered and kissed their uncle and Grandmother. We all shook hands with each other. Grandmother smiled.

"I wish I could fix you some apple pancakes to celebrate," I said, "just like the ones on the ship. You missed such a lot being sick. I got the recipe somewhere. I sure could make you them. Gilbert wrote it down in my book for me. I'll go and find it. I think it's under my bed somewhere."

"Righto," Peter replied, ignoring my suggestion, "I agree that there's a call for celebration, yes, let's celebrate this momentous occasion. But, how about I invite you all out to tea this afternoon in town. How about going to 'Dorothy's' on Trinity? Very nice teas there, very nice. Good scones, lots of cream. Jam just right, never too runny. No, just right. Good place. Excellent 'Chelseas' too, very treacly, very sticky. Just what's needed, yes, just what's needed."

"Yes please," the girls chorused. "But please, Uncle Peter, could **you** drive us there?"

15

It was May 1936. I was enrolled at Polstead Primary down in the village as a nine year old. My birth date had been decided upon for me. It was to be the tenth day of March, 1927 – the day, but not the year, we'd arrived in England. I suppose it was as good a day as any other. Peter declared that having one's own special day was a good thing, yes. Letters were written on my behalf and, one day in June, a woman arrived at the house carrying a leather briefcase. She was shown into the morning room and, to my horror, she asked to speak to me. I was terrified. The image of the 'rat-woman' school's inspector came raging back. I scrambled behind Stella on the sofa. I didn't want to talk. I couldn't talk. Burying my face in a cushion, I pressed my nose deep into the fabric. The woman asked me about my past. She called me 'dear' but I still didn't want to tell. I couldn't. I wouldn't. The past was a world away, a time and a place I had left far behind, long before. I'd closed the memory off. I had locked the cupboard door on that part of my life. Everything was hidden within its walls. I wanted to forget, I did not want to remember. But, wrapping me in her arms, Stella reassured me, over and over again, that I was safe with her. She rocked me to and fro against her body, to and fro. She stroked my hair and hummed close to my ear. Everything would be all right with Stella. She would always be there for me. She and I were one. So, hesitantly, with head bowed and sobbing into her chest, I answered the woman's questions. She smiled when she finished and shook my hand. It was going to be all right.

Not long after the visit an official birth certificate arrived. It came by courier and was signed for with great ceremony. I felt re-born. The past, it was gone for ever. Stella and Peter had become my legal guardians and, that night, in the dining hall at Polstead, we celebrated all my birthdays in one big, joyous party. Under the candle lit chandelier we dined. The oval mahogany table was laden in its finery with silver dishes and a glitter of glassware. Peter and David wore satin waistcoats with bright bow ties. Hala wore a mink stole and a string of pearls. And Stella wore a flower behind one ear and laughed a lot. She handed me a little box. Inside within the tissue I found an amethyst-jewelled butterfly with a golden chain. "It was mine," she whispered. "It was from my mother and now I hand it to you." Everyone clapped and cheered. The girls were balancing party hats and they blew paper whistles and snake trumpets. The air was frothy with bubbles and balloons bounced about the carpet. Stella sat down at the grand piano and with a grand fanfare of opening notes sang:

'Happy birthdays to you,
Squashed tomatoes and stew
You act like a monkey,
And you smile like one too!'

Everyone cheered and laughed. I was feted. My first birthday party.

✳ ✳ ✳

"So are you telling me you could be much older, or even younger, than you think?" Delphine asked.

"I am indeed. Sometimes I feel older, especially round the knees, but normally I act much younger!"

"I think you're younger too. Everyone thinks so; you've got such a good memory. Wish I could think as clearly as you can. I'm just feeling my age more and more every day. They say youth is wasted on the young. I go right along with that. So, tell me, what happened to the twins? Did they settle into that fancy school of theirs?"

"Actually, they did. It wasn't too bad after all. The Spruce was a good school. They made friends there pretty quickly. That was some achievement! I think it helped that they were Americans. To the other girls in their class they probably seemed quite glamorous and worldly. Being different helps in some situations. It was quite surprising, really, as generally they weren't that outgoing. Looking back, I think, probably, it was the right thing for them. It brought them out of their shells. And once Stella had sorted out Polstead they started inviting school chums back for tea and tennis matches. There was a tennis court in the gardens behind the house. Stella had got the grass trimmed, rolled flat and even got the net on the straight. Soon you could hardly tell that Margaret and Marion were even American. Such posh English accents! They were good looking girls, too. They could have been princesses by the time they finished that school. Unlike me! Even now, after all these years, people still recognize that I'm coming from the States. Can you believe it?"

"I never lost my accent either."

"But then the girls did have their elocution lessons at school ... and come to think about it, etiquette and deportment coaching as well. I remember them walking around with piles of books on top of their heads. They were good at it. I think, like me, they needed to re-invent themselves. They needed to belong to elsewhere. It did them a whole load of good being there.

"On Saturdays I accompanied Stella when she went to fetch the girls home from the Spruce. First of all we'd drive into town and do the week's shopping. Stella never quite understood speed limits or bends. I think she may have scared a lot of people in her path but I, like her, absolutely loved the thrill. You know what, Delphine, I think if I ever come back on this earth I might take up being a rally driver. And what's it called, the one where you drive around a track in an old banger?"

"Banger racing."

"I think I quite fancy the fun of that. Can you remind me, if I forget, that's what I'm going to do in my next life?"

"Sure will."

"Anyhow, where was I?"

"Shopping in town."

"So after doing the shopping Stella and I would wander around the old town. Maybe we'd wander down to the river and watch the punts or rowing boats from a bridge. Did I ever take you to Cambridge to see the punts?"

"No."

"More's the pity! Never mind. They're a bit like gondolas, but someone stands at the back and quants them along with wooden poles pushing off the river bed. I used to dart from one side of the bridge to the other in the hope that the pole would hit the bridge's low underside and knock the punter into the flow. They did sometimes too! It was just great hearing splashing and spluttering and not to mention the giggles and yells of their becalmed passengers left aboard.

"School was good for me, too. It was a one classroom school and we went up in stages rather than ages, so I suppose it didn't really matter how old you were. The teacher, Miss Caruthers, was such a lovely lady. And, you know, she took a particular liking to me and my odd little ways. She was firm, yes. And most of the other children were a bit wary, but she had her way of encouraging talent from all of us and, for me, that was, as you well know, my painting. Did I tell you that when I held my first art exhibition in London, Miss Caruthers was the one who came down? And the first person to buy one of my pictures?"

"That was a good investment!"

"Yes, but she didn't know it then! She did it to make me feel good. That's what teaching is about, making children feel good at what they're at. – I remember it was snowing heavily that day, yet she travelled on the slow train down to London, just to see my show."

"Those picture shows! I remember them well. My goodness, you were some busy lady back then."

"I never stopped, did I?"

"No, you did not ... and we didn't, either!"

"The setting up of those exhibitions, the work that went into it! And organising all those guests to come along for the opening nights."

"And the press! Everything had to be just right for them, didn't it? You were such a perfectionist. You wouldn't rest until it was just so."

"That's right. That was me all over."

"George was always hanging things up here, and up there, then next moment down again from up there and shuffling them back over to up here. I'm sure sometimes those pictures often ended up where they started off."

"Poor George! He has the patience of a saint."

"He had to! And what about the mess afterwards! Do you remember? Empty glasses everywhere, ashtrays overflowing on to tablecloths, cheese and pineapple trodden direct into rugs, cocktail sausages on sticks down the side of chairs, half spilled bottles lying behind sofas, vols-au-vent crushed on the stairs! "

"Sorry about that ... but they were good parties, weren't they? Sold loads, too."

"And do you recall how George would drive you about town at all hours of the night and day?"

"Yes, I do. I forgot I'd lost my license. Naughty girl, I was!"

"And some of the places you went to! They definitely opened my eyes wide. What a life you led. Not to mention some of the shady characters you dragged back home often. Sometimes we couldn't get shot of them for days after."

"You and George certainly put up with a lot. But, you know, I think I needed all that. Got rid much of that pent-up anger of mine. You were my saviours. Always keeping an eye out for me, weren't you? Feeding me, cleaning up, sorting things out, seeing I was safe. I even remember George not letting me take a taxi back at night. He said it wasn't right for a woman to be out that late. Can you believe it? I was older than him yet he still treated me as if he were the parent."

"Well, he was right, Kitty. You weren't old enough, not up here in the head, to be out alone. We worried something about you."

"I did appreciate it. You know, you kept me going. I was like your little girl."

"True, you were a little girl. Sometimes in the early hours of the morning we'd find you dozing in the studio, with the turn-table whirring silently around and surrounded with half-drunk bottles. And all over the furniture cigarette stubs would be smouldering away in ashtrays. George would lift you up off the floor, or wherever you were strewn, and carry you off to bed. I'd go and tuck you up tight, switch off the lights and even give you, if I was in a good mood, a kiss good-night."

"George would probably break his back if he tried to do that now! But, I got through it all. I'm so glad I'm still hanging on here. There's been some wonderful years since. Thank you for all that."

"Glad to hear it. But remember, we wouldn't be here without you so don't you forget that either."

"As you like."

"Good."

"Is there any chocolate about, Delphine? I just fancy a strawberry cream."

❋ ❋ ❋

The summer of 1936. A happy time for me. A happy time for Stella. Sunlight bounced through the windows in Polstead. Glasses glittered, silver shone and floors sweetened with lavender wax gleamed and glowed through day and night. With a flourish of feathers, webs were wafted away, carpets revealed their patterns and curtains freshly crisped proudly displayed their flowery garlands. In the garden, lying on my back hidden in the long grass, I watched clouds drift over. I saw their faces smile down upon me and sometimes laugh. Now and then, they came along herding sheep. And odd times dragons passed by with smoky breaths, and mountain ranges grew deep in ice-cream snow. I danced after butterflies, counted time on dandelions and cradled ladybirds in my hands. I twisted through the ancient limbs of mulberry, biting into its gorge of murrey-red fruit. Here I was in my majesty. From high in the tangle of branches I could scan my kingdom. I could see as far as I ever wanted to see. I could see the church steeple, to me a princess's tower. I waved to passing hats and coats that bobbed along the top of the boundary hedge. And glancing down into the gold-green wavering depths of the undergrowth I stalked numerous cats who stalked numerous birds who stalked fat wiggly worms. I trailed harvest mice, and wished them luck in life.

Cleo was the tabby who regularly came a-mewing. Sometimes she'd let me stroke her velvet-like coat whilst she fed but, other times, I got a hiss or a clawing for my trouble. I understood that. I didn't mind. I didn't like being interrupted at my feeding either. I was pleased she had a home to come to.

"Why've you called her Cleo, Uncle Peter?"

"Cleo, yes, good question. Cleo's short for Cleocatra. Ha-ha! Should be Cleopatra, just my little joke. Ha-ha!" He loved his jokes. "Cleopatra, yes, now, fine woman, very intelligent. Last of the Ptolemeics in Egypt. Long ago, long, long ago in Egypt. Fine queen but had a, had a bit of an encounter with Caesar, a Julius one, not a good idea, no, no never is. Caesars generally not good. Better not to mix with them. Always cause trouble in the end. Egyptians good, though. Loved cats."

"Me too."

"Glad to hear it. Loved cats, yes. Good, good. Me too, yes."

"I think I'd be a good Egyptian, because I love cats and I don't mind queens."

"Splendid, yes, splendid! I'll have look along the shelves. Yes, see if I can dig you out a book on pyramids and camels and things. Oh, and cats. Yes, cats, of course."

Peter was spending whole days working in his study. I'd only see him on his occasional cat-feeding session or his errands to the Post Office. Often times he'd have a large bundle of envelopes, clasped close to his chest, ready for the posting. If I spied him wandering along the garden path I'd dash over and, skipping alongside, chatter away. For a man without children of his own, he showed much patience. I was always asking him the names of things and demanding answers to all sorts of, what must have seemed, bizarre questions. I was fascinated by the colour blue and I remember haranguing him, over and over, with questions such as 'who painted the sky blue?' and 'how many colour blues are there?' and 'when does blue become green and stop being blue?' He would consider my questions with seriousness and try to provide an answer suitable for a child of my age. I never really understood his answers but I just liked to hear the gentle growliness in his voice. A bit like, I imagined, a friendly bear would sound; not that I'd ever heard a bear growl, not even 'Canute the Shy'.

Visitors from the university and other places would call at Polstead, particularly in the evenings. I was allowed to answer the door and announce their presence. I took my job very seriously, courteously greeting, taking hats and gloves, removing umbrellas or bicycle spats and rain-wet coats. Once disrobed of their fripperies, I'd accompany the guest, with great aplomb, to the study. Having knocked firmly and awaited a call of, "Come in, yes yes, come in, yes," I would swing open the study door with great flourish, often causing loose papers to take off in flight (and possibly fright) from the pile on his desk! Some of the guests smiled at me, some praised me for my personal attention. Others seemed more taken aback by my propriety and cordoned slowly around me as if I were some dangerous beast. Nobody was allowed into the study unless invited so I would hover about outside in the hall. Every now and again I would peep through the keyhole and spy on Peter. Unfortunately a floorboard outside the door had an irregular creak. Suddenly Peter would look up towards the door. Once he waved to me and said, "Yes, Kitty? What is it?" In embarrassment, for having been caught, I scarpered.

Peter was very good to all of us. We were family. That first summer he introduced us to strawberry picking. After a day in the fields we came back suntanned and laughing with clothes stained and baskets spilling over with the richest ruby-red fruit. He took us to garden fêtes, donkey derbies and to fairs where we won coconuts with hairy skins and goldfish, magnified large, in glass jars. He showed us how to capture, in our hands, clouds of pink candy-floss escaping the vendors' barrows. He sailed us down the river with hefty hampers full of cakes, thick bread sandwiches and bottles of pop; the twins were ever squealing, ever worried that the tonnage might sink the punt. They sat gripping everything, including each other, anxious lest the punt should tip into the stream's murky depths. Mindful of their fearful shrieks, Peter glided us gracefully along the Cam, rustling through curtains of willow to picnic on the banks of meadowsweet at Grantchester. I thought it a great disappointment that he did not deign to wobble the boat or pretend to fall in as I'd seen others do. I liked the idea of being adrift and, ungraciously, I thought it would be such a hoot if the girls tumbled into the stream. I could rescue them. I was a good swimmer. They wouldn't drown. I'd save them, and instead of shunning me they would be ever grateful for the rescue. So, at every sweep of leaf that brushed past and under every stone bridge we slithered, I kept my fingers crossed hoping for ship wreck. Unfortunately nothing untoward ever occurred. Peter was captain of his craft and his passengers always safe.

Best of all were the garden parties. These were held in college courts or on their sacred lawns. Proudly Peter would introduce us to Professor 'This' and Lord 'That' and we'd shake their hands as if we, too, were worthy beings. Politely we would chat away to their wives and children and munch scones heaped high with creams and jams. Nobody seemed to notice, or care, how many you ate! Tiny petals of flowers floated in little glasses of fruit punch served on silver trays by college maids dressed in white lace. A time so wonderful it could have been a story. Margaret and Marion laughed and smiled. They looked so pretty dressed in their florals and sporting their satin-bowed straw hats.

Autumn soon followed and with it came the sad news. In October Peter received a telegram from America informing us that Esther had died.

❉ ❉ ❉

"They say everything good comes to an end," sighed Delphine. "I know Esther dying was expected, but still! Those girls must have hurt. It's when a girl needs a mother most. So, Kitty, did they treat Stella more like a mother-figure after that?"

"No, not really. They never did, before or after. Don't get me wrong. They were nice enough girls but they didn't warm, not to Stella or to me, or anyone else come to think of it. I never felt as if I was their little sister although others believed we were related. They never jelled, not even with Uncle Peter who, of course, was real family; not in the way I did. I don't know, maybe that's normal for twins? I don't think the girls ever got over losing their mother. I s'pose the distance didn't help. You know, they never went back to see Esther's grave, or anywhere else."

"They never went back to the States?"

"Don't think so, not that I know of. You see, war broke and the dangers of crossing the Atlantic were far too risky. Nobody crossed unless they really had to."

"Not surprised! So many ships went down. The war turned everybody's life upside down and inside out. I was too little to remember much about what went on back in St Elizabeth. But I do remember my mamma telling me about the nightly curfews we had. You try keeping nine children happy inside one room from dusk 'til dawn!"

"Especially in that heat."

"No air conditioning or freezers in those days."

"Times have changed."

"They were some real hot nights. Don't know how Mamma coped. Jamaica's only a tiny island. A lot of the time we were just cut off from the rest of the world. There were all sorts of shortages going on. Feeding us little ones couldn't have been easy going. You know, George's two older brothers, Leonard and Kenny? They volunteered their lives, without second thought, to fight for King and country. They were only boys themselves when they sailed off. They were so happy to go. They were singing."

"What a terrible waste of life."

"Sure was indeed. But England, they'd been taught, was their mother country and they put that before anything else. Not that it did them any good! As you well know, neither came back."

"Yes, I remember. So very, very sad!"

"And d'you remember how George and I went to that place, where was it now? ... Oh yes, Anzio. Saw their names carved deep on the memorial. We took some snaps and sent them back home. Mamma never got over her loss. Mothers never do. They were her first and second born. The war so changed the world. We all changed. However much you wish it, those clock hands back just can't be turned back. But, poor

Mamma, she wouldn't believe that one day her boys weren't going to walk right back into her kitchen. You know, until the day she died, she kept their places set at table, just in case."

16

Stella was crying over some onions, her pinafore blotched with splodges of dried-on food. The kitchen was fogged with steam and smoke. I was making pastry cut-outs and dusted white in flour. Vegetable peelings piled high in the sink were hiding yesterday's pots and pans. Residue from previous meals peppered the floor and the smell of burnt porridge lingered unhappily in the air. Hala and David had departed for a new life in Palestine. Stella now was in charge of the kitchen.

Peter beamed into the kitchen. "I say," he announced, "I've some jolly good news! A new family are coming. They're joining us here for a bit. Not for long, though, only until they've got themselves sorted." Stella raised a hand to her forehead and muttered something.

"No no, don't worry, Stella," Peter continued. "No extra mouths to feed. We'll put them up in Gardener's Cottage, unless, that is, you two prefer to live there now. I don't mind, no, not at all, who lives where. They're very nice. Very nice people. Yes, very nice indeed. Italian family from Turin. Had a bad time of it with Mr Mussolini. Bad time for all. Anyhow, I've sorted things out and hopefully, fingers crossed, we can set them up and get them going again. They'll be standing on their own two feet in no time. No time at all, no time at all."

"Good for you, Uncle Peter."

"Yes, sorry, of course," agreed Stella. "It's just that I'm a bit overwhelmed, Peter. Cooking isn't my thing at all, sorry about that. When can we expect to meet them?"

"Not sure, not sure, but soon. Soon as they can."

"Have they got any children?"

"Got two, yes, two boys, about twelve, thirteen, I think. Yes, around about fourteen or fifteen. Nice family. Father, university man. Economics, history, that sort of thing. We'll have a lot in common, yes. Known him for years, you know. Great writer, talks a lot of sense. To me, anyhow. Bit of a 'Commie', you know. Yes, bit of a 'Commie' but very, very nice. I say, how about we get things ready for them. Would you be offended, Stella, if I took the liberty of asking you to choose the furnishing for me? Put you at the helm. You know, being a man I'm no good at that type of stuff. Sizes and patterns and kettles and talc and all that, no good at all. Have no idea whatsoever about these things. Maybe you could have a look around and make a list. Bits and bobs they may need in the cottage. Don't suppose they'll have anything with them, I assume nothing at all ... apart from the clothes on their backs. They'll need furniture and things, but good solid furniture, please. And nice curtains, comfortable beds, dinner plates, irons, tea plates, bed stuff, curtain rings, armchairs, and an electric toaster of course. Very useful, yes, toaster, good for crumpets. Chairs. Yes chairs, too. Both types: some with arms, some with legs. You know, that type of thing? Make it nice for them. They deserve a bit better than utility. Get the best you can. Had a rough time, yes very rough. Are you able to pop off down to town and sort it out? Much obliged if you could."

"Well, when I've sorted this kitchen out, I'll be pleased to be of service."

"Good, good. I'll help you out on the kitchen front. Not recommended but I'll do my best. Shopping-wise I suggest 'Sayles' or 'Josh Taylors'. Good stores. Or, of course, wherever you think best. You're the boss. Much obliged. You know what's what. A sofa. Get them to deliver. Soon as convenient. Get whatever you need. On account of course."

Several months later the phone rang. It was quite late. I was in my dressing gown about to go to bed. "Stella?" Peter called up the stairs. "Have to go out. I'm off to the station. Got to go immediately. The

Della Setas, the Italians we're expecting. They're here. They've made it. They're in Cambridge now. Waiting at the station. I need to pick them up."

"Can I stay up and say hello?" I asked Stella.

"As long as you don't chat too much. I should think they'll be pretty tired after such a journey."

"I promise not to chat too much but I can say something to them, can't I? I want to be friends straight away."

"Is that a good idea or not, Peter?"

"I'd say so, Stella. Yes, jolly good idea. Yes, but not too much chat. Not just you, Kitty, none of us, that is. They'll be tired, very very tired. Very tired indeed. Had an unbelievably rough time. Can I leave you now to warm the rooms and heat up some soup or something for them? Probably famished."

"Yes, of course, leave it to us, Peter. We'll manage. Just go!"

I scampered into the entrance hall when I heard Peter pull up outside Polstead. Peter guided them in. In front of me I saw three coats hanging loosely under grey faces. Shadow darkened their eyes. Their cheeks hollowed out pits. My cheer of welcome suddenly silenced as dark clouds raged inside me conjuring up images from times long gone.

Stella coughed. "Welcome to Polstead, I'm Stella. Hello." She walked towards them holding out her hand. They didn't look up.

"This is Professor Eli Della Seta and this Signora Sara Della Seta," Peter announced, "and this young man is Vitale." Silence. "Bad time of it. Very bad. Let's get them warmed up. Get some food going and then, I think, they'll probably be wanting their beds."

"Hello," I said. "I'm Kitty. I live here, too." I sidled up to the mother and twisting my head to the side I looked up into her face. I felt I was approaching a scared animal. She stared, then smiled back at me and nodded. Nobody said anything.

"Come on into the kitchen now. Come come." Peter beckoned them through. "Leave your bags there. We'll sort it out later. Just leave it. Come. Sit down and have something hot." I passed over bowls of soup and handed them chunks of bread. They ate quickly but silently. Their mouths low to the plates. Eyes cast downward.

"We made up the fires in the cottages," Stella said brightly when they'd finished their fill. "The coals should be glowing away and the water will be hot soon enough. It will be lovely and cosy for you in there. I think you look as if you need to get to your beds." Hearing this, the father nodded. "You can have one of my nightgowns, Signora Della Seta, and I have some fresh clothes for you for the morning, if you would like. Peter, could you possibly lend some pyjamas to Professor Della Seta, and for Vitale?"

"Of course! Should have thought of that myself. Yes. Do it straight off. I'm afraid my things may be a bit on the large size but tomorrow we'll see what we can do about that. No problem. I'll just hop upstairs. No problem, whatsoever."

"Uncle Peter," I piped up, "where's the other boy? Isn't there s'posed to be two children?"

"Ah, sore point, Kitty, but yes, you're right. Talk about it tomorrow. Shush for the moment about that. Anyhow, I'll go and fetch those things so you can all get off to your beds and have some kip."

Stella and I had laid out some tomatoes, milk, bread, jam, cheese, coffee and a few other things in the cottage. A few slices of Stella's cake lingered in a tin. She looked at the dried-up cake and seeing me raise my eyebrows said, "Well, if they're hungry they'll eat it, whatever. Just you see." I knew that to be true. When Peter returned with the clothing we shepherded the Della Setas down the path to the cottage. It was frosty outside and they were shivering. Inside the front door of Gardener's Cottage they stopped and gasped aloud in amazement. They stared at the food laid out on the table, the fire glowing in the grate, the white sheets and the piles of warm Witney blankets, and the radio and vase of flowers on the dresser. They carefully picked up the welcome pictures I had painted for them and held them close to their bodies as if they were treasure. And turning to Stella they nodded and smiled. "For us, for us?" the mother whispered. I nodded. She reached for Stella's hand and kissed it to her mouth, thanking her over and over again. "It's nothing. It's really nothing," Stella repeated. I was so proud of her. "It's your home now," she said softly to them. "You're safe. You're home. You don't have to run any more. Now, sleep well. It'll be all right, you'll see."

❋ ❋ ❋

"Some beginning!" said Delphine.

"They were such lovely people. I wished you'd met them."

"You were fond of them, weren't you, Kitty?"

"I adored them, particularly the mother. I called them Mamma and Pappa. They wanted me to. They liked the idea of family and, of course, I liked it too. Mamma always had a smile for anyone she happened to bump into. You'd have loved her too. Not once ever did I hear her raise her voice to anyone. Strife was just carried along with her in a slow shrug of her shoulders and a quick pout of her lip."

"And she certainly had some strife!"

"She certainly did."

"So, tell me, what about her other son? What happened?"

"Oh, that was Luccio. Terrible. Nobody really knew what happened. Like so many others, I suppose, he'd been imprisoned, disposed of somehow. Maybe Dachau, but nobody ever knew for sure; Italians were often sent to Dachau. Peter, of course, pulled out all the stops. He really tried, he really did, but he just couldn't get anywhere. He was always phoning some office or other, or writing letters but, sadly, on that occasion he was not successful in his quest."

"He saved loads of people, didn't he?"

"That's right, Delphine, but you know, it was only after Peter passed away did we actually find out the number of people he'd helped over the course of the years. He never talked of it. It was something personal to him, very private. Some of those folks came up to Polstead and some stayed on there awhile, but others we never knew about. Peter never let on what he was up to. He was quite secretive."

"Why was that?"

"Don't know! Probably there's still things I don't really know about him. Of course, we knew a little because we lived with him for all those years. We couldn't help but see some things ... especially me with my nosiness! But, you know, even after the war ended he was still doing his bit; in fact, I don't think he ever stopped until the day he died."

"So going back to the Della Setas, Kitty. How did they actually get to Polstead?"

"That's some story! Believe me, it took them months. It was no mean feat. I don't think they would've made it without the help they encountered along the way."

"Sometimes, I've found, it's those you don't know that can be the most generous. That's always heartened me knowing that; strangers can be so kind. They're not gaining anything by helping you out, in fact, sometimes they lose a lot more. You don't hear about that side so often. What I don't ever understand is why some people are good and others downright wicked? I've never fathomed that one. But, Kitty, you were like that yourself, good that is, not bad!"

"Well, I don't know. I often think, I should have left you both sitting miserably on that cold wet bench! You know all this stomach here is George's fault, I'm getting so plump these days. Look at this here roll of fat. Look how it wobbles! I would've still been slender thing if it hadn't been for George's cooking. I should have left you both there! Can you believe that once upon a time I was a skinny little thing? Anyhow, how about another sip of tea?"

"No buns today, then?"

"No, I'm too fat. Well, maybe, what's on offer?"

"That's better. Nothing like a cup of tea, thank you, Delphine. Now, getting back to the Della Setas. You know, they couldn't talk about what had happened to them. They kept silent about it for ages and ages. As the years passed stories came out in snippets and Vitale told me a few things. It's sad about Vitale. He couldn't open up about the past. Not to his parents, anyhow, not one bit. He wanted that period in his life blanked out. It's understandable. Too much pain to be rekindled. I understood that. It distressed him even to be near his parents. In their eyes he could see the past mirrored. Eventually, when he spoke to them, he couldn't even look them in the face. In the end he ran away from us. Funny, he and I both runners. We just ran in different directions."

"You've stop running now, thank goodness."

"Yes, these wobbly old legs won't take me far any more, not that they would want to go anywhere nowadays. In some ways, you know, Mamma and Pappa lost both their sons to the war. First Luccio, then Vitale. As you know, Vitale went back to Italy after the war. He needed to detach himself physically from his past unhappiness."

"So, Kitty, what was their story, then?"

"The same old thing! You know, Italy was just like everywhere else in the 'so-called' Christian world. Excuse me, Delphine, but, by now, you know my feelings about religion well enough. I know it's hard to imagine Italy being like that, knowing our life here now. But, sadly, Jews in Italy had been outcast for centuries. The Popes made sure of that! Of course, there were a few good popes around, as well as the bad."

"Glad to hear it."

"The Della Setas came from Torino and generally all was well there. Then, in the twenties, the Fascists came to power and, boy, how things changed! The Fascists decided that Jews were not fitting to their ideal model. They expelled them from public office, took away their passports, denied them citizenship."

"Just like the blacks were treated. Still are, in places!"

"That's right. Anyhow, Jews and other sympathisers were attacked, mainly by unruly gangs of youths. They ransacked homes, beat people up, smashed shops. They were just louts, really, fuelled by ignorance. It was the same the world over. Of course, the authorities did nothing. Turned a blind eye. But then, the law changed and it actually became legal to discriminate against those who didn't 'fit in'. Pappa was expelled from the University for being a Jew. Torino, you have to understand, was one of the most prestigious universities in Italy. It was shocking that Fascists were controlling academic and intellectual thought."

"Back to the middle-ages!"

"Exactly. But Pappa was also involved, like many other Italians, in Communist activities; he was an anti-Fascist. So he was doubly censored: his books burnt, papers destroyed, ideas scorned. Once fired from his job, his livelihood was gone. On top of that, Mamma told me how he would disappear, sometimes, for days on end. He would return broken in spirit, and often in body as well. Their only hope of survival was to escape."

"But without passports?"

"Exactly, it wasn't easy at all."

"You're looking a little tired now, Kitty. You can go on with the story tomorrow."

"I know, Delphine, but sometimes, even in antiquity, it helps to pass things on. Get things off your chest."

"Uh-ha, you're telling me!"

"But, Delphine, it's not a nice story. It's not my story to tell but it upsets me even to this day, so it is my story in some ways. It's terrible to think what Mamma went through. I can't get it out of my mind but I don't want to burden you with it as well."

"Now, Kitty! I want to know, as long as, that is, you want to tell. 'A problem shared ...' and all that. I'll bounce back. We've cried together before now. We've been holding each other's heads up high for years."

"True, but it's different when it's somebody else's life which you can't do anything about, you can't change. I could never mend Mamma's heartache, although she mended mine on many occasions. You see, I loved Mamma and Pappa so much and I can't stand their suffering. I can cope with my own, well I can these days, but not that of others. You know I'm just an old softie."

"I do indeed. You are an old softie and there's nothing wrong with that. There's no point, Kitty, bottling things up for all these years. Time to let it go. Let it out."

"All of it?"

"Hook, line and sinker."

"You want the whole can of worms?"

"Yes, the whole can, particularly the sinker."

"With a Grappa?"

"A Grappa it is, then. I'll join you."

"Bring the bottle."

"It's bad for our health."

"I've not noticed."

"Here goes, then: Well, if Pappa didn't arrive home Mamma would storm up to the police head-quarters. She told me that she would take Luccio and

Vitale along with her; she was too frightened to leave them at home. At the police station, Mamma would stand her ground, desperately arguing for Pappa's release. The police often threatened her, ridiculed and insulted her. Sometimes she got Pappa's release, other times not. Often, for the sake of Luccio and Vitale, she would have to accept defeat and, heavy in heart, retreat homeward. She remembered that Peter was one of Pappa's old colleagues from Cambridge, so taking the initiative she wrote to him asking if he could find work for Pappa in England. Without his invite they were doomed."

"Like David and Hala."

"Exactly, except by then it was even harder. Somehow Peter managed the arrangements and Pappa was invited over to Polstead as a research assistant."

"So that's how they got out."

"Uh-ha, but things got even more complicated. Their exit papers were approved, but they still had to cross France. It wasn't safe to travel, not for anyone. It was Vichy France. Vicious France, Peter called it. Transport was policed. There were stop-checks everywhere. Passengers were awoken during the night to have their papers scrutinised. There was no respect for anyone, neither the old nor the young, man, woman or child. People were thrust from carriage doors as the train sped along. People were kicked, for a whim, down the corridors and punched in their seats where they sat."

"Is that what happened to Luccio?"

"Possibly. I often wonder who really suffers the most; is it the victim, or is it the onlooker, the ones who are left behind to remember?

"Their train stopped at the border. At gunpoint the passengers were ordered out of the train. All their documents double-checked. The Della Setas had one document for their family group. They handed their papers over. A scrupulous German officer noticed that Luccio was over fifteen. He was not entitled to be included in the family's papers as he wasn't considered a child at sixteen. Of course, he didn't have any documents of his own. Peter had thought Luccio much younger and therefore able to travel with the family. A guard singled out Luccio and started yelling at him, and Luccio, being a young man, argued back. The guard hit him with his rifle. He didn't have the sense to shut up, or grovel, and Luccio was forcefully marched off. Pappa, of course, started to remonstrate. He was also rifle-butted. The remaining passengers were shoved back on board. Mamma cried out to stay with Luccio but the soldiers threw her back inside the carriage. The train moved off, without Luccio. I can't imagine what she must have felt!"

"There are no words to describe anything like that happening."

"No, but that, of course, wasn't the end of it. The train kept stopping. Starting again. Going forwards, going backwards. Going nowhere in particular. At one halt several families were pushed out of the train. The soldier lined the fathers up in front of their wives and children and got ready as if to shoot them. They counted down slowly, 'three, two, one', and then, they lowered their rifles, and laughed. It was a mere game to them. A slow torture just for their amusement. People were down on their knees, crying, begging, praying, the old as well as the young. Do you want me to go on?"

"Yes, I want to know, Kitty. I thought we had it bad but it was nothing. Nothing compared to what those people went through. Makes me wonder if there is a God!"

"Me too. But as you know I gave up that notion of God years ago. Who'd want a God who turns away at times like that!

"After that Mamma and Pappa knew they just couldn't remain on that train. There wasn't any food or water. Toilets were overflowing across the floors. The stench must have been unbelievable. As the train trundled on Mamma and Pappa could make out, in the dusky light, that they were probably not too far off the Swiss border. From the windows they could see snowy peaks and thick forests along the horizon. They made a decision; they were going to jump. Once in Switzerland, they reasoned, Pappa could go back and search for Luccio. They knew some people living near Lausanne with whom they may be able to hide. Their chance came. It was nightfall, the train came to a halt in an area of dense wood. They clambered down between the carriages and made a run for it, escaping through the dark of trees. They ran and ran but exhaustion caught up. An empty barn came into sight and thinking it was their last night on earth, they huddled down on some soiled straw and prayed."

❋ ❋ ❋

The sound of straw snapping under foot and heavy breathing. It was light. Numb with fear. Waiting for a kick, a bang from a gun. Nothing. Trembling and hugging Vitale, Mamma opened her eyes. A man was standing looking at them. Not a soldier, just an ordinary man. A farmer. He beckoned them to come. They followed. Terrified. Grasping at each other. The man waved them into a house. Inside there was warmth. He told them to sit. He poured them coffee. He gave them bread and cheese. Pappa explained they were lost and looking for the border with Switzerland. The man nodded knowingly. He got up, left the house, and went away.

"Shall we go now while we have the chance?" Mamma whispered.

"No," Pappa replied, "I trust this man."

"I do, too."

Hours later the farmer returned. "Have you money?"

"Only a little," Pappa replied.

"Tomorrow is market day," the man continued. "There is a little town, St Gervais, about a dozen or so kilometres away. I can get you to the station in my cart but you must hide under the crates of cheese. From there a little train will take you through the mountains over the border into Switzerland. Leave the train at a village, it's called Vallorcine, and walk north through the forests. Keep from the road. There are plenty of tracks but, even then, wait until nightfall. It's the best I can do to help you."

"Won't they stop us getting on the train?"

"Maybe, but I think it's your only option. Buy a ticket from the conductor. I can't think of anything else to help. I'm sorry. It's the best I can do."

"Let's try it," Mamma said. "A chance is better than no chance. Thank you, Sir, for your help."

Next morning the farmer drew into the station yard. He got out and walked away from the cart. Peeping through the wooden slats they could see, with horror, that the farmer was gibbering away to a uniformed officer. The two men were shaking hands and laughing. They were being turned in! Vitale started to whine in fear. The officer was looking back at the cart. Slowly he and the farmer strolled back. They stopped to admire the horse and the farmer reached over and pulled out a cheese from one of the crates. He handed it to the officer and herded him, chatting, into the station bar. At the door he stopped and coughed deeply. That was the signal! Trembling, they climbed out under the cart and scuttled across to the back of a waiting train. Cautiously they stepped over the rails and clambered up between the carriages and crept inside. Soon the train shunted forward on its onward journey to Switzerland.

At every halt more passengers got on. At Bossons a young woman sat down opposite them. By her side was a little boy and a shopping basket full of vegetables. The woman kept glancing across, staring at their shoes, at their bags, at their faces. Their fear grew. They crouched lower in their seats. They felt she was going to denounce them. A conductor got on board. "Tickets, please," he was shouting. "Any more tickets?" Several soldiers were standing on the platform, smoking, laughing. The woman opposite was now staring fully at them. Mamma trembling. Vitale hiding his face in his father's coat.

"Morning, Henri," the woman opposite spoke. There was cheer in her voice. "Four to Le Buet. We got on at Bossons, today, and I need a ticket, too, for little Maurice. I'm afraid he's old enough to have to pay. No longer my little baby boy." She gave the boy a big kiss.

"Morning, Germaine? How he has grown! You're feeding him up well. You want five tickets? But there's only the two of you? Did you want returns, then?"

"No no, father's friends from Le Midi are with me today." She nodded her head towards Mamma, Pappa and Vitale.

"Oh, excuse me, my dear. I didn't notice you'd got guests with you. How's little Maurice, then?"

"Like little boys always are!"

"How's business?"

"Not bad for this time of year. The weather is in our favour."

"Pleased to hear it. Regards to your father. Tell him I'll come up one of these days for a jar or two."

"He'd like that, Henri. I'll let him know. He may need to open a new barrel if you're coming over for a drink! I think he's got some special Cognac in. You may need to try it out for him!"

The conductor continued on his way. Mamma and Pappa were speechless. They dared not look at the woman. At last Pappa reached over and whispered, "Thank you, Madame, thank you so much." They sat silently until the train started to slow. The woman stood up. "Follow me, now," she whispered to them. "When we get down, walk with me as if we were old friends."

Once on the platform Mamma held the little boy's hand and Vitale swung the woman's shopping basket over his arm. Chatting and laughing they walked slowly along a path towards a hotel. Mamma and Pappa were swinging the little Maurice backwards and forwards between them. The woman led them through a back door into a kitchen. Once inside she said, "I can see you have trouble like many of those who have passed along this route before you. If you want I can help you. My name is Germaine Chamel."

"Thank you, Madam, for your great kindness," Pappa replied. "We need all the help we can get. We need to get to Lausanne. I have friends near there. They will help us."

"Okay. Rest now. I'll get you some food but you must leave here tonight. I know someone. When it gets dark he will show you a way across from Barberine. From there you can get to Lausanne by following the river to the Rhone. Tell me," she said looking at Mamma, "do you have other shoes with you? You won't be able to walk far in those. You'll slip. No? Let me see if I can get some boots to fit you. Leave those here."

❋ ❋ ❋

"Did they make it to Lausanne?"

"Yes, no map, no compass! They followed the river along the Trient valley to the Rhone and then towards Lake Leman. After a week of walking they arrived cold and hungry, and having 'borrowed' a little fishing boat they completed their journey without incident. Sometimes you have to do these things!"

"Yes, indeed. The woman in France ... what was her name again?"

"Madame Chamel, you mean?"

"Yes, Madame Chamel. Did she survive? If she'd been caught, I suppose she would have been shot. She took some risk!"

"Yes, she survived, and so did her family. Years later Mamma and Pappa returned to the hotel at Le Buet. They took me along, Vitale didn't want to go with them. As soon as Mamma saw Madame Chamel she recognised her immediately. Madame Chamel, of course, didn't know them from Adam! There were so many people she'd helped over the years; she couldn't be expected to recall all of them. And, by then, Mamma and Pappa had put on rather a lot of weight. Did they love their food! Over the years we revisited Madame Chamel several times. She was always pleased to see us. And I think, Delphine, if I'm not mistaken, that the hotel at Le Buet is still run to this very day by the same kind family."

"Really! So, did Pappa go back to look for Luccio?"

"No. They realised, by the time they reached Lausanne, they wouldn't be able to make it back. It was far too dangerous. It was a terrible decision."

17

Stella wasn't the only person who felt relieved when Mamma Della Seta took charge of the cooking. Overnight the kitchen was restored from smoky battlefield to a preserve of delectable sweetness and fragrant harmony. The Della Setas worked their magic in the garden once spring arrived, transforming it from a wavering water-colour of wilderness to a summer vibrancy blooming with magentas, sun-rich yellows and pulsating pinks and mauves. A trail of orange exploded across the beds like flowing lava, and geraniums and nasturtiums cascaded from terracotta pots and rusted watering-cans. Squares of cabbage, cauliflower and lettuces stood to attention, their faces smiling respectfully skyward. And to Stella's delight nodding heads of rosy tomatoes winked from under their greenery. Exotics of peppers, pendulous aubergines and furry courgettes bathed under sparkling tents of glass. Herbs potted around the sills and curls of squash and pumpkin dozed in scattered cushions of leaves. Mamma and Pappa presided over the digging, the sowing and the pruning. A couple of hens came to live with us and then a few more joined.

Polstead was complete with men, women, children, chicken and tomato.

❋ ❋ ❋

"We had plenty of fresh eggs. I became 'Chicken Monitor'. My role was to feed the hens and stop them pecking at each other. Could they fight! You can't believe how vicious they were to each other."

"I s'pose that's hen-pecking for you!"

"I know how they felt," George added backing away from Delphine. "I've been hen-pecked most of my life."

"I'm going to ignore that comment, George! Go on, Kitty."

"Anyhow, Vitale and I never fought over anything. Vite was just what I imagined a big brother to be. He was perfect as a brother. We'd sit next to each other in the kitchen, sometimes for hours on end, watching Mamma cook or scribbling little pictures at the table. Mamma never made use of a recipe book but she loved dictating her recipes for me to copy down. She was a wizard cooking. She'd simply wave her spoon over the cooker and before long a dish, wondrous to behold, would appear. I was always ready to be her food-taster."

"So, not like Stella's cooking then?"

"No, nor mine!"

"I have to confess," Delphine laughed, "I never took well to the kitchen, either."

"I'll second that," George nodded in agreement.

"Much of our time was spent happily: reading, drawing, painting, going on forays along the river and along the paths. We both liked climbing trees; that was fun. Like me, Vite just loved to paint. It was so nice to have a companion. And before long, Peter recognized Vite had artistic talent and enrolled him at the Ruskin Art School in town. I'd passed my 'eleven plus' exams and got a scholarship place to the high school in Cambridge. Stella and Peter were so proud of my achievement."

"I bet they were."

"Quite often Vite and I would travel together into Cambridge. The old bus would chug along the leafy lanes and we'd sit, sometimes in silence, trying to see through the scratched windows or, when wet, finger drawing pictures in its mist. Other times we'd chat away and, under my enthusiastic tuition, his knowledge of the English language improved. I also gained something worthwhile from our journeying together. Other girls from Cambridge High spotted me in the regular company of a tall, dark, handsome young man and, importantly, someone who was not my brother! My social standing in the classroom attractiveness stakes soared! Vite, as you know, had movie-star glamour."

"I do remember that. He was definitely good-looking! Here," Delphine said, blowing off dust from a photograph. "This is him, isn't it, when he was a youngster? Yes, he was certainly a looker."

"Not as handsome as me, though, Delph?"

"No one could be as handsome as you, George."

"Let me see that picture again, Delphine? Pass me my specs, dear. Thank you. Yes, wasn't he just!"

"And this photo here," George added, "isn't it one of Grandmother?"

"Yes, that's her. Funny old thing! She died, I think, the spring of '41 or thereabouts and was buried with great ceremony. Loads turned up to the funeral. In her time she'd been a popular and unusual lady. She's been a suffragette; did her stint in jail. I believe she was quite a character. Lots of people loved her. Because of the war Henry couldn't come over for the funeral. By then, it was raging throughout Europe. Terrible time it was. The war didn't bother me too much. I felt safe with Stella. I knew nothing could happen to me with her around. I always felt safe. I knew that Stella would always be there, keeping me from harm. I can even hear her saying, 'It'll be all right, you'll see.'"

"So, did Henry ever come over to see the girls?"

"Yes, once peace was declared he came over; in fact, he came over several times to visit. And on one occasion ... he brought over his new wife and baby daughter. You can imagine Marion and Margaret were not too pleased but, as you know, they were never too pleased about anything much. By that time, they'd grown up and were living away in Edinburgh. Trained to be nurses. Didn't come back to visit very often and never went back home to the States."

"Am I right in thinking that Stella went back in the end?" George asked. "Why've you never said much about that, Kitty? I always wondered."

"George, don't pry! Kitty will tell us what she wants, when she's right and ready."

"No, don't worry, that's all right. Sometimes I need a bit of a poke to get me to open up about certain things. It was a bad time for me, yes, but you know, time heals ... or so they say."

"So it was a real bad time for you?"

"It was indeed. Yes, sirree, it certainly was some bad time. Just thinking about it now makes me shiver ... even after all these long years. Oh, don't worry, dears, I'm alright! But, how about putting the kettle on and then, if you're offering, I wouldn't say no thank-you to a little slice or two of some cinnamon toast. I feel autumn's walking this way."

✳ ✳ ✳

The war had ended. There were parties in the streets. There was dancing and music and shouting and singing and food and drink. The news came through and we all gathered and galloped about the house. We cavorted out through the kitchen door into the garden, down the lane, around the village and back again. Other people joined us along the way, making a daisy-chain of happy, laughing bodies swirling around and around each other. Even Peter joined in and broke open a vintage champagne delved from the depths. "Cheers," he said raising his glass. "Cheers to a new world! Cheers! Let's celebrate the end of war, the end of destruction. L'chaim! Never again! Never again! Salute! Celebrate, that's what we'll do. Yes! Raise your glasses to the future. Peace to one and all!" We all raised our glasses. I had never tasted champagne before. It tasted good. Before long Stella and I were giggling away like two little school girls. We hugged everyone and everyone came and hugged us. Mamma and Pappa kissed us many, many times on both cheeks. I was nearly eighteen, still at school, so happy, so very happy.

Then my world changed. My world changed. Again.

I was sitting with Mamma and Pappa in the kitchen. I was reading. Peter slicing tomatoes. Pappa at the sink. The door opened quietly and Stella stepped in. She closed it carefully. She cleared her throat.

"There is something I want to say. Can you all give me a moment, please." We looked at her. She was gripping her hands together tightly, her feet aligned straight and close together. Unusually her normal rush of hair was combed neatly into a pleat. She coughed again. "Please hear me out. It's as difficult for me to say as this may be for you to hear." Mamma stopped stirring. Pappa stopped scrubbing the carrots. Peter stopped searching under the dresser for the runaway tomato he'd dropped when she'd walked in. Even the steam clouding above the boiling potatoes seemed to hover uncertainly. The room slowed. Eight astonished eyes stared back at Stella. Mamma's over her glasses, Pappa's under his, Peter's from the floor. Mine from my book. This isn't a Stella way of talking. Why is she looking like that? Why is she acting so strangely? What is she doing? What's happening?

I studied Stella's face and saw her skin reddening; it smouldered up her neck and spread like wild-fire across her cheeks. I felt a creep of fear sidling up inside me. I saw her quiver.

"I have made a decision." She stopped. "I have come to a decision. I have decided to return home, home to Colorado." For a brief wondrous moment I hoped Stella meant she was going home to visit her parents. How nice for her. How very nice for her. How nice for them. "My parents, you see, are now getting on in age." She coughed again. "And they will need my help, more and more, as time goes on. You see, I'm an only child. I have to go. It's my duty. There's no one else."

I was stunned into silent horror. Muted with pain. I couldn't really believe what she was saying. So contrived, so artificial. Ridiculous! Why? Of course, I understood that Abi-Laura and Christopher must be quite old but Stella hardly ever spoke of them, never with much affection. In fact, I hadn't seen her receive letters except, maybe, on birthdays and possibly a small parcel at Christmas. She didn't speak about them. Not for years had she said a word about them. No! What is she on about? That was a life past. The other world. You go forward in life, not backward. My heart ached from grief. It couldn't happen.

Silence.

Outside a bird sang its call to dusk. And the old clock, on the mantel, continued its tock, tock, tock.

Peter clambered up off the floor. "Gosh! Bit of a shock there, Stella! Wasn't expecting that. No, not at all. You know, I always thought of Polstead as your home. Permanent home. I thought you understood that you are welcome here for ever. Has something upset you, my dear? You are still happy here, aren't you?"

"Yes, Peter, of course I am happy here, but, as I said, I'm needed back home. I'm now required to care for my parents. I've commitments with my own family."

"Oh, yes, I see, yes. It's just that ... it's just, er, that I've come to see you as a member of our family. You and Kitty are major parts of our lives. Is there, is there another reason, Stella? Is there something else? Has something happened?"

"No!"

"If it's your parents, then, I assure you, it wouldn't be a problem to bring them over here. Yes, get your parents to come over. Yes, yes. They could live here at Polstead. Very happily, yes. Sort them out some rooms. No problem to me at all. You know that. Always welcome."

"I know."

"Yes, always welcome. I can arrange for them to fly, that is, if they don't care for the sea. Easily sorted nowadays. My word, I only read in 'The Times', a few days back, that Pan-Am are about to start regular passenger flights across the Atlantic. I can sort it out. Yes, good idea, get them over here. My pleasure. Yes, my pleasure. A great pleasure to assist."

"Thank you, but no! They just wouldn't like that. Peter, you've always been so very kind and I'm sorry about this. I have been thinking it over for quite some time and I've come to this decision as being the best solution. I thought about it long and hard; it wasn't an easy decision."

"Oh, I see."

"My work here is done," she continued. "The girls are now grown up and living their own lives. You, Peter, are being very well cared for by Mamma and Pappa." Mamma smiled and nodded. "Vitale is settled back in Italy." Mamma pouted but continued to nod. "And Kitty, dear," – she didn't look me in the eye – "Kitty, you've nearly finished school now and, in a couple of months, you will be off to college. You will have your own life. You don't want to be tied down by me. You can do what you want, now." She raised her eyes from the floor and looked at me.

"Stella!" the voice from inside me raged. "Stella, for crying out loud, what the hell are you saying? Have you gone nuts? Are you bonkers? You can't just go like that. You can't just go and leave me. You're my family. You can't just go away. What's going on? You can't leave me. What's wrong with you? What have I done wrong?"

"Kitty, you know perfectly well you've not done anything wrong. But you've got other family now, not just me. You've got a really good home here. There's Peter and there's Mamma and Pappa. You're part of their family. Peter's just said that."

"But, you can't just leave me like that, not now. Please don't go, Stella, please."

"Don't cry, Kitty."

"I still need you. I always will. You gave me my life. I wouldn't be here without you. I wouldn't be alive without you." Mamma came over and encircled me in her arms.

"No, Kitty," Stella continued, "your parents gave you life; I just helped you live. Now you've grown up you can do it on your own. You don't need me. My work's done here. I'm really very sorry you're so upset. I didn't mean to upset you so. I didn't want to make you cry. Oh, sweetheart. I truly am. Please. I don't mean to hurt you, or anyone else, but that's how life is. I've been thinking long and hard about it. It's not a sudden decision. I've thought it through. My mind's made up."

"And you never bothered to talk it over with anyone ... not even me, ha? For God's sake, Stella! What's wrong with you? Can't anyone say anything to make her see sense?" I yelled. "Please, Uncle Peter, stop her going, please. She's crazy. Stop her going. Don't let her go."

"Kitty, I can't stop her. I know how you must feel, yes I do. I don't want her to leave us either, no. But I think Stella has to make up her own mind. And, yes, she is right in what she says. She knows you're safe here with us. She knows I'll always look after you. Remember, this is your home. A home here for ever is what I said, yes, for ever. And, yes, before you know it, just like Margaret and Marion, just like Vitale, you'll be off doing your own thing. People grow up, go away, start a life someplace else. People move on, it's normal, yes, people move on."

"Oh, so is that it, then? I s'pose you'll be upping and moving on too, Uncle Peter," I shouted back. My chair fell over as I reared up in anger. I yelled in Stella's face, "You lied to me, you lied to me. How could you? I hate you. I really hate you!"

Mamma opened her arms wide. "You, my darling Kitty, will always be my daughter, wherever you are I am here. I don't go anywhere. And Stella, I know, will love you wherever she is in the world."

"Yes," Stella nodded. "That's true. I will love you, Kitty, for ever, and ever."

"You cow!" I yelled, escaping the room. "You bloody cow! I hate you; I'll hate you for ever"

❊ ❊ ❊

"I know how you must be feeling," Delphine said holding my hand. "It's real hard to lose a mother. I know she wasn't your real mother but she gave you mother-love. And like all good mothers she just had to let you go, let you spread your own wings and fly off into your own blue sky."

"But, Delphine, the point was that Stella flew away from me! I was still only a girl and not as brave as I made out. What she did hurt me, hurt me so much. Terrible! It still does, as you can see." Delphine wiped away the tears from my face. "After all these years the hurt is still lodged right here inside me, here. Silly old thing I am! Sorry Delphine, sorry George."

"What you sorry about! It's okay to be upset about things like that. There now. Here, have a tissue. Now, tell me, did she ever write?"

"Yes she did; she went on writing for years and years. I never read her letters. I was so angry that I just ripped them up as soon as they arrived. I never ever wrote back. Not even a birthday card. But she kept on sending me post."

"She must have been really sad about that. So what happened to her? Did you ever find out?"

"Yes, but not for many a year. Well, eventually I pulled myself together and went down to London.

I got a place at the Slade. I did well there. I had a busy life in London, a good life; thanks to good old Uncle Peter. He made sure I had somewhere to stay and, of course, I was always welcomed back to Polstead whenever I felt like coming back. I held exhibitions of my work down in London, as you know. Sometimes Peter would visit, and Mamma and Pappa would rattle down in their little 'bubble' car to see my shows. That little blue car of theirs was such fun! I worked hard in London and made some good friends, but I missed Vite. As soon as the war finished he'd scarpered back to Italy, to Florence. He went to study architecture there. He did well, too. But, sadly for Mamma and Pappa he hardly ever came back to England to visit them.

After that I lived on my own. Never really got over that feeling of being abandoned; I don't think I ever will. I liked being with people but, generally, I didn't really trust them enough to have any sort of permanent relationship. I don't know what it was. I flitted in and out of friendships. Friendly in the passing. That was me! Then the day came when Peter left me. He died. All quite sudden. A heart attack, they said. He was only in his early sixties, you know."

"Pretty young."

"Of course, we all came back for the funeral. And that was when I came to appreciate what a great man he'd been. I mean not just to us, but to so many. People came from all parts of the world. Many who wouldn't have been alive without Peter's intervention. They brought their children, and their children's children. There were also people there who were totally unknown to us. But they knew who we were and, respectfully, came up to express their condolences. They had such great admiration for Peter. I remember Alan Turing coming up and shaking my hand. He recognise me as Kitty. I s'pose I was such a funny little thing when I was younger! I think Peter must have talked a lot about me. He was always so very proud of my achievements."

"I'm not surprised. You did really well. Made something of your life."

"And, you know, Peter of course was as good as his word. In his will he left Gardener's Cottage to Mamma and Pappa. They could live there for the rest of their days. And Polstead House itself was left to be shared between me, Vitale, Margaret and Marion. I don't think the girls were too pleased that we'd been included in the will! But I didn't feel bad about that. I knew, in my heart, that was what Peter wanted. So I ignored their little jibes. They'd never seen me as part of the family, not like others had done. I don't know what it was with them. But, anyhow, none of us wanted to stay at Polstead. It wasn't the same, not without Uncle Peter there. And, of course, the house was far too big for us to look after. So we sold up, took our share of the profit and went our separate ways. In the end, it was quite amicable. The girls were okay. I used my share to buy the flat in Hampstead; the one where I was living when we first got together. And, of course, I knew whenever I came back up I could always stay in Gardener's Cottage with Mamma and Pappa. They liked that; I did too. It was a bad time, you know, losing Peter. It was so unexpected. Once more I'd lost a parent. A part of me died."

"Not surprised. Your loss was doubled. Not only had you lost your own mother and father but also Stella and Peter. They were parents to you too."

"Exactly how I saw it. However, a letter arrived, a year or so later. It was posted in America, but it wasn't from Stella. When I moved down to London, you see, I'd lost touch with her completely. She didn't have my forwarding address. The letter was from Sybil. You know, the little friend I had had all those years back when I lived in Quivering Creek."

"Uh-huh, little Miss *Anne of Green Gables* herself. So, what did she have to say? That must have been some blast from the past."

"It was. If you recall, Sybil was Henry's niece through Esther's side of the family. By then, I'm ashamed to say, I'd forgotten all about her and our 'eternal kindred spirit'! But somehow she had got hold of my London address, probably from Margaret or Marion. They were cousins, of course."

"That must have been a nice surprise!"

"It was. But anyhow, Sybil wrote that she'd heard Peter had passed away and once again I was out on my own. She said if I ever wanted to come back to Silverton I would always be made welcome and I could stay with her whenever I wanted. Wasn't that nice of her?"

"Did she still live in the same place?"

"Yes. By then, her lovely mother, Lois, and that nasty husband of a doctor were long gone. Sybil, however, still lived in Silverton House. I could stay, she wrote, as long, or as briefly, as I wanted. She even left me a phone number. At first I 'poo-pooed' the idea. I couldn't think why anyone would want to go back to that God-forsaken place. I had a drink, and then another. Then I thought, why not? I could visit for a holiday, maybe lay some ghosts to rest. I was torn; didn't know what to do for the best. I couldn't come to a decision. It wasn't a matter of money any more. I had my own income, so it was my fears of the unknown."

"You mean it felt like it could open up a can of worms?"

"I s'pose that's one way of putting it, Delphine. Maybe. I went up to see Mamma and Pappa that weekend. As usual, they were overjoyed. Fed me, like usual, up to my eyeballs! Now that rationing was long past, Mamma's cooking skills just rocketed. She could concoct the most wondrous things. I remember it was a summery day and the wind blew warm. We strolled arm in arm out into the garden and, while I sat on the wall thinking things over, she gathered courgettes flowers, handfuls of spinach and bunches of tomatoes; and, Delphine, you should have seen her apron pockets. They were overflowing with aromatic herbs and shiny leaves. Back in the kitchen, where the sun was always shining, she stuffed the flowers with ricotta, basil and other things she'd nurtured over the weeks. She fried them crisply in olive oil and smiled, happily, as she watched me enjoy the feast. She was always worried that I didn't eat properly."

"I remember that. I used to worry, too. You were a lazy eater."

"True. I'd never bothered with cooking so I'd got kind of skinny again. If Mamma could only see me now, she'd be so happy! Anyway, we talked while she whipped up a dessert made with fresh with eggs from the chickens that ran the orchard they'd planted years before. And, like as if I was a little girl again, I licked out the bowl in front of her. She laughed with pleasure. We even talked about Luccio. She never did find out what had happened to him. Of course, we also talked about Vite. By then, he was living in Italy with his friend, Jacques. She missed her Vitale; she missed him such a lot. When my courage was gathered, and my stomach full, I casually mentioned I'd received a letter from Sybil. Without hesitation, she held my hands in hers and said, "Darling, you must go. Take chances when you can, 'gather your roses while you may'. Don't let fear hold back your life. Go. See where you came from. I'll still be here, for you, when you come back. I promise." And she hugged me and rocked me and she let me cry. You know what a soppy old thing I am!"

"So you went. That must have been some big step for you to make! Did you go by sea?"

"No, that novelty had definitely long passed. That would have been too sentimental a journey. Anyway, it wouldn't have been the same not being able to dine like royalty! I flew. It was the first time I'd ever flown. That was quite an experience in itself. Flew into Denver."

"Is Denver near enough your home town?"

"Not really. Nowhere was near my home town. But I got myself a rental at the airport and drove as far as I could. No stopping except for gas. I was heading straight towards Quivering Creek. I thought I might be tempted to turn around if I stopped so I kept on going. However, as the light started to fade, tiredness got hold of me and I had to suffer a sleepless night in some down-trodden motel. Not ideal! In the morning I perched on the end of my bed with Sybil's number in my hand, but, I couldn't get up that courage to dial that number. I just couldn't. I just couldn't do it."

"Oh, so she wasn't expecting you?"

"No. I hadn't replied to her letter. She didn't even know I was in the States."

"We do the strangest things when we're stressed."

"We do indeed. Next morning I headed south again. I felt drawn towards Elkhorn. I needed, once more, to check if 'she' was there ... just sensing Ma's ghost would've sufficed! I needed to ask why she'd gone; why had she'd gone and left me? What had I done so bad?"

"You'd done nothing wrong, Kitty."

"I know that now! As things happen I took a wrong turning; you know what I'm like with my lefts and rights! I passed a bleached limb of a signpost near a turn-off and as I drove by, the name 'Brigham' drew my eye. It called me over. I backed up and, as if summoned, the car dragged slowly up the track. I felt it being pulled along. I had no choice. Not much had changed. The land still scarred. The same dirt. A scratched epitaph of a road."

❀ ❀ ❀

The sun high. No wind. A starched brightness. Everything lurid and over exposed.

The land carcass-like and scavenged.

I survey the lasso of rough-torn mountains. I follow the endless wires which mark out the scope of my parent's and grandparent's world. In my mind I see how they had been yoked like cattle to this ranch, their future culled by years of exploitation and deprivation.

Too spooked to move, I hunch low behind the steering wheel. Fear grazes my skin. I feel as if not alone; some ancestral force is demanding my due. The prairie lays parched. Dilapidation crouches low on its haunches. On the horizon withered trees and skeletal bushes stoop as if begging alms. Where once the mighty ranch house stood, in a garden green and gurgling with the sound of fountains, I see, in its hollow, a graveyard of decay.

I make out the rusty-rib remains of our little shack. I glimpse the collapsed porch where Pa's life was ripped away from me.

The squealing of a lone shutter draws me from the car. It is swinging, pathetically, off a limp shoulder of broken wood. I feral my way across and, picking up a rock, shatter it, separating it from it's painful past. Splinters scatter across the dirt.

I kick my way through a scour of bramble. The dust rises from the dead earth. There is nothing left, not even a bone.

A place of exodus.

The black wings of great birds wave me a final good-bye as I speed away.

I pull in warily at the sign saying, 'Elkhorn welcomes you. Drive Safely'. The sign has been bullet-holed. No station yard, no rail to tie up your horse, no tracks. No tracks! Ruby's little shop is buried under a clatter of hoardings and peeling promotions for coming rodeos and travelling circus. I sit staring at the posters. I linger, just in case 'she' bursts through their ballyhoo like a performing lion. The store where Pa and I shared our last soda of happiness is gone. It is now a compound littered with burnt-out cars. Abandoned sofas and wheel-less prams lay scattered in front yards. A skulk of bruised caravans loiter behind dried-out scrub and the boom of 'too loud' music sounds out, unpleasantly, through the weight of air. A neon light flashes *'Beer'*, on off, on off. I get out of the car and walk inside the roadhouse. A bloat of pony-tailed men are hunched around the counter smoking and swilling their time away. They stop their talk when they see me enter. A cold-air fan twirls precariously and erratically from an old meat hook. I sit down underneath the neon sign. A server heads my way.

"Hi, my name's Rhonda. What can I get you, Ma'am?" she smiles.

"A coffee, I guess."

"Okey-doke. No pie, or nothin' else? Just coffee?"

"Yes."

"Can't tempt you with somethin'?"

"No. I'm just fine, thanks." I sit staring out the window. I swallow a mouthful or two. The neon light keeps flashing above me. One of the men puts money in the jukebox and some inane song comes blaring out. I pick at a chip in the red Formica.

"Would you like a top-up, Ma'am?"

"Okay."

"Not seen you in here before. Not from round these parts, then? Where you coming from?"

"Here, I come from right here. I was born round here; born up at the Brigham's."

"You don't say! That's been gone quite some time, now. Great you came back to visit us! You from England?" She turns to the counter. "Hey guys! This lady was born here, up at the Brigham's."

"So?" they snigger. "S'pose somebody had'a be born up there. Enough begetting went on!" There's a snarl of laughter.

"Well, I think that's real int'resting, Ma'am. Most folk round these parts are just passing through. They don't stay long. Nothing to stay for. To be honest," she whispers, "most of them stay round because they have some gripe, you know what I mean? Nice you took the trouble to look us up. Now, sure you don't want any pie?" I shake my head.

I must have sat there for several more hours. Rhonda kept topping up my coffee and eventually she placed some pie in front of me. "As you're a local, the pie's on the house." I left it. I couldn't eat. I sat staring under the glaring light. I could feel a shuddering within my skin. I didn't know what to do. I felt I could no longer move.

Rhonda came back. "How you doing, Ma'am?" I couldn't reply. "It's okay with me, but we'll be closing soon, so ... can I get you anything else?" I knew I was shaking. I knew it was visible. "Ma'am," she continued, "excuse my rudeness but you sure you're all right, you feel okay?" I fiddled in my bag and shook out my address book. "Have you got a phone I can use?" I faltered.

"Yeah, sure have, right in the counter at the far end. Over there by the cooler. See it?" I tried to stand and walk the distance between my table and the counter but it seemed immense. I gyred along. I felt as if I was walking backward.

"Let me give you an arm," I heard Rhonda say. She guided me to the phone. I could hear the men at the counter snickering. I tried dialling but I just couldn't manage to get the numbers right. My fingers kept missing the holes. "Here, let me do it," Rhonda said. "Give me the book and the phone. Is this the number here you want? Sybil Cummings?" The phone rang and I could hear a cheery voice answer.

"Hi, is that Sybil?" Rhonda asked.

"It is. Who's that speaking?"

"Hi, my name's Rhonda. You don't know me. I'm phoning from the diner at Elkhorn. I've got a lady here with me who, I think, is a friend of yours. She's not feeling too great and I wonder if you can come pick her up." There was a silence.

"What's her name? I don't think I know anyone 'round there."

"What's your name?" Rhonda whispered.

"Kitty." I could hardly utter the word.

"She says her name's Kitty, but she's not speaking too good. I think she's got a bit of an English accent."

"Kitty! ... You don't mean Kitty Wardle?" I heard a voice shriek at the other end. I nodded to Rhonda.

"She says yes."

"My Goodness! I'll be over as soon I can. Oh, my Lord! It'll probably take an hour or so. But I'll be there, hold on. How wonderful! Oh my!"

Rhonda sat me down. The other customers, heavy with drink, were slouching out by then. The roadhouse closed its door for the night and Rhonda, having swept the floor and wiped the surfaces, came and sat down opposite me. She held my shaking hands in hers. I don't know what she said to me but she kept on talking. Suddenly a car screeched to a stop out front and there was a rattling at the door. Sybil flew in. I recognised her immediately. She threw herself down by my side and, like in days so long gone, put her arm over my shoulder and hugged me close.

Sybil and Rhonda emptied my car and put the luggage into her trunk. Both agreed I was in no fit state, whatsoever, to drive back to Silverton that night.

"You silly girl," she said with another hug. "I would've come and picked you up from the airport.

I would've picked you up from anywhere." Turning to Rhonda she said, "Is it okay to leave the car here overnight?"

"Well, to be honest, Ma'am, I wouldn't if I was you," Rhonda murmured quietly. "You may not have tyres by the morning, let alone lights! Hey, I know you don't know me well, but I'll give you my address. I think it may be a good idea if I drive the car back to mine. Then I can keep my eye on it overnight. You never know who's around these parts any more. I'll give you my number and when you're back to pick it up, give me a shout. I'm always around. There's no place else to go!"

18

Sybil nudged me through her front door and into the living room. She tucked me up on her sofa and spoon fed me soup. I didn't want to eat but she made me. She slept in an armchair through the night by my side. When I awoke, the next morning, she was gone. I sat up and wearily contemplated my surroundings. The piano was still standing in the very same place where I remembered it to be. I recaptured an image of Stella playing the piano with Lois Cummings, by her side, warbling away ... well out of tune! Lois was no singer. Sybil and I would lurk behind the door giggling at Lois's attempts to screech the highest.

Bookcases bulged against the wall of Sybil's living room. They leaned precariously, heavy and unbalanced, their contents spilling out. I studied the pattern in the rag rug lying on the floor and could make out materials from Sybil's clothing from all those years back. It brought back memories of happy times spent. Framed photos of Lois, Doctor Cummings and a youthful Sybil sat on the mantelpiece. They jostled with half eaten packets of cookies and a host of postcards and dog-eared letters. I focussed my attention on a more recent picture of Sybil. She was smiling, proudly dressed as a nurse, holding up a certificate to the camera. I heard the pad-pad of footsteps outside the room. The door was opening very slowly and very quietly. Suddenly, Sybil's face shone around the edge.

"Oh good, you're awake," she cried, "I'm so glad you had a good nap. It's probably what you needed after such a tiring journey. If only I'd known! Now, listen here, my Kitty friend, what I suggest is that I bring us in some lunch and, if you're up to it, we can have a good old natter. If you want to, that is." I nodded. "You were awful shot-up yesterday so, I think, maybe a quiet day would be my recommendation. Then tomorrow we'll see how things go."

"Thank you, Sybil. That's nice of you. I'll take your advice because I can see from that photo over there you're now a trained nurse."

"Good idea. I like my patients doing what they're told. Not that they normally do! I'll rustle us up something to eat now. By the way, don't worry about the car. I've sent someone to fetch it back for you. That Rhonda was a very kind lady. I'll drop her off some flowers or something when we're next passing by."

"Sorry I caused you trouble."

"Not at all. I'm just unbelievably overjoyed that you made it. Now, I'll be back in a tick. If you feel like giving yourself a bit of a wash and brush-up, the bathroom is, if you remember, just down the corridor. Same place as before, just a bit more up to date, even got hot running water now. All mod cons! What would Pa say to that? So much extravagance! I've left towels and soap and things out for you. Use whatever you want."

I felt strange wandering down that hall again. I walked along dragging my fingertips along the wall. I looked through to the old garden area. It was all gone, all paved over. Only a few small flowerbeds remained. The tree, and its den, had disappeared.

Sybil and I chatted. I still felt choked; couldn't say much, couldn't really eat. I just listened quietly to the gentle soothe of her voice. She described how she'd gone off to Denver and done her training. Stayed twenty years and never bothered about marriage, or anything like that. All that romance and sentimentality we'd gleaned from *Anne of Green Gables* had swept right over her head. "I saw," she confided, "how easily men could change once they had a little 'wifie' tucked up back home. I didn't want any of that. I didn't want to end up like Ma." I nodded. "You know, she was a bright button. She was a great writer. Wanted to be a journalist. Even got herself a job on the *New York Herald* when she was about eighteen. Not many women got that far in those days. But then, of course, Ma goes and meets someone who is her 'knight in shining armour'. And that was that."

"You mean your pa?"

"Uh-huh! About ten years ago Pa suffered a stroke. Happened it was a bad one. Being the dutiful daughter I came running home and helped out with the caring. Then one night, all a sudden, he just collapsed and died. Ma didn't know what to do with herself. She'd been ordered about for so long that, when he was gone, she couldn't cope. So I stayed on. I couldn't leave Ma alone. She deserved more."

"Your ma was a lovely lady."

"She was indeed. But it was like, as if somewhere along the line, she just lost whatever was 'her'. She became resigned and withdrawn. You know, I've my suspicion that, over the years, Pa used to administer her drugs to keep her muted. He said it was for her nerves! Sometimes she acted like an automaton. Anyhow, that's enough about that now. Sorry about the tirade, Kitty. It's just a little, or rather, big, hobby-horse of mine!

"Anyhow, after he died, Ma and I decided to open up a nursing home right here. Some folk haven't got family close by to help them when they fall ill. Since the war lots of youngsters have left for the cities so many of the older ones don't have a soul about to help them out.

"Been open now, probably going on seven, eight years. Time flies! We've only got four ladies in at the moment. I got room for a couple more. So tonight, if you'd rather, you can have your own room here, no problem; as long as you don't mind a Zimmer and commode in the corner. Now, Kitty, I can see you're worn out. I don't even need to be qualified to know that. Have a snooze. I've got a bit of work I have to see to. Too much talk, too soon, I think. How about we have a TV supper, in here, tonight? And then tomorrow I'm sure you'll feel more like yourself."

❋ ❋ ❋

"So what was the old place like, Kitty? Had Sybil changed much?"

"Not so different. You know, by breakfast next morning I felt so much better. Sybil was a tonic in herself. Always was. Anyhow, the previous evening, we'd curled up on the sofa, snug with a box of chocolates, switched on the TV, and watching 'Golden Oldies' laughed the night through. '*I Love Lucy*' was on. Do you remember her, Delphine?"

"Lucille Ball?"

"What a scream! And then, '*The Brady Bunch*' came on, and, oh yes, '*Beat The Clock*'. We cried and cried with laughter. We ate ice-cream straight from the tub, read some *Anne of Green Gables* aloud to each other and giggled the hours away. It did me a world of good. After that I slept solidly through the night.

"After breakfast, Sybil showed me about the house. What a change for the better! Her Pa's grim old surgery was now shiny bright. She'd painted it pink! He would have been mad if he'd known."

"A lick of paint makes a big difference."

"Sure does."

"Then what d'you get up to?"

"Well, she showed me around downstairs and took me out to the garden. Then we went upstairs and she introduced me to some of the residents. Nice folk they were, too. We chatted with them for a while."

"Nice chatting to old folks."

"It sure is, but ... then, Delphine, I got the shock."

"What shock? — You okay, Kitty?"

"Yes, I'm fine. Just taking a breather."

"We went room to room visiting, and then we got to this door. Sybil knocked. She turned to me and said, very gently, "Kitty, you know the lady in this room." Before I could react I was ushered inside. A face lay on a pillow. A face I knew, only too well."

"Stella?"

"Yes Ma'am. It was indeed. Stella was lying there. She reached out her hand to me. My heart felt as if it wanted to beat right out of my body. I wanted to run but I couldn't. My feet felt as if they were part of the floor. I couldn't move. I couldn't breathe. Her hand stayed stretched out."

✳ ✳ ✳

Sybil shepherded me across to the bed. I felt the warmth of Stella's hand on my arm. I felt the warmth of her breath on my skin as she raised her head to kiss my cheek. I felt the warmth of her voice. But the ice inside me did not melt.

"Kitty," she murmured, "Kitty." I looked up. "Kitty, I have to tell you something straight out before you say anything. Kitty, I was wrong. I was wrong in what I did to you. I was wrong. I shouldn't have left you when I did. You weren't ready. At the time I thought I was doing right by you. I admit now I was wrong. But, I meant you no harm."

"I know that, Stella," I whispered, looking down again. "You were always so good to me. You were so wonderful."

"No, Kitty — you were wonderful for me. You were my inspiration, you kept me going. You know, without you I didn't have a part to play in life. Having you to look after set me on the right track again. I adored you. I still do."

"I know you did."

"Anyhow, there's something I need to tell you," she continued quickly. "You remember that old box? The one I used to keep in my room? The one I wouldn't let you play with?"

"The special box, you mean? The one you said was full of memories."

"That's the one. Well, there's something in it that I want you to know about. It's over there on the table. Can you fetch it over?

"Let me explain something first, Kitty. Years ago, back in Quivering Creek, I got a letter. Lois brought it around. It was when we were planning that train journey to New York. You remember that?"

"Of course I do."

"We broke our journey at a place called Grand Bend. We ate out that night, in town?"

"So?"

"There was something I didn't tell you."

"What?"

"Can you sit me up a bit more, Sybil. Thank you, dear." Stella took a little key from a chain around her neck. She unlocked it. The box was crammed full of all sorts: fading photos, quartered letters, browned cuttings from the newspapers, a knot of gold and silver trinkets, and envelopes. Stella handed me a letter. I opened it out:

Dear Mrs H

I heard you got my little girl Kit with you. My friend Ruby let me know. I'm real sorry I ran away and left her but I couldn't stand it no longer. I was a sick gal then but the preacher has put me straight now and I go to church real regular. I got a job in town and when I have some cash spare I'll make sure I send you it to help raise the child. I got no home of my own or I'd do it myself.

God Bless

Ellie Wardle

PS I call myself Liza now

I gave Ma's letter straight back to Stella. My teeth were clenched. Stella passed me another with the same handwriting.

Dear Mrs H

Sorry I haven't sent no money but things haven't worked out as I hoped. I heard you're taking my Kit to England. I'd be so sad not to see her again and I want to see her badly. It hurts so much. I got a job in a road diner now. I'd be mighty grateful if you would let me see her before you go. I won't tell her who I'm. I just want to look at her one more time just for a minute. Come soon. I work at 'Bert's Burgers' every night that God gives me. It's in a place called 'Grand Bend' just off

the main drag down in Kansas. Cross my heart I won't touch
her just want to look at her once more. Then you can have her.

> *Bless you both*
> *Liza*

"So, I s'pose, that's why we went to see 'your friend' in Grand Bend. Did my ma see me?"

"Yes, she was the server who came across. She wanted to give you extra sprinkles. I should've told you before."

"Yes, you should have," I snapped. I was shaking with anger.

"I'm not asking your forgiveness, Kitty. What I did was unforgivable. I just want you to know."

"Great, but a bit late now."

"I did try, in the past, Kitty, but you didn't answer my letters."

"So, Sybil, you were in on this too, were you? So that's why you wanted me to come across here. It was for Stella's sake. So she could clear her conscience. Silly me! There's me thinking you wanted me over here because you actually cared about me."

"I do care about you, Kitty. You needed to know things."

"So, Stella, why didn't you tell me at the time."

"Because I was so frightened she'd grab you back from me. If you knew it was your ma you may have

wanted her more than you wanted me. I wanted you
for my own. You were all I had. She had every legal
right to take you from me. Yes, it was wrong."

"Are there any other letters?"

"No. Those were the only two she sent. I never
heard from her again."

"So there's nothing else you know of her. Do
you know if she's still alive?"

"No. Sorry, I don't know any more than
that."

"What else is in the box? Anything I should
know? What are the cuttings about?"

"Oh, different things from over the years. Rum-
mage through if you want. You may find something
of interest."

"So you think I'm now old enough to be
trusted?"

"I think so, Kitty-Kat. Me too."

❊ ❊ ❊

"I stayed on at Silverton a couple of more weeks
and spent the time with Stella."

"Did you forgive her, Kitty."

"I forgave her."

"I'm glad you did, Kitty. It's not good for the
soul to keep carrying such a burden."

"Anyhow, as soon as I arrived back in England I immediately hurried to visit Mamma. She threw her arms around me and kissed and rocked me. I cried my pain out. She fed me and warmed me. I stayed in the cottage with them for ages. I don't know how long it was but, eventually, I healed and went back to the studio.

"The following year another letter arrived from Sybil. Stella had died and had willed me her 'box of memories'."

"Is that where it came from? I always wondered what was inside. I always imagined precious jewels!"

"No, 'fraid not. Do you want to see inside?"

"Of course I do."

"Pass it over, then. Pretty heavy, isn't it?"

"Shall I unlock it?"

"Thank you. Let's see. Look at this."

"What is it?"

"I need my glasses. Now, here we are. It's a poem – not actually a good poem – but still, a poem she wrote about me."

To Kitty

Like the wind through an aeolian harp
She brought music to my life.

She blew in with the breeze and
With both hands she did seize

My heart
Forever.

Her tune was to dance,
To laugh, enhance

And bring notes of colour
To the grey haze of days.

The breeze has now dropped
The song now cropped.

Days seem flat and
pain feels sharp

Without the wind
In my wondrous harp.

"Pretty, isn't it? I didn't really know how much happiness I'd brought her until I found that poem. It was nice of her to write it for me."

"Those are real pretty words."

"Of course, I read Ma's two letters over and over. I tried to see what else I could find within the words. I tried to feel her through the writing. It was something material with which I could still connect. I traced the pencilled script with my finger, feeling the paper as she must have done all those years previously. I kept her under my pillow, sleeping with her for months until she faded out of my life again. Gone, forever. But never forgotten. She was my ma, albeit from another world. Don't get me wrong, Delphine, I felt right sorry for her. She was a woman I hardly knew but the impact she made on my life was everlasting. Too late now!

"Amongst the letters and papers I also found tiny pictures I'd drawn. Look at this one, '*My Favrit Cake*' and '*My New House In Ingland*'. Aren't they just sweet? They were rolled up tight with neat little bows. And there was a little folder of pictures and recipes I'd collected over the years."

"How pretty they are, Kitty. You drew beautifully even when you were just a little thing."

"Look, here are some recipes from Lois Cummings, and look, these are from Abi-Laura. I'd always wondered what had happened to these. So pleased I got it back. It gives me a connection, a pretty ribbon to my past."

"Let's see, I wonder if George can follow any if those instructions. He could bring you back a genuine taste of the past. Now, that would be something."

"Well, I wouldn't rely on them. I was only little. They're probably full of mistakes. And see these news cuttings. Stella kept reviews of my exhibitions."

"Show me."

"I was so surprised! I think she must have got them from Peter. I didn't realise how closely she followed my life. I think at the bottom, Delphine, underneath some loose jewellery, there's a large brown envelope. Let's see if I can find it. On it was written 'Morten Hurtigrutensson 1902-1931'. Inside was a framed photo of Stella and Morten holding hands. She looked so young, so happy. Oh, here it is! Look, the cutting announces Morten's 'premature death from wounds sustained from an attack on his person by members of the Canon City, Ku Klux Klan whilst defending some Negroes.' Shocking times! According to the paper he was a 'foreigner himself having only 'latterly' arrived in the States from The Faeroe Islands'... 'New immigrants are meddling in situations that they do not fully comprehend, causing problems for themselves, as well as others.' What times they lived in! But I know things like that, probably, still go on in places."

"Sure do."

"But the best of all was this. Here, Delphine, open the bag. Mind, there's something sharp inside."

"Why, it's a little blue cardigan. It's only half knit!"

"She never did finish it!"

"After I got back from the States it took me a while to get myself going again. But eventually I settled down again ... they say time heals."

"It sure does."

"I was soon back painting. Then I bumped into you and George and, I dare say, you know the rest of the story! You can tell me! Now, how about a nice cup of tea? And what d'you say to a little Grappa?"

Epilogue

Vite, or Vitale Della Seta, died following a car crash in 1977. His parents were heartbroken. Both passed away the following year. In his will, Vite left his architectural practice and home in Florence to his companion of many years, Jacques Gianotti. His country house, Casa Luccio in Umbria, he left to Kitty.

Kitty Wardle died peacefully in her sleep in 2010. Her true age was never discovered. In her will, Casa Luccio and its contents were passed on to her dearest friends, George and Delphine Hale. The rest of her estate including her art work was donated to the charity 'Refugee Aid'. Her ashes were scattered to the wind.

Mamma and Pappa Della Seta are buried in the Jewish section of the churchyard at Polstead. Peter had made provision for this special section to be created. A memorial also stands to the memory of Luccio Della Seta and to those other Jews who did not survive the war years.

Peter's contribution to the war effort has not been officially recognised. His records are withheld from the public domain under acts concerning national security. Access should become available in 2058.

George and Delphine continue to be happy in Casa Luccio. They miss Kitty terribly. They now work as volunteers for the charity.

Further information concerning Ellie Wardle's background and whereabouts was never pursued.

An envelope found in the 'treasure box' contained Stella Hurtigrutensson's certificates and diplomas. One was an adoption certificate. Stella had been adopted at the age of six by Abi-Laura and Christopher Matthews of La Junta. Parentage unknown. Luggage none. Only item found on person: amethyst butterfly necklace.

A second stamped envelope addressed to 'The Holy Cross Orphanage', dated 1948, was also discovered in the box. It had not been posted. It contained a letter of enquiry from Stella concerning her own parentage.

In the 1970s, Germaine Chamel received an 'Order of Merit' from the Israeli government in recognition of the many people she had saved from the Nazi regime. She is one of *The Righteous Few*. Hotel Le Buet is now run by Germaine's son, Maurice, and her grandchildren. It is open for business to this very day.

POSTSCRIPT

Dear George and Delphine,

Your name and address was passed on to me by the charity 'Refugee Aid'. I recently attended a fundraising event they organised in Cambridge. The organisers thought that you may be able to help me.

I am a freelance journalist and art collector. Last month I was saddened to read in the obituary section of 'The Guardian' and 'The Independent' that Kitty Wardle had died. I have been an avid admirer of her work and over the last few years I have collected several of her prints. Until I read the article I had no idea that she had led such an unusual life. I would like to research her background further and write up her biography for publication.

I am also an established writer and biographer. My recent publications include ' Hannah Snell: The Female Warrior' and 'Dancing on the Edge: The Life of Mary Lamb'. In conjunction with Linda Grant I have also written the story of Halinka, a Polish child, who by using her own initiative and courage survives to become a victor rather than victim of The Holocaust.

I understand that you may be able to help me with my research. I wonder if you know anything more about Kitty's history. I am travelling to Italy next month and I would like, if I may, to call to see you and ask you some questions about her life. If this is not convenient please let me know at the above address otherwise call, my mobile number, 07801554940.

Thank you for your time.
Pauline Whitaker

Dear Pauline

George and I would be greatly delighted to meet you. We loved Kitty and we are happy to share our memories of her with you. We know a lot about her background.

Would you like to come for lunch? George is quite a good cook. And I'm pretty good at chatting! Let us know nearer the time.

Looking forward to meeting you.
Take care.
Delphine Hale

Some favourite recipes from Kitty's little note book

❋ ❋ ❋

Amy's Juggling Lemon Cake

I. Weigh out 4 eggs. Put into a large bowl and give it a quick whisk with a fork.

2. Weigh out the same weight in butter (never ever, ever use margarine in cakes!), white caster sugar and white self-raising flour plus two extra large heaped spoons of the flour.

3. Sieve (most important) it all together with I levelish teaspoons of baking powder into a bowl (if you add more it will taste real bitter).

4. Add 4 level tablespoons of any old milk (remember not to heap it high!).

5. Beat all together so that it is light and shiny looking.

6. Grate (with a finer grater than the one I use for cheese) the yellow skin of two large lemons directly into the bowl. Mind your fingers.

7. Juggle the bare lemons for as long as you want. It's good for the soul and keeps your wrists nimble. Cut the lemons in half when bored and squeeze all the juice out and put aside for later.

8. Scrape the mix into a 10" or 26cm cake tin, or thereabouts. Preferably lined with cake tin paper. In fact that's real important so the juice don't escape.

9. Put it in a medium hot oven at about 160 (or three logs and a pine cone if you happen to be in The Yukon or similar, at the time. Nice place).

10. Lick the bowl out if you want. Otherwise wash out.

11. Put timer on for about 45 minutes.

12. Open oven and carefully press in cake top with fingers. Mind you don't burn yourself. If top springs back remove cake. If fingers sink in put back in oven for another 5 mins. Keep repeating process as necessary.

13. When happy remove cake from oven.

14. Important now! Get a bowl and pour in half a cup or more of granulated sugar or coarser if you have it hanging around. Pour over the squeezed lemon juice from earlier. Mix vigorously with a fork (good for the wrist again) and pour slowly over the still warm lemon cake. It doesn't matter if it's not dissolved.

16. Leave for at least three hours, or eat immediately if desperate. Nice with ice-cream if still warm.

✳ ✳ ✳

Stella's Tomato Stew

Just chop up a handful of vegetables with lots of squashed tomatoes. Put them in a large pan of salted water. Boil. Then add a small handful of rice. Cover and simmer. After half an hour add a can of beans, or your own freshly cooked ones. They'll be all right. And some herbs. Keep simmering till you're ready to eat. Add more water if people drop in for lunch and boil up again. If you don't finish it all keep it in a bowl in a cold store until you ready to reheat. It'll be all right, just you see.

✳ ✳ ✳

Lois Cummings's Blueberry Shortcake

Pick a good handful of blueberries or raspberries and wash the dust off. Leave to drain.

Make your shortbread by mixing together one cup of flour and one cup of cornmeal and a teaspoon of baking powder. I always rely on 'Royals' but use whatever you have. Add a handful of sugar and a pinch of salt. Then chop up about half a cup of butter and rub into the mix with your fingertips until smooth. Get half a cup of cold milk and stir into the mixture until its soft enough to all stick together.

Then squash into a buttered pie tin and bake in a hot oven for about 10-15 minutes until it's golden and crisp to the touch. Leave to cool.

Grind a handful of skinned almonds with a handful of sugar and mix in a shallow pan with some melted butter until golden and smelling good. Make sure they don't burn. If they do start again. Careful, don't burn your fingers.

Then go back to your blueberries and mix them with a handful of sugar so it's all stirred up evenly.

Get some cream cheese (or thick cream if you have no cheese) and mix in as much as you want, or don't want, to the blueberries. Personally, I think the more the better.

Put the cooled shortbread base on a plate and spread over the blueberry cream cheese mix.

Dot, or pour over, the almond mix depending on how thick it is. Finally sprinkle with some sugar.

Now you can lick the bowl.

❋ ❋ ❋

Abi-Laura's Peanut Cookies

First put Mordi down.

Wash your hands and put on a pinny. Heat oven to gas mark 40.

Put 5 ounces of soft butter into a bowl and beat with 4 ounces of white sugar and 4 ounces of light molasses sugar or Demerara.

Then add one fresh beaten egg, one teaspoon of vanilla extract and 5 ounces of crunchy Peanut Butter and mix.

Sieve together 7 ounces of flour and a teaspoon of baking powder and half a teaspoon of ground salt and add to above.

Add a handful of dried fruit of your choice. I like dried melon or cranberry but you can choose whatever you like. You can even make them spicy if you want. Mix it all to a soft dough.

Don't touch the cat.

Roll into 28 ping-pong ball size pieces and squash each one flat about the size of a jam-pot lid.

Put on to about three separate baking trays and cook for 15 minutes until the cookies are a light golden. Cool and keep in a tin.

Nice with milk.

Make sure you wash and dry everything up afterwards.

It's okay to pick Mordi up now.

❋ ❋ ❋

Breakfast Apple Pancakes from Royal Dining Room on SS Brittic

4 ounces self raising flour
1 teaspoon of baking powder
2 beaten eggs
Half a cup of milk mixed with a teaspoon of lemon juice
3 tablespoon of melted butter

An apple sliced thin
2 tablespoons of caster sugar mixed with cinnamon
Corn oil

Mix the first four ingredients together in a large jug with a fork or whisk. Add a spoon of the melted butter and mix into a batter.

Put the rest of the butter in a pan with the apple mixed with some cinnamon sugar and cook for a couple of minutes on a medium flame.

Cool. Then mix the apple into the batter.

Heat a tablespoon of corn oil in a large fry pan. When hot pour in a puddle of batter about 12 centipedes wide. When risen, after about 15 seconds, turn over with a spatula and do the other side.

You may need to add more oil for the other pancakes.

Keep warm on a plate in the oven.

When ready to serve decorate with sliced strawberries or other fruit dipped in sugar.

Serve hot with soured cream.

(enough for one Kitty or two adults)

✳ ✳ ✳

<u>Hala's Cherry Cheesecake</u>

First light the oven to gas mark four. Be careful you don't burn your fingers. Open a jar of cherries and take two tablespoons out and drain as much juice as you can out through the strainer into a bowl. Pour juice from bowl carefully into a glass and say 'ler hime' and drink. It is better than the finest wine. Then get a big bowl off the shelf and put in two pounds of curd cheese or one pound of cottage cheese and one pound of cream cheese. Add 8 ounces of fine white sugar. Break four large eggs into a smaller bowl and beat up and then add to the cheese mix and stir with a big wooden spoon. Add a teaspoon of almond essence and four ounces of ground almond. If you haven't got ground almonds, use potato flour or corn flour. Or if your prefer use vanilla essence instead. Mix it slowly but strongly. Get a cake tin, not too big, not too small and line it if you can with baking paper. Then poor mixture in. Now add the cherries over the top of the cake. As they cook they will sink and colour the cake so pretty. Bake for about an hour until the top is golden. Remove and cool. If you want you can sprinkle over crushed biscuits or crushed toasted almonds when it is cool. It is good every way.

✳ ✳ ✳

Mamma Della Seta's Potato Latkes

Get some potatoes from the garden, about four. Wash them, then peel them and wash again. Wipe dry. Chop a little onion very fine. Be careful, the knife is sharp. Grate the potatoes and mix well with the onion. Put in a tea towel and squeeze tight. Like this....ooooou! Try to get as dry as possible. Put them in another tea towel and rub. Get all the moisture out. Keep going till it is as dry as possible. Then, my darling, get fresh eggs from the chicken, two maybe. Whisk eggs with a big pinch of salt, a pinch of white pepper, a pinch of baking powder, some grated nutmeg and a handful of breadcrumbs, flour is good too if you prefer.

Mix all up until it is thick enough to make a little flat cake in your hands. You understand? Good. Put good oil like corn oil into a pan, a good thick layer and then heat it, not too hot, but hot enough to fry gently. Put the Latke cake gently into the fat. Squash a bit with the fish slice. Put two in at a time. See, they are bubbling around the edges, nice and gently. Look there's room for another little one. Now, listen darling, this is the secret; my Mamma taught me this. Remember. Do not turn the Latkes over until one side is cooked golden and crisp. It makes a difference, believe me. Some people they turn them over and over. It's no good. For the best Latkes leave them be until they are ready to be turned. They will wait for you and you wait for them.

Then when you are sure they are crisp you can turn them over and when both sides are really golden you can gently take them out of the pan with the fish slice and wrap in a warm tea towel until you are ready to eat. Then put them on a warmed plate: a little bit of apple sauce and a little soured cream on the side. Make them like this and you'll always have friends at your table. All right my darling? A good taste of life.

Made in the USA
Charleston, SC
29 March 2013